HIS CURVY WIFE

A SMALL TOWN CURVY GIRL ROMANCE

BOOK BOYFRIENDS WANTED
BOOK TWO

MARY E THOMPSON

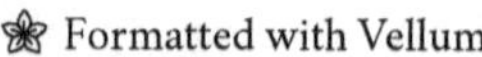 Formatted with Vellum

BOOK BOYFRIENDS WANTED

Welcome back! We're glad you decided to join us for another adventure. Never miss out on anything happening in MacKellar Cove and sign up for Mary's newsletter.

Romancing the Curves comes with subscriber exclusive freebies, sneak peeks, and a first look at everything Mary has to offer. Be the first to know about new releases and sales and all the curves ahead!

SUBSCRIBE NOW AT MARYETHOMPSON.COM

Happy reading!

For Alex...

1

MELODY

I've learned there are two kinds of plus sized women. The first one is like my sister, Willow. Willow was chubby growing up. She had those cute, chubby, baby cheeks, and those adorable chubby thighs, but when she outgrew the baby stage, they hung around.

Girls like Willow were lucky once they became adults, though, because by that time they'd developed thick skins. They took all the name-calling and teasing and turned it into armor to protect them against the people who thought they were less than simply because the scale said they were more than.

Willow was sarcastic and sometimes mean, but she wore her weight like a badge of honor. She no longer cared if she didn't get asked out because she knew how to take care of herself. It didn't matter if she was overlooked because she threw it back in their faces. Willow, and women like her, were powerhouses in the chubby girl world. They were the champions telling the rest of us to stand up and be proud. The ones wearing tight clothes and two-piece bathing suits and showing off all their assets whenever they felt like it.

The other kind of plus sized women were like me. Average, or even thin, growing up. I never had a date ask me if I wanted salad instead of pizza or was told I shouldn't eat that extra cupcake at a birthday party. I could sit on the couch and read a book or watch TV and no one ever suggested I go outside and get some exercise. I was invisible because I was what the world accepted as normal.

But as an adult, I had to learn not to be mad when those things happened. When a waiter raised his eyebrows when I ordered extra cheese on my burger. Or when a mom pursed her lips when I grabbed the biggest piece of cake at her daughter's birthday party. Or when no one looked my way with interest when I walked into a bar, but everyone turned and stared at the woman in the blue dress, devouring her with their eyes.

Not that I blamed them. The woman was stunning. She had long legs and one of those Pinterest-worthy butts, and she was all perky and perfect.

I sighed and swirled the straw through my drink. It was so easy for women like her. I envied them. The ones who knew how to flirt and could dress up and look sexy without even having to think about it. I didn't even want to imagine the layers of Spanx and slimmers I would need to look like I was twice her size.

"I need lessons on how to be sexy," I said to myself.

"No, you don't," someone said from behind me.

I spun on the bar stool and sucked in a breath. "Sorry. I didn't know you were there."

"Then who were you talking to?" Hudson Grant was the owner and bartender at O'Kelley's. The bar was also one of only two bars in MacKellar Cove, the town in the Thousand Islands of upstate New York that I called home.

I grew up in MacKellar Cove, fell in love in MacKellar

Cove, and had my entire life in MacKellar Cove. I loved it here and couldn't imagine ever living anywhere else. But there were definitely things I didn't like. For example, the best bartender in town was close friends with my soon-to-be ex-husband.

I shrugged. "Myself, I guess."

Hudson leaned on the bar and smiled. He was a good looking guy, and a good man. He was four years older than me, so we didn't grow up together, but we'd become friends over the years. The shaved head under his baseball hat and the full beard he hid behind gave him an edge of badass, but if you looked closely, his eyes were far too kind to be an ass. "Melody, you don't need lessons on how to be sexy. No woman does."

"Not one who looks like her," I said with a nod toward the woman who'd captured the attention of all the men in the bar. Three were walking toward her, and the rest of the bar watched, waiting to see if they'd get a chance. Even the women stared at her. No one was immune to how attractive she was.

Hudson followed my gaze. His trailed down the woman's shapely legs to her red heels and back up her blue dress to where she was almost falling out of the top. She was gorgeous, and she was flaunting what she had. I didn't hate her, but I was jealous as hell of her. I'd never looked like her.

"See, this is the problem. Women don't have any idea what sexy really is," Hudson said, wiping his towel across the smooth wooden bar top.

I scoffed and spun back to him. I tilted my head, my dull brown hair falling over my shoulder. "Are you honestly going to tell me that woman isn't sexy?"

He shook his head. "No, I'm not. She is. But not for the reasons you think."

"Oh, really?" I asked with a laugh, propping my chin up on my hand. "Enlighten me."

"When you look at her, what do you see?"

I turned on my stool and looked at the woman again. "Long, thin legs. Killer heels. A sexy dress that hugs her slim body and accents her boobs and her ass. Gorgeous hair. Pouty lips. Bright blue eyes. Shall I keep going?"

Hudson shook his head. "You just described her. You told me what she's wearing and what she looks like."

"So?"

"That's not what makes a woman sexy," Hudson said.

I spun on my stool, but he held up a finger to me and walked a few people over to serve drinks to the customers waiting for their Friday night relaxation.

I turned back to the woman and tried to see something else. What else made her sexy? What else made any woman sexy?

"Have you figured it out yet?" Hudson asked a minute later.

I faced him again and shook my head. "Nope. I think you've been drinking tonight."

Hudson chuckled. He never drank, and everyone in town knew it. At least, not while he was working, and he was always working.

"It's her confidence. That's what makes her sexy."

"What?" I blurted.

"That woman could be wearing jeans and a tee and every man in the room would still want her—"

"Yeah, because she's hot."

Hudson nodded and gave me one of those smiles he gave people when they'd had too much to drink and thought they could drive. Right before he took their keys and called them a ride home. "She is. I agree. But it's the way she presents herself. She's not hot because she has a nice body or is wearing a great dress. Personally, I think she looks a little silly in that dress when it's snowing outside, but she didn't ask me. She has confidence, and she's sure of herself. That's why every man in the room is looking at her."

I turned back to the woman and looked more closely. She was beautiful, but Hudson was right. I'd seen other women just as pretty as her but with half her confidence who didn't command the attention of so many men. I'd also seen women who looked nothing like her and had men drooling because they knew they were hot.

"You see it now, don't you?" Hudson asked.

"Yes," I grumbled. "I was hoping it would be easier than that to feel good."

Hudson patted my hand and walked away. Guess the good advice from the bartender was over. Of course, he was also one of my husband's best friends, so he probably didn't want to get in the middle of it. Of any of it.

I sipped my drink and looked out at the crowd again. Willow was still on the dance floor with some guy. It always amazed me that she could meet a guy, sleep with him, and part ways without a second thought. And even more shocking was that she met men she didn't already know. Whether they were guys who were older or younger or guys who didn't live in MacKellar Cove, my little sister managed to avoid awkward hook ups in a way that made it almost look like it could be fun.

I shuddered. Just the thought of sleeping with someone else made my skin crawl. I fell in love with Ramsey when we were in high school. He was it for me from the day we first met. Not that he felt the same. I was in the background for longer than was sane, but I loved him.

We started dating in high school, but when he went away

to college, we broke up. The break up didn't last, but it was long enough that I decided to try dating other guys. I went to homecoming with a guy from my math class. He was cute, and smart, and funny, but when he touched me, I felt like I was going to be sick. He wasn't Ramsey. No man was Ramsey.

I told myself I had to find a way to get over it, but I never did, and when Ramsey and I got back together a few months later, I thought I'd never have to. I knew I was going to marry him.

But now, I was thirty-five and staring down a divorce from the only man I'd ever wanted. Life sucked.

"Hey," Willow said, taking the seat next to me and my drink. She drained my glass in one gulp and exhaled. "You should come dance."

I shook my head. "I don't really want to get in the way of you two."

Willow shook her head. "He left. His friend's wife freaked out."

I fought the urge to roll my eyes. It sounded like code for his wife, but I wasn't going to lecture my sister. "I'm getting tired."

"You are not going home," Willow said firmly.

Even though there were five years between us, Willow was always my best friend. When she was born, I acted like she was my baby, protecting her and caring for her. As she grew up, I stayed close, wanting to protect her still. I will always regret that I couldn't keep her from developing that thick skin. That I wasn't in the same school as her to defend her against the Kathy Rogers of the world who thought it was funny to torment my little sister forever.

Willow was also the only one I talked to. She knew I wanted to go home because Ramsey was there with Amber. We worked out a visitation schedule, and when it was his turn to spend time with her, I did everything possible to give them space to play and talk and be together in the only home Amber had ever known. Which meant I left.

"I'll go in the other room," I whined. Willow was right. I hated to admit it, but I'd become like a junky lately, desperate for any little piece of Ramsey I could get.

I really thought the holidays were going to be the hardest part about getting divorced. Surviving Thanksgiving and Christmas without my best friend and partner by my side was easy compared to what came after.

The holidays were all about Amber. That was how it should be. She was spoiled rotten by both of us, and she was the one who made everything easy. Focusing on her made forgetting what was missing easier. Not foolproof, as evidenced by my Christmas Eve meltdown when I realized the gigantic play castle I bought her was something Ramsey would have been able to put together in about five minutes but took me the better part of three hours.

But after that, it was easy. She was overjoyed with her presents, and her first long break from school was a chance for us to spend time doing silly things like snowball fights and dressing up like our favorite princesses.

It wasn't until after the break, when she was back in school and I was back to the boring life I'd adopted over the last few months that I realized just how wrong I was when I thought getting through Thanksgiving and Christmas was going to be the hardest part about getting divorced. Oh, no. Those holidays had nothing on Valentine's Day.

Damn Valentine's Day. The day Ramsey and I always got a babysitter, usually my sister, and went away. A night in a hotel, a luxurious dinner alone, and an opportunity to reconnect.

When we were first dating and then first married, those nights were a luxury, a chance to spoil each other. Once

Amber was born, those night became our best chance to have sex. To rekindle the fizzling romance that held us together for so long. It never mattered what was going on with us when Valentine's Day rolled around. We were in love, and we put everything else aside to show each other how special and important our relationship was.

And for the first time in more than fifteen years, I was going to be spending the holiday alone. I'd already spent our tenth anniversary alone, crying myself to sleep and praying Amber didn't wake up and ask why I was so upset. Spending Valentine's Day without Ramsey just might kill me.

"You're not leaving," Willow stated firmly. "You're staying here with me, we're going to drink and have fun, and then you're coming home with me tonight."

"But—"

"No buts! Ramsey is with Amber. There is nothing you need to go home for. He left you. He moved out. He didn't want more kids. You've always wanted a huge family. That's why you two bought your house. That's why you let him walk away. That's why you're going to find someone else and give my perfect niece some brothers and sisters. Because you deserve it."

I took a deep breath and nodded. Willow was right. I knew she was right. I hated it, but it was true. I always wanted a big family. After our own less than stellar upbringing, I wanted to have a boatload of kids and make them feel special and amazing and perfect, things Willow and I were never given permission to feel.

"Another drink, Hudson!" Willow shouted toward where Hudson was serving drinks at the other end of the bar. If he wasn't there, two to three bartenders handled things, but with him tending bar, he kept the other employees on the floor running drinks and serving food.

Hudson nodded to Willow as she walked behind the bar

and grabbed a bottle. Vodka. Willow and I both liked vodka. She poured a healthy two fingers into my glass and grabbed one for herself. She added a splash of Sprite and enough cranberry juice for the drink to turn pink, then pushed mine toward me.

We lifted them and clinked our glasses, not needing words to know we were both thinking of the other's happiness with every wish we'd ever made. I turned the glass up and let the alcohol fill my mouth. The fizz threatened to come back out of my nose and the sour cranberry juice made me pucker, but I swallowed it anyway.

Willow's drink was gone in two gulps, and she stood behind the bar encouraging me to finish mine. She refilled them as Hudson headed our way, then she led me onto the dance floor.

I drank and laughed and spun and danced. I let the freedom of having zero responsibility take over and let me enjoy my night off with my sister. We sang at the top of our lungs to the songs we knew, and swayed together when a slow song came on. And for just a little while, I let myself forget my heart was broken and the love of my life had left me.

Two guys watched us as we danced. They were cute, and I didn't think they were locals. They smiled at us, and when Willow winked at one of them, they both approached us.

"Hey," the one guy said to me. He was the taller of the two with dark eyes, full lips, broad shoulders, and a narrow waist. Ramsey had the same shirt the guy was wearing. I'd gotten it for him for Christmas a couple years ago.

I forced a smile. "Hi."

"I'm Mitch," he said, extending his hand.

I stared at it for an embarrassingly long time then shook my head and reached for it. He smiled at me, and I went back to tugging on my fingers, a nervous habit I'd done forever.

"Oh, sorry. I, uh, didn't realize," he said.

I narrowed my eyes at him, trying to figure out what he knew that I didn't know. He was staring at my hands. I looked down, but they were the same hands I'd always had. Sure, they weren't smooth like a twenty year old's hands, but there wasn't anything wrong with them. Short, painted nails. Proportional fingers. And…

Oh.

My rings.

"Um, yeah," I said, trying to figure out if it was a good excuse or if I should play it off.

"You're married?" Mitch asked.

I hesitated for a second then nodded.

"Well, I mean, if it doesn't bother you…" He shrugged.

Was he serious? "If what doesn't bother me?"

He shrugged again. "If it doesn't bother you that you're married, it doesn't bother me either. We can still hook up."

"Are you kidding me?"

He shook his head. "Married women never ask why I didn't call or when they're going to see me again. I didn't know, but if I did, I still would have come over."

"Why?"

"Um, what?" he asked, confused now.

"Why would you have still come over? If you knew I was married. Why did you come over at all?"

"Um, well, I, uh…"

"Go away, Mitch."

"Yeah, okay," he said, racing away.

I shook my head. My buzz was gone, and I was tired. I motioned to Willow that I was going to get a refill and reclaimed my bar stool.

Willow kept dancing with Mitch's friend. I sat on my stool and watched them and the other people in the bar. Enjoying their Friday night. Blissful. Lucky.

I just wanted to go home and hide under my covers. Hide and never come out again. That way I didn't have to face creepy guys who wanted to sleep with married women and sexy women who could sleep with any man and my husband…who was never going to sleep with me again.

Dammit.

2

RAMSEY

$\mathcal{I}$ smiled at my daughter and checked my phone for the thousandth time since my wife walked out the door. I knew she was at O'Kelley's, and that she was with her sister, but my mind was on overdrive thinking of all the other people there. People with cocks who would take one look at Melody and want to take her home. People who were smarter than me and wouldn't let her go.

"Daddy, look!" Amber said in her too loud voice.

I turned back to her, shoving my phone into my pocket, and grinned. "Good job, honey. That was great."

I had no idea what she actually did, but it was harder than I could do. I'd never taken a dance class in my life, but that was irrelevant. My daughter was insanely talented, even if all she was doing was spinning in a circle with her hands in the air.

"Ms. Emily says I'm the best spinner in class," Amber said proudly. Her red hair floated around her as she spun again, showing off her new skill.

"I bet you are. No one could be nearly as good as you," I told her with a smile. "Do you want to play a game?"

Amber abruptly dropped to the floor and nodded. She loved games. Board games, games on my phone, games we made up. She was easy to please.

We picked Candy Land to start with. Amber won, as always, then she got to pick the next game.

We spent an hour playing games before she yawned. She wasn't old enough to be able to tell me when she was tired, but it was getting closer to her bedtime. The only thing Melody and I talked about anymore was Amber, so I knew the school year wore her out. She conked out earlier on the weekends than usual, and she fell asleep faster during the week. All the excitement was good for her, but it definitely left her exhausted.

"Why don't we take a bath and read a book?" I suggested, hoping she'd go for it.

She nodded and lifted her arms when I stood. I scooped her up and my knees nearly buckled when she wrapped her arms around my neck and rested her head on my shoulder.

I'd missed that. A lot. Of everything I'd missed by moving out, the day-to-day with my family was the hardest. Amber was growing up quickly, and it made sense for Melody to be the one who had her full time, but it meant I missed out on a lot. Bath time, nighttime cuddles, story time, and everything that used to come after that.

I drew in a breath and pushed those thoughts out of my head. Amber cuddled on my lap while I ran her bath. Once I made sure it wasn't too hot, I told her to climb in. She was too tired to splash and play, so she washed quickly, then got right back out, cuddling back into me once I had her wrapped in a towel.

She sleepily pulled on her pajamas and crawled under the covers. I laid down next to her and opened the well-worn copy of Charlotte's Web. It was Melody's favorite book as a kid and she started reading it to Amber when she was pregnant. We'd continued reading it, re-reading the book at least twice every year.

I softened my voice and started reading where they left off. Amber yawned and curled against my side. I wrapped my arm around her little body and held her close, inhaling the sweet scent her of fruity shampoo.

It wasn't long before Amber's soft snores filled the room. I kept reading until I finished the chapter, then set the book on the nightstand. I curled around my daughter and held her for a minute, wishing I would be able to sleep under the same roof as her again.

She wiggled against me and turned over, and I sighed. She never liked to cuddle at night. During the day, she'd crawl in my lap and play with my hair or Melody's, but at night, she needed her space. I eased out of her twin bed and turned off the lamp, then left her room, closing her door like we'd always done.

I checked my phone once I was in the living room again. No messages from Melody. It wasn't late yet, but she didn't say what time she'd be home. She'd never been one for going to bars or staying out late, but I wasn't sure I knew her anymore, so maybe she was now.

I felt like a creeper walking around the home I'd called mine until a few months ago. Was it okay if I watched TV? Was the food in the fridge saved for a future dinner? Hell, I wasn't even sure where I could sleep if Melody didn't get home until really late.

It sucked being a guest in my own home, but I was the one who left. I was the one who said we should get a divorce. Yeah, I felt like we were over, but she never said those words.

I leaned my head back on the couch I'd found so comfortable when I lived there and told myself it was for the best. Melody wanted more kids, and the only way to stop that was to lose her. At least she would live. If I gave in and we had another child, she could die. That was what the doctor said. Mel didn't care. She wanted to have another kid, more than one. And she wasn't giving up. Which left me only one option. I had to.

Walking out the door was the hardest thing I'd ever done. Mostly because there was a part of me that honestly believed she'd tell me not to go. It hurt my pride almost as much as it hurt my heart that my wife would rather have another child than me, but if we weren't together, she wouldn't have another child. She wouldn't die. She would live and Amber would grow up with her mother.

That was what really mattered to me.

I made some popcorn around eleven and wondered if I should call Melody. If I did, was that going to make me look like a desperate ex? What if she was with someone?

Just the thought had me clenching my fists and ready to punch something. She was still my wife, and until we signed divorce papers, she belonged to me.

SOMETIME DURING THE NIGHT, I passed out on the couch. I woke up with a stiff neck watching infomercials about cleaning the house.

I got up and walked down the hallway to my old bedroom. The lights were off, but I could tell Melody wasn't there. I walked into the bedroom, not turning on the lights, and just stood there.

Melody's scent filled the room. Her perfume, the same one she'd worn since high school, floated around me. Her shampoo drifted out from the bathroom. The bed was made, but the indent on her side was more pronounced. Or maybe that was just because my side was covered in pillows.

My old side. It wasn't my side anymore. Nothing in the

room was mine anymore. My clothes were out of the closet, my personal items out of the bathroom. Every trace of me had been erased from the house.

I went down the hall to one of the guest rooms, the one next to Amber's room. When we bought the four bedroom house, we planned to fill it with children and laughter and love. We had a guest room so friends and family could stay, but the second nursery became a second guest room instead of a second nursery once we lost Steven. I hadn't been able to bring myself to go into that room.

The bed in the guest room was comfortable. I'd slept on it more than once when I still called the house my home. I stared at it like the death sentence it felt like it was. Melody didn't come home. After a night at a bar, she didn't come home. And she didn't call or text me to say she wouldn't be. Which left me with only one possibility of where she was.

I tossed and turned on the once comfortable bed until the sun forced its way through the curtains. I wanted to pull the covers over my head and forget about the outside world, but footsteps raced down the hallway and told me I had a job to do.

Amber was standing at the end of the hallway, looking around. Melody was always the first one up. She let me sleep in whenever I wanted, but she was up early, making breakfast, drinking coffee, and getting ready for Amber to wake up.

"Mommy?" Amber called out softly, a hint of fear in her voice.

"Hey, baby girl," I said, drawing her attention.

"Daddy!" her brown eyes lit up with joy and she rushed to me.

I bent down and scooped her up, holding her close. The fear inside her gave way to excitement as my regret ramped up and made it hard for me to breathe. I wasn't around. I wasn't there for so much, and Amber was excited to see me, but it also reminded me how rare it was for me to be there in the morning, or at all.

"What do you say we fix some breakfast?" I suggested, carrying her to the kitchen.

"Where's Mommy?"

I shook my head and pasted on a smile. I was not going to show my daughter how upset I was that her mother didn't come home. That she spent the night with a stranger instead of home with us.

Us. What a joke.

"Mommy isn't here."

Amber's face paled. "Did she leave me like you did?"

That was it. That was the moment I knew I'd never recover from walking away from my family. My daughter thought I left her. She was so young that we never sat her down and explained it all to her, but she drew her own conclusions and thought it was all her fault.

Instead of continuing to the kitchen, I took her to the couch and sat with her on my lap. "First of all, Mommy will be back. She just spent the night out with Aunt Willow. She didn't leave you and she never will. She loves you."

Amber's bottom lip wobbled and her eyes filled with tears. "You don't love me?" she asked in a shaky voice that shredded me.

I hugged her close and shook my head. "No, Amber, that's not it at all, baby. I love you. So much it hurts. I hate not being here with you all the time."

"And Mommy?"

I nodded and swallowed the lump in my throat. "And Mommy. I wish I could still be here with you guys."

"Then why can't you? In school, Mrs. Anderson says we have to be nice to everyone, but we can be friends with whoever the people we like the most. If you like me the most, can we be friends still?"

I smiled through my pain and tucked her wild hair behind her ear. "We'll always be friends. And I'll always love you. You will always be able to tell me anything, and I'll always be here for you. Me leaving has nothing to do with you."

"So, you don't love Mommy?"

I drew in a breath and smiled again. "I do love Mommy."

"Then why don't you live here?" she cried.

"Because…" How do you explain to a child that leaving was about loving the people you left when you didn't even understand it yourself? How could I tell her that if I stayed with them, Melody would wear me down until I gave her anything she wanted and it could mean losing her forever? How did I tell my daughter that?

"Why don't you live here, Daddy?" she asked again.

"Because Daddy and Mommy want different things," Melody said from behind us.

I didn't hear her come in. I didn't know how much she heard. All I knew was she was there, as always, with the right words to put a smile back on Amber's face.

"Mommy!" Amber shouted, jumping off my lap and rushing toward her mother.

Melody took a step back when Amber barreled into her. She wrapped her arms around our daughter and smiled, then dropped to the floor to scoop Amber up. "Hey, sweetheart. How was your night with Daddy? Did you guys have fun?"

Amber nodded. "We did. Daddy let me play games and I showed him my dance. He said Ms. Emily is right and I am the bestest spinner in class. And we ate dinner. And Daddy read some more of Charlotte's Web to me before I fell asleep."

"That sounds like a great night," Melody said. "I'm so

happy you had fun with Daddy. And I thought you'd still be sleeping this morning. How early did you wake Daddy up?"

Amber shrugged, and Melody finally looked up at me. Our gazes collided and the guilt in her eyes made my gut swirl. Her not coming home sent my imagination into a tailspin, but seeing the guilt in her eyes and knowing she was with someone else was more than I could handle. She avoided looking at me, but the second she did, I knew. I knew she wasn't with Willow like I hoped, even though I knew every second she spent with her sister was taking her farther away from me. No, my wife spent the night in the arms of another man.

"We haven't been up long," I finally managed.

Melody nodded and focused on Amber again, breaking the connection we had. "Why don't we get breakfast started?"

"Daddy was going to make breakfast. He's going to have breakfast with me."

Melody's eyes went to mine again. She gave me a tentative smile and nodded. "Sounds great," she said to Amber a little too brightly. "Why don't you two get started while I go change?"

Amber happily skipped to the kitchen, and when I didn't immediately follow, she said, "Come on, Daddy."

I wanted to talk to Melody, but I couldn't in front of Amber, so I followed my daughter to the kitchen while my wife changed out of her sex clothes.

Amber and I made French toast for breakfast, with bacon and sausage because, why not? Melody and I drank our coffees and pretended everything was fine. Amber didn't notice Melody and I didn't speak to each other. She simply chattered happily about everything going on.

After breakfast, Melody told Amber to change out of her pajamas. Amber argued, but Melody pointed out the syrup on them, and Amber finally agreed.

As Amber left the kitchen, Melody started cleaning up. I stayed at the table, the one we picked out together when we were first married. It was old and worn, but it was sturdy, a fact we'd tested out more than once before Amber was born.

I stared at the table and tried to think of anything other than my wife testing out the table, or another table, with another man. The longer I stayed silent, the more pissed off I was.

"Do you do this often?" I asked her.

"Do what?" she replied, not facing me.

"Stay out all night?"

She spun around and glared at me, one eyebrow raised. "Excuse me?"

"I was just wondering if you usually spent the night with someone else when Amber is home wondering where you are and if you're coming back."

She crossed her arms over her chest, and dammit, my gaze went there. Because she knew me so well, she noticed and dropped her arms to her sides. Her fists clenched, and I ground my jaw to keep from opening my mouth. I wanted an answer.

"No. I've never spent the night out. I've never done anything. I'm home, raising our daughter night and day, like I've done her entire life."

I scoffed. I couldn't help it. I was pissed off. Furious. I hated that my wife screwed someone else while I was home with our daughter, and she didn't even have the decency to tell me she wasn't coming home.

"Who was he?" I asked.

Her eyebrows went up. Her hands lifted, like she was going to cross her arms again, but she dropped them back to her sides. She pursed her lips together and drew in a breath. "Who was who?"

I stood up and stalked over to her. I waited until I was

close enough to feel the heat from her body and smell her scent. She must have put more perfume on when she changed because I couldn't smell another man on her. "Who was the man you went home with last night? The one you spent all night fucking while I was here with our daughter? The one you were so wrapped up in that you couldn't be bothered to tell me you weren't coming home?"

She flinched like I slapped her, then straightened, raising herself up. She squared her jaw and glared at me. "You haven't spent a night with Amber in months, Ramsey. Months. You walked out of this house and decided you didn't want me anymore. You made that choice, not me. And you don't ever get to walk back in here and tell me what I can or can't do, or who I can or can't sleep with."

"Just tell me if you're screwing someone I know. Just so I'm prepared that when I see him again I know if he's seen my wife naked."

She scoffed and shook her head. "I didn't realize you were this big of an asshole. I really didn't."

"You're my wife, Melody."

She shook her head again. "No, I'm not. You said you wanted a divorce. You walked out on me. You left. So, no, I'm not your wife, I'm the woman raising your daughter."

"Tell me who you were with last night."

"Screw you, Ramsey. Get the hell out of my house."

"I still pay the bills. It's my house, too."

She laughed and finally broke eye contact. She turned back to the sink and ignored me. But I was too upset to let it end that easily. I needed to know who she was with, so I could kick his ass and tell him not to ever touch my wife again.

"Who was it?" I demanded.

She turned around and slapped me, all in one motion. It

happened so quickly, I didn't realize what she was doing until I felt the sting on my cheek.

I looked at her, ready to light into her, and saw tears running down her cheeks.

"I spent the night with Willow, you ass. I wasn't with some random guy. I was with my sister. For the record, I have never once asked you about who you bring home at night. I have never once accused you of sleeping with someone else. You have your own place and you get to do whatever and whoever you want, and I don't ask. So, you don't get to come in here and accuse me of anything. You don't get to judge me. You don't get to say anything about the way I'm living my life since you walked out of it. Fuck you, Ramsey."

Amber's footsteps raced down the hall, and Melody pasted on a bright grin and pushed away from me. She swept Amber up and carried her into the living room. I heard them talking and laughing and playing, and I felt like an outsider. I wasn't a part of their lives anymore. And I was just making it worse by being there.

I accused my wife of sleeping with someone. I made her feel like shit. All because I was jealous. Because I wanted her to be mine again. Because I couldn't accept the fact that I let her go.

I didn't deserve them. I never really had. So, I snuck out the back door like the fucking coward I was and vowed to give Melody what she needed. Space from me.

3

MELODY

The door closed so quietly I almost didn't hear it. Amber was talking, but when I realized what it was, I stopped listening to her. I hated myself for it, but I strained to hear some sign of Ramsey still in the house. Something that told me he didn't sneak out the back door and leave me to explain to our daughter why her father disappeared.

It wouldn't be the first time I'd done it, but it sucked. When he first moved out, he couldn't face her. He told me he'd talk to her, but he never did, and after two days of her constant questions about when he was going to be home, I admitted to our daughter that her daddy wasn't coming home. He didn't want to live with Mommy anymore, and because he didn't want to live with Mommy, he wasn't going to live with her.

Every word out of my mouth felt like a gut punch.

Amber was mad at me then, but after a few days, she was okay with how things were. She was always okay. It was one of the things I admired about her.

I dragged my focus back to her after a minute and

stopped worrying about my husband. Until Amber asked where he was.

"Daddy had to go, sweetie. I'm sorry."

"But he didn't say goodbye to me. Is he mad at me?"

I shook my head. "No, sweet girl. He forgot about something and had to go. I'm sure he'll call later so he can talk to you."

Amber nodded, but she didn't bounce back like usual. This whole thing was weighing on her as much as it was me, and if Ramsey's weird, angry behavior was any indication, the three of us weren't going to be a family again.

I sent Ramsey a text later that day and asked him to call Amber when he had a chance because she was upset he left without saying goodbye. When he called, I handed the phone to her without even answering it. I'd had enough of him for one day.

Amber and I spent the rest of the day inside. We watched movies and had a dance party and curled up in her bed at night to read another chapter of Charlotte's Web. When she fell asleep, I went through the house cleaning up.

I walked into my bedroom and immediately knew I forgot something. I turned on the light, expecting to see my bed a mess from Ramsey sleeping there, but the covers were exactly how I left them. Amber said when she got up no one was there, so I knew he didn't sleep on the couch. That left one place.

I went down the hall to the guest room. One of the rooms I'd hoped to turn into a nursery one day. We had just started planning Steven's room when I lost him. It remained storage, a room full of items for a child who would never be born. But the guest room...that was only a nursery in my mind.

I painted it a soft green color when we moved in. It would have been easy to add pink to it and make it suitable for a girl or add blue and fix it up for a boy. Instead, it was a guest room. Another room in a house that was too big for a family that was too small.

I took a deep breath and stripped the tangled sheets from the bed. Because I was weak, I pressed my nose to the pillowcase and breathed in the scent of my husband. Tears sprang to my eyes and heat pooled low in my gut. I hated that I still wanted him as much as I did. Walking in that morning and seeing him, rumpled and sleepy, reminded me of all the times he'd woken me up before he went to work. Times when he was late to work because he didn't leave the bed until much later than he should have.

I choked back the tears and shoved the sheets into the corner of the room. I'd deal with them some other time. I wasn't strong enough when I was hurt and angry and horny.

Damn him.

"You should start dating," Sharon said kindly.

My eyebrows went up. "What? Did you hear what I just said? I was sniffing the sheets my husband slept in."

Sharon nodded. "I heard you, Melody. That's why I think you should start dating. You need physical contact. You want someone in your life."

"I don't think I'm ready for that."

Sharon smiled. "You're never going to be ready."

Sharon had been my therapist since I lost Steven. The depression almost killed me. I had no desire to live for a while. Even knowing Amber was there wasn't enough for me. I hated myself for not protecting my son when he was still inside my body. The doctors said I had a medical condition that made it impossible for him to thrive, and I felt responsible.

Which was why I was talking to Sharon. She helped me to

see that losing Steven wasn't my fault. She was trying to convince me losing Ramsey wasn't either, but I knew that wasn't true.

"It's only been six months. We aren't even divorced yet."

Sharon nodded, her braids sliding over her shoulder as she leaned forward. "Melody, you're never going to be ready. Women whose husbands die or cheat or something happens that tells you there's no coming back will sometimes be ready. You and Ramsey, the two of you had a disagreement. It was a big one, but it was still a disagreement. No one cheated. No one did something unforgivable. Nothing happened that said your marriage is over and can never be recovered. That's harder because you're holding out hope."

"I'm—"

"You know you can't lie to me," Sharon said with one dark eyebrow up.

I laughed and nodded. "Fine, you're right. He was so mad Saturday. What if he was jealous?"

"What if he was? Are you going to give up your dream of having more kids?"

I sighed. "No."

"Then nothing has changed."

I nodded and choked back my disappointment. I wanted to believe Ramsey would come around. That he would see things my way and know I was right. We had the big house. We always talked about a big family. And I was fine.

But he…He left. He didn't agree with me, and he left.

"I've been with Ramsey since I was in high school. I have no idea how to meet someone."

"Online," Sharon said simply as though I was foolish for not knowing.

"No. Online dating? No. That's for people who can't get a date."

Sharon chuckled. "No, it's not. It's for people who want to

meet someone. Sure, there are people on every site who just want to hook up, but there are also a lot of people who want to get to know someone they wouldn't normally have a chance to get to know."

I sighed again. Online dating. I'd gone from marrying the only man I'd ever loved to online dating. My life sucked.

"Fine. I'll try it. But I'm not going out with someone if he's creepy."

"Of course not," Sharon said with a laugh. "I would really hope you have better sense than that."

I chuckled and tried to think of dating, and online dating, as a good idea. None of it was a good idea. But I had no choice in the matter because what I really wanted wasn't going to happen. Ramsey was not coming back.

I DIDN'T HEAR from Ramsey the rest of the week, and by the weekend I decided to sign up for online dating. I hated every minute of filling out the endless questionnaire for Karissa's Book Boyfriends Wanted app. Of all the options out there, hers seemed to be the best. I hated the idea of Karissa knowing I was using it, but I also felt a little better that she wasn't going to rip me off.

Sunday afternoon Amber had a birthday party for one of her classmates. The mom and I had become friends, and I offered to help her with the party. Amber and I went over there an hour before the party was supposed to start armed with supplies to turn their house into party central.

I carried my bin to the door and smiled when Casey opened the door with wide eyes.

"Um, what is all that?" she asked, clearly scared.

"Hi, Makayla," Amber said brightly.

"Amber!" Makayla shouted. "Mommy, can I show Amber my room?"

Casey nodded. "Of course. But when I call you, you need to come down."

"Okay, Mommy. Let's go," Makayla said to Amber.

"That's okay, right?" Casey asked me as the girls raced up the stairs.

"Yeah, of course. We'll get everything set up faster without them trying to play with all of it," I told her. She led me to the kitchen and motioned to the table for me to set the bin down.

"Okay, so what is all this?" Casey asked again.

"It's a party in a box. Games, decorations, tableware, everything."

"Are you serious? I was just going to let them run around the house and play. And I have plates and stuff."

I nodded. "I know. And you can use whatever you want from here. Amber helped me pull it all together, so it's all stuff she thinks Makayla will like. But it's totally up to you."

"Let's see it."

I smiled and opened the bin. I had collected items for years from dollar stores and party stores and clearance racks and everywhere I could think of. I had three more bins at home with similar items, but Amber chose the colors she thought Makayla would like. Pink, green, and white but no specific theme so they could add in whatever they wanted.

"Wow, this is…wow. I don't have anything like all of this."

I nodded and started pulling things out of the bin. I had games that went on the floor, games that sent them through the house, and games they played on the wall. I had decorations that could quickly transform any room including balloons, streamers, and centerpieces. I even had a few bags of candy in the same colors so we could create a treat bar or topping bar for the girls, depending on what fit with the party.

"How do you have all this stuff?" Casey asked, trying to take it all in.

"I really like throwing parties. I buy stuff when it's on sale or when I have coupons and when Amber wants a party, we have whatever we need. It makes everything a lot easier."

"I wouldn't even know what to get. I mean, who thinks about this stuff."

I smiled.

"Okay, fine. You do. This is really just blowing me away," Casey said. "All right, what do we do first?"

"I'd suggest we start with games. We can always set the table when the kids are here, and decorations are optional. But games will keep them from destroying your house."

Casey nodded slowly. "Sounds good."

I could tell she was overwhelmed so I picked two games and handed her one to set up in the living room while I set the other one up in the kitchen. When she was done, she looked a little more relaxed.

"Are all the girls from class coming?" I asked as we started to hang streamers in the front hallway leading kids to the kitchen and living room.

Casey nodded. "Yeah. And so are all the parents."

I rolled my eyes and groaned. Casey hummed in agreement. All the kids were sweet kids, but the same couldn't be said for the parents. One of the moms was constantly trying to take over everything. I volunteered with her for the first class party and thought she was staff because of the way she directed everyone. It wasn't until Casey told me she was a parent that I realized.

"Well, I guess we're going to have to kill her with kindness because we can't kill her for real," Casey said.

I snorted and shook my head. "You're trouble."

"That's why we're friends."

I nodded. Casey and her husband went through a separation before the school year started. They ended up in counseling and managed to tape things back together, according to Casey. When Ramsey showed up to meet the teacher separate from Amber and I, Casey quickly picked up on our situation and said she was willing to listen if I needed a friend.

"So, my therapist said I should start dating," I told her, knowing I needed another opinion.

"Good. You totally should."

"Really?" I asked her.

She nodded. "Absolutely. You can't stay single forever."

"I'm not single."

Casey drew in a breath and sighed heavily. "I know. And I'm sorry. But you kind of are. I know you don't want to hear that."

I shook my head. "No, I don't, but that doesn't mean it's wrong. I am single. My husband left me. He decided he doesn't want to be with me."

"It's time you remembered how amazing you are. You know what? I think I might know someone I could set you up with."

I shook my head again. "I don't think that's a good idea."

Casey put her hand on my arm. "He's in a similar position you are. He's still married but he's separated. He isn't sure what's going to happen with his marriage. He's someone you could talk to. You don't have to fall in love with him and marry him, but I think he's a good person for you to go out with. Easy."

I sucked in a breath. "I'll think about it."

Casey nodded. "I totally get it. Let me know. And for the record, I thought about dating when Kyle and I were separated, but I didn't have the guts. I give you a lot of credit for considering it."

"I signed up for online dating," I confessed.

"What? No."

I nodded. "I don't know if I'll go out with a stranger, but maybe it'll be easier than someone I actually know."

"Except you could end up matched with someone you do know," Casey said with a wrinkled nose.

I shrugged. "I'll see how it goes. This would all be so much better if I didn't have to do it at all."

Casey hugged me from the side and put her head on my shoulder. "I know. And I'm sorry."

I forced a smile and thanked her. We had just enough time to finish the streamers when the doorbell rang.

"Makayla! Come down and greet your guests!" Casey yelled as we walked to the front door.

The girls rushed down the stairs and yanked the door open before Casey and I made it. They all squealed, and the girls ran down the hall, leaving Casey and I to say hi to the mom.

The rest went pretty much the same. Makayla, Amber, and whoever else was there answered the door, screamed, and ran away, and Casey introduced herself and led the parents into the kitchen where finger foods and snacks lined the island.

By the time the last guest arrived, I was in the kitchen with the parents who were already there, and Casey answered the door on her own. I was smiling at something one of the moms said when Robin, the difficult mom, walked in.

My smile slid from my face as Robin took in the decorated room with pursed lips. She forced those lips into a smile when Casey asked if she wanted something to drink.

Casey rolled her eyes at me as she walked by, and I could have kissed her for taking away some of my tension. I had always been a people pleaser. I shied away from conflict and tried to make sure everyone liked me. I'd gotten better since having Amber, especially when she needed protection, but inside, a part of me was still that shy teenager who desperately wanted the boy I liked to notice me.

It always came back to Ramsey.

"This place is…cute," Robin told Casey.

"Thanks," Casey said brightly. "Melody is a genius with this stuff. She set it all up in about thirty minutes. Makayla loves it."

Robin turned toward me and smiled. Her eyes scanned my curvy body then immediately dismissed me, leaving me to relive another part of high school when the cheerleaders found me not good enough to be friends.

There was a big part of me that knew I was better off not being friends with girls who had no interest in being friends with me, but back then I couldn't see that. I just wanted people to like me.

Amber came rushing into the room with the other girls and threw herself at me, distracting me from Robin. I focused on my daughter, her pale skin flushed with the excitement of having a good time with her friends. "Mommy, we're going to play a game. Can you help us?"

I nodded and brushed her hair back from her face. "Of course. Which game does Makayla want to play first?"

"Ring toss first. Right, Makayla?"

Makayla nodded, and I led the girls to the living room. We had a station set up for each kid and paper plates cut to form the rings so nothing in the house would get damaged.

"This is a great idea," one of the moms told me.

"Thanks. It's cheap and easy to do, and the kids like it."

"Is this what you do for a living? Plan parties?" she asked.

I shook my head. "No, I'm a stay at home mom."

"I am, too. We should get together sometime while the girls are in school. Coffee or something. If you're interested.

I'm Carly, by the way. It's hard to keep up with who all the parents are. My daughter is Charlotte."

I smiled. "Melody. Mine is Amber. And coffee would be great."

We exchanged information and agreed to check our calendars and be in touch during the week. I was riding high until I noticed Robin staring at me.

4

I was not interested in a confrontation. I just wanted to watch the kids have fun, enjoy talking to some of the other parents, and go home.

But Robin clearly had other plans.

"You did all this?" she asked when she walked over.

It wasn't the question that bothered me, it was the tone. The one that said not only did she not believe I was capable of doing it but that she didn't think I'd done a good enough job. I really wanted to remind her the party was for a six year old, not a clubhouse dinner with the MacKellars, if any of them ever returned to town. And the guest of honor loved her party.

"I did," I said with a smile. "Makayla really likes pink and green so we decorated in her favorite colors."

Robin pursed her lips and looked around the room again. "Where did you come up with these silly games?"

I locked my grin in place and promised myself a glass of wine after Amber went to bed if I didn't rip Robin a new one in front of all the children. "The games are easy to make games that are good for indoors. Since it's cold outside, we knew the kids would be indoor. And since Casey didn't want her house destroyed, I picked some games that would be fun for the kids but we could set up a few different ones so they wouldn't get bored waiting for someone else to have a turn."

"They need to learn taking turns," Robin said snidely.

I nodded. "I agree. But the excitement of a party is a time when kids usually forget their manners. They prefer to just be kids and have fun."

Robin nodded sharply and pursed her lips again. Thankfully, before she asked me anything else, Casey called me over.

"I thought you could use a rescue," she whispered when I reached her side.

I groaned quietly. "She's such a…I don't even know what."

"Yes, you do. You just can't say it with twelve six year olds running around."

I chuckled. "True."

"What did she even say? You looked like you were going to rip her head off."

I rolled my eyes. "She wanted to know if I helped you plan the party and where I came up with the *silly* games."

"The girls are loving the games. If you can't be silly when you're six, when can you be?"

"That's what I said. She's just too uptight. Everything has to be perfect in her world."

Casey nodded. "I almost feel bad for her."

"I feel bad for her husband and her daughter." I paused then added, "Actually, no I don't. She has a husband. I'm not going to feel sorry for him. If mine can walk out, then hers must be happier than Ramsey was."

Emotion swelled up inside me at the realization that a horrible, uptight woman was better equipped to hold on to her husband than me. I was standing there judging her when I should have been asking her for advice.

"I'm mean," I confessed.

Casey laughed softly. "We all are. Robin is mean to us, we're mean to her. I don't know anything about her. Maybe she's a nice person, maybe she's not, but—"

"I'm being petty. That's not fair."

"You don't mean it," Casey said soothingly.

I snorted. "I kind of do, but that doesn't make it better. I just don't deal well with people who judge others, and I'm standing here judging her. Wow, no wonder my husband left me."

"He'll be back," Casey said.

I smiled at her, but she was trying to placate me. Ramsey wasn't coming back. He was done with me. I always backed down when we fought, but this one time, I wanted something. I wanted to win. And I didn't let him have his way, and he left. In truth, I wasn't sure if that was the kind of marriage I should be in.

I STAYED out of the way for the rest of the party, having my own pity party while the kids ate cake and Makayla opened her presents. Robin glanced at me once in a while, but she didn't approach me again.

When the party was over, I helped Casey clean up and collected the stuff I brought that was still usable. Amber and Makayla played with all her new stuff while Casey and I made their house look normal again.

Casey offered me a glass of wine before we left, but I declined and told her we needed to get home. We didn't, and I think Casey knew that, but she didn't push.

At home, Amber was still bouncing off the walls. She wanted to have a dance party in the living room, so we pushed the couch against the wall and turned up the music. I resisted, but seeing how happy Amber was made me smile and I started to dance.

"This is fun, Mommy!" Amber shouted as we shook and spun and danced to the crazy music she picked.

I had to admit she was right. I laughed with her and let go of all my tension. My life was changing. Gone were the dreams I grew up with, the dreams I'd held on to for the last twenty years. Ramsey wasn't interested in being married to me, and that hurt, a lot, but it didn't mean my life was over. Everything I needed was right in that room.

Amber kept dancing and giggling. I wished she never knew the pain I was going through. Hopefully she'd choose the right person to be with when she was older. The person who made her happy and never wanted to spend a minute away from her.

That was all a parent could wish for their child. Happiness. And I wished it for her. Hard.

When Amber was worn out and collapsed dramatically on the couch, I turned down the music and we put on a movie. Sundays were our lazy days. We sat around and did as little as possible, and after a busy party, we needed extra lazy time. Which meant ordering delivery.

Amber decided on pizza, so I called in the order while she sang along with the movie. I grabbed paper plates and two cups of water and settled in with her to watch and wait for the pizza to show up.

When I looked at my phone, I saw a notification from Book Boyfriends Wanted, the dating app. I pulled it up and was surprised to find I had two matches. Wow. I looked at both of them and read the details the guys wrote in their bios.

Who was I kidding? I wasn't picky. I just wanted companionship at that point. I wasn't desperate for sex yet, which was why I went off my birth control, but someone to talk to who wouldn't get in trouble for swearing and wasn't delivering me food would be nice.

The doorbell rang, and Amber bounced up, rushing for the door. "You know you don't answer the door without me," I told her.

She paused and waited for me to catch up. I looked through the peephole and nodded to her to open the door. The pizza guy smiled at her then focused on me. We traded cash for food and said goodnight while Amber closed the door.

She sniffed enthusiastically when I opened the box. "Yummy."

I chuckled and put a slice of pizza on her plate. She blew on it for about two seconds, then took a bite. She spit it right back out and fanned her mouth.

"Is it hot?"

She nodded. "It burned my mouth."

"Drink some water and blow on it before you take a big bite."

I watched out of the corner of my eye as she ignored my advice and went back for another bite after two more seconds of blowing on her pizza. She didn't spit it out, but she chewed with her mouth open.

I couldn't really blame her. I was just as excited about the pizza as she was. Ordering in was a treat for us. I felt guilty being a stay at home mom and not having dinner ready every night, so I worked to make sure everything was done. And since Ramsey left, I tried to watch our money even more. I knew I needed to get a job, and soon, but Ramsey hadn't said anything yet. Aside from his comment about the house still being his because he was paying for it.

The pizza was gooey and delicious and I loved every bite of it. A part of me knew I shouldn't reach for a second slice, but I told that part to stop complaining and enjoyed the second slice just as much as the first. I seriously considered a third, too. Because I was hungry, and no one was going to judge me for the amount of food I ate.

When we were done with pizza, I put the leftovers in the fridge and settled on the couch with Amber again. She continued singing songs and mouthing along with the actors as they spoke their lines. We'd watched the movie so many times I knew most of the lines, too, but I let Amber sing along by herself.

Amber started yawning not long after the movie ended, so we cleaned up and she got in the bath. She barely made it through the first page of the chapter, so I kept reading but put the bookmark at the beginning so we could read the chapter again.

Then I poured myself a glass of wine and sat down on the couch with my phone. I wasn't sure what I was more afraid of, the men on the app or the phone call I needed to make.

I looked at the time and sucked down a healthy gulp of my wine, then tapped the screen and called my mother.

Shudder.

"Melody," she answered cooly.

"Hi, Mother. How are you?"

She huffed. Nothing was ever good with her. Nothing was ever bad with her either. She just existed. "I'm fine, Melody. How is Amber?"

"Amber is good. She had a party today and helped me set it all up. They had a great time. Lots of kids running around and being kids."

"Kids shouldn't be allowed to run wild. They should be taught the proper way to behave."

I stifled my groan and pursed my lips. "Amber is being taught the proper way to behave. And when she's with her friends, she should be silly and have fun."

"You can have fun without being out of control. Or

maybe you've forgotten that since you no longer have a husband who is helping you raise your child."

The barb was a good one. My mother knew exactly what to say to make sure I knew what she thought of my life choices. Talking to her once a week was an exercise in self control because God forbid I actually showed some damn emotion. People weren't supposed to get upset about silly things like their parents not caring if they were sad or mad. All that mattered was not upsetting my mother.

"How's Dad?" I asked, hoping for nothing more than a subject change.

"He's fine," she said with the same tone she used for every word she spoke. "He went to dinner with a friend tonight."

"You didn't want to go?"

She huffed. "And listen to them talk about fishing and golfing and spending time on their boats this summer? No."

Sometimes I wondered how my parents ended up together. My mother was so cold and indifferent to the world, and my dad had friends and went out and enjoyed life. He told me once he'd been in love with her forever, and that she wasn't always so uptight, but I didn't know that side of her. I only knew the woman who told me emotions should only be shown when no one is around to see them.

My childhood was not much fun.

"What are you doing this week?" I asked her, again trying to find a topic that wouldn't upset her.

"I have lunch on Tuesday and my knitting club on Wednesday. You know this already, Melody."

I rolled my eyes at myself. She'd had the same schedule for years. She always met with the same women, and they were all the same uptight and cold women. I really didn't understand them at all.

"I do. I was wondering if you had anything different going on this week."

"Most of us don't have the luxury of free time. I still work every day. Grocery shopping and cleaning the house and preparing meals for your father and me. The things you should be doing if you ever want your husband to come back."

"Oh, sorry, Mom. Amber is calling me. I need to go."

"You should let her learn to self-soothe, Melody. She's old enough that she shouldn't be waking you up at night."

"Okay, thanks. I need to go. Love you."

"Good night, Melody."

I hung up the phone and sank back against the couch, almost feeling guilty for lying about my daughter to get my mother off the phone. It was a wonder I ever felt anything for Ramsey after a mother like her. She'd been berating me for letting my husband walk out the door, and I was tired of hearing it. Mostly because all the things she said were the same things I thought.

If I'd been a better wife, he wouldn't have left.

If I'd let him have his way, he wouldn't have left.

If I'd given up on my dream of a big family, he wouldn't have left.

Of course my mother saw each of those as bigger sins than murder. Killing someone who deserved it was okay in her book, but letting your husband walk out the door was not.

I was pretty sure her priorities were screwed up, but she was the one with a husband at home every night, just like Robin, and I was the one wondering what Ramsey spent his nights doing.

I ignored my phone, and the messages on the app, and started cleaning up. There wasn't much out since we spent most of the day at Casey's, but I still wanted to make sure the house was picked up by the morning.

When I was done, I went back to the couch to watch a

movie. About halfway through, I poured myself another glass of wine and tried to pretend my life had actually turned out the way I hoped it would.

A bunch of kids running around, my husband curled up next to me in bed every night, and happiness for all of us.

My fantasy only got me so far. The romantic comedy on the screen made me want to yell at the heroine that she had no idea what she had when she told the hero she was done with him. Thankfully, she had a friend who was willing to call her out and make her see where she went wrong. She apologized, and they were able to live happily ever after.

Too bad it wasn't that easy for me.

I turned off the TV and put my wine glass in the sink. I looked in on Amber then went to my room alone.

Dammit, I hated that.

"MELODY?" a male voice said from behind me Monday morning at drop off.

I turned and smiled at Amber's friend's dad. Scott, maybe? Or Sean? Something with an S.

"Good morning," I said with a smile.

"Morning. How are you? I haven't seen you lately."

I helped Amber hang up her coat and set her sneakers on the floor so she could change out of her boots. "I'm great. Thanks. How are you?"

He grinned. "I'm doing good. Really good. I'm running off to work, but I wondered if maybe we could get dinner. Tomorrow night?"

"Um, tomorrow?" I stammered, wondering how I was going to get out of it. It wasn't that he wasn't good looking, or that he wasn't a nice man, but he wasn't my husband.

"You said Aunt Willow is coming over tomorrow night,

Mommy," Amber provided. Then she turned to Scott and said, "My Aunt Willow likes to babysit me because she doesn't have any kids. Maybe Gina can come over, too, and Aunt Willow can play with both of us so you and Mommy can go out to dinner."

Scott, I was pretty sure it was Scott, grinned widely and met my gaze. I tried to think of something, but there was nothing I could say to put him off.

"That sounds like a great plan, Amber. I love the way you think."

I smiled and forced myself to nod.

"Is six okay?" he asked.

"Sure, that sounds good. Is there anything Gina doesn't eat or any allergies she has?"

He shook his head, his grin taking over his whole face. "Nope. She likes pretty much everything."

I nodded. "Sounds good. I guess I'll see you tomorrow night then."

He nodded. "Definitely. I'm looking forward to it."

I smiled, then turned to Amber again. She had one shoe on, so I helped her with the other one and made sure she had what she needed from her backpack before going into her classroom.

I thought I was home free until I realized Scott was standing there waiting for me.

"Can I walk you out?" he asked.

I smiled and nodded. I really needed to figure out how to act around other adults. Especially adults that were men and wanted to date me.

"What are you up to today?" he asked as we walked down the hallway.

"Cleaning the house, cooking, grocery shopping. Stuff like that."

"That's nice," Scott said. "I wish I had time to do more of

that. I always feel like the bad parent when Gina stays with me. I do my best to get foods I know she likes, but it's hard to stay on top of everything. Sara used to do all that."

I nodded and remembered he went through a divorce a few years ago. I didn't know either of them well, but since MacKellar Cove was so small, I knew who they were. Gina was a few months older than Amber, but until they were in kindergarten together, I hadn't met Scott or Sara.

"The adjustment was tough. That's something people don't tell you before you get divorced. Losing the person you thought would be with you forever is hard enough, but the complete upheaval of everything you got used to was a constant reminder that nothing would be the same again."

I nodded. "I'm learning that. Nothing has been easy, and for us it's only been a few months."

"It'll get better. But there will always be things about divorce that are hard. For me, the hardest part was accepting I won't have more kids."

My ears perked up. "You wanted more kids?"

He smiled. "I did. I always imagined having a big family. It was one of the things we fought about. One of the reasons we ended up getting divorced."

"I know the feeling."

"Yeah?"

I nodded.

We reached my van and paused. Scott reached for me and for a second, I froze. Then he flattened my crooked collar and smiled. "I'm really looking forward to tomorrow, Melody."

I nodded. "Me, too," I told him honestly. Because if I was going to date, a man who wanted more kids was definitely going to top my list. "Me, too."

5

RAMSEY

I walked into O'Kelley's and glanced around. For a Tuesday night, it was busy. Unfortunately, I'd gotten to know how many people were usually at O'Kelley's each night. I spent far too much time there over the last six months. Far too much.

Ian waved at me from the far end of the bar. I nodded back and headed his way, barely noticing the women between us. I wasn't interested in any of them. They weren't Melody.

Hudson had a beer in front of the stool before I made it over to Ian. I nodded at him, and he jerked his chin back then served more customers.

"You doing okay?" Ian asked me.

I shook my head. I'd stopped trying to hide how bad things were, but it was still tough to admit I couldn't make my marriage work. Ian and Blake were new and shiny and perfect. Nothing could touch them. He smiled without even realizing he was smiling.

I used to have all that. I used to have someone who loved

me as much as I loved her. Someone I could talk to about anything and everything.

"Have you talked to Melody lately?"

"Not since I walked out Saturday morning," I admitted. Might as well confess all my sins.

"Why were you there on Saturday morning?"

"I was spending time with Amber Friday night, and Melody never came home."

Ian's brow darted up.

I nodded. "That was my thought, too. Nope. She was at Willow's. But I lit into her and accused her of sleeping with someone I knew. She told me off—"

"Good for her."

I shrugged and nodded. "Yep. Then I left."

"You left? What do you mean? You apologized and said bye or…"

"The second one. I snuck out the back like a spineless fucking wimp. I couldn't face her. The pain in her eyes…I keep hurting her. I keep saying and doing things that hurt her. I can't keep hurting her, Ian. I have to distance myself from her."

"Or maybe you should apologize and try again."

I shook my head. "She deserves better."

"Better than someone who loves her?"

I scoffed. "You've been with Blake all of five minutes. I've been married to Melody for ten years."

Ian breathed a laugh. "And who's the one who'll be sleeping alone tonight?"

I growled.

"Listen, I told myself Blake deserved more than me for years. I convinced myself that she should have someone who had more to offer her. I still feel that way. She deserves the world. But I love her. And she loves me. And we're happy together. I'm going to marry her, and we're going to have a family and build a life together. But none of that would be true if I hadn't apologized to her and gotten over myself."

"It's not that simple for Melody and I," I grumbled.

"Is he being whiney again?" Hudson asked, grabbing our glasses and refiling them with ease.

Ian nodded. "Yep. He wants to bitch that he doesn't have Melody, but he's not willing to do what it takes to keep her."

"I lost her," I shouted.

"No, you threw her away," Hudson said pointedly. He focused on me, his dark eyes holding me captive until he decided to speak again. "You couldn't handle having a conversation and acting like an adult. You didn't get your way, so you said fuck it and left. You didn't lose her. She still exists. She's still on this damn earth. And if you were half the man you could be, you wouldn't be sitting here crying into your damn beer about losing her. You'd listen to your friend who's going to get laid tonight and do something to get your family back."

Ian just nodded along with Hudson, but me? I was pissed. Because I knew he was right.

"She doesn't want me. She'd rather have another kid than me," I complained.

"You haven't given her a reason to change her mind about that. Did you talk? Did you tell her why you were scared? Or did you just demand she do what you say then cut and run when she refused?" Hudson asked.

His questions were frighteningly close to their target. Me.

"She wouldn't listen," I said quietly.

"So you blew it up," Ian said. "How many times did you tell me I should have told Blake I was the guy she was matched with on Book Boyfriends Wanted?"

"About a hundred."

Ian nodded. "Exactly. Why do you think things are any different for you?"

I really didn't like it when they were right. It did not make me feel better.

Hudson opened his mouth to say something, but the front door opened. He froze, rooted to his spot. I turned and felt the same paralysis lock me in place.

Melody was standing just inside the door. Her red jacket, the one I helped her pick out, was sliding down her arms. With each inch, a black sweater and jeans were revealed. But it wasn't my wife I was staring at. It was the man behind her, smiling at her, helping her with her coat.

I started to get up and go over to them when two hands grabbed me. I glared at my friends, but they didn't back off.

"You will not do any good going over there," Hudson said harshly. "Trust me."

"He's right," Ian said. "You're the one who asked for a divorce. You can't rush over and act like a jealous husband when you told her you were done."

"I never said I was done."

"No, you just said you wanted a divorce. It's the same damn thing," Hudson said. "You can't expect her to sit around forever. She's going to date, and you are, too. Back off."

I shrugged them off and settled back into my seat. "Fucking hell."

I turned my back on them and tried to pretend they weren't in the same room as me. I couldn't look at her. I didn't want to. If I did, I'd know instantly if she was enjoying herself. Were her eyes sparkling? Was she leaning toward him? Did she touch his arm?

"What's going on at work?" Ian asked.

He was trying to distract me. Nothing would work, but I appreciated the effort. "I have a new client coming in Thursday. He's the new owner of Jones Family Maple Farm."

"Really?" Ian asked. "I thought that place was locked in probate court."

I nodded. "It was, but it's been settled. Good thing, too. It's been too long since I've been there."

"Remember when we first went there on that class trip? What were we? Fourth grade?"

I chuckled. "Yeah, I think so. That was the first moment I hated you."

Ian laughed. "The feeling was mutual."

"I still can't believe you told Mrs. Adams that I was the one who broke the tap."

Ian shrugged. "I wouldn't have broken it if you didn't shove me."

"And I wouldn't have shoved you if you didn't try to kiss the girl I was holding hands with."

We both laughed. Neither of us remembered the name of the girl, but she was the first one we fought over. It only got worse as we got older. The stakes were higher, the women more important to us, and the threats bigger. If I hadn't settled on Melody, I wasn't sure Ian and I could have become friends at all. We stopped fighting over girls because I found her. Really, she found me. She was it for me.

I turned on my stool and searched the bar until I found her. They were at a table, but she was facing me. I didn't recognize the guy she was with, which made me wonder who he was and where she met him.

"I can't believe she's here on a date," I mumbled.

The weight of my situation landed hard on my chest. I fucking hated it. She was my wife, the love of my life, and she was laughing at something another man said. A man who would try to kiss her. A man who would think he could call her. Who would want more with her.

Because what man wouldn't. She was fucking perfect.

Except she wanted another kid, even if it killed her.

"Maybe you should start dating," Ian said quietly.

Hudson just walked up and jerked back when he heard

what Ian said. He spun on his heel and walked to the other end of the bar.

I wished I could get away that easily.

"I don't want anyone else."

Ian nodded. "I get it. But if Melody is moving on, maybe you should think about it. If you're sneaking out of your house and avoiding talking to her, you're not going to fix things."

"Weren't you just telling me to apologize to her."

Ian nodded again. "And I still think you should. But if she's dating, it might be too late."

I pulled out my phone. "What's the name of that app you used? That one Karissa made?"

"Book Boyfriends Wanted. Why?"

I tapped the screen as Ian figured out what I was doing.

"Not a good idea, dude."

"Why not? You just told me I should date."

"Yeah, but—"

"But what? My wife is sitting across the room with another man. My fucking wife, man. She's here with someone else. And she's laughing and talking and flirting. She's not sitting around waiting for me to apologize to her. She's moving on. I should do the same. You just said so."

Ian held my gaze for a long minute then looked away. I ignored his disapproval and signed up for an account. There were a ton of questions to answer, but I sat there and answered them all.

Sometime while I was focused on the app, Ian slapped my back and left. I kept working. I wouldn't have the guts to do it another time. It had to be right then, when my wife was on a date with another man.

I tapped to publish my profile and finally looked up from my phone. Hudson was serving beer. Piper was smiling at a customer at a table. And Melody was gone.

I swallowed the rest of my warm beer and tried not to imagine where Melody was. Or what she was doing. Or how much happier she was without me in her life.

Yeah, I was the one who walked away. I was the one who said we should get divorced. I was the one who was an ass. But I did it all so she would see how much I loved her. So she would see that I'd rather lose her and let her live than sit by and watch her die.

I was debating ordering another beer and some food when someone climbed onto the stool Ian vacated. I turned to see who would sit down next to me and instantly scowled.

"It's so great to see you, soon-to-be-ex brother-in-law," Willow said with a grin.

Willow never liked me. I wasn't sure why, but she didn't. She did everything she could to get under my skin, and everything she could to drive a wedge between Melody and I. There was a part of me that wondered if Melody and I would be having so many problems if Willow wasn't around to stir the pot.

"What do you want, Willow?" I demanded.

She smirked and tossed her red curls behind her shoulder. "I was just going to get a drink."

"And you had to pick the stool next to me to do it?"

She shrugged. "Drinking alone isn't good for you."

I rolled my eyes at her and reached for my wallet. It was better to get the hell out of there before she said something that made me mad than to sit there and wait for it. I had beer at home, and I'd done enough drinking alone to stop caring if it was bad for me.

"Are you leaving? I thought you might want to know how Amber's day was," Willow said with a sad look.

Amber. The bitch knew exactly what she was doing. If she said Amber, she knew I wouldn't leave. I'd sit right back down and listen because it was about my daughter.

It worked, dammit.

"What happened to Amber?"

Willow shook her head. "Nothing. It sounds like she had a pretty good day at school. And we had pancakes for dinner. A friend of hers came over."

"On a school night?" I asked. Melody and I were always clear. No playdates during school. We agreed.

"Well, Melody had a date with the girl's dad, so it worked out better for them if I watched both girls. And Gina was crazy cute. Her dad is, too."

"I don't want to hear this," I said, getting up again.

Willow chuckled. "No, you probably don't. Because my sister is happier without you in her life. She can do the things she wants to do. She can go out with men who aren't going to tell her what she can and can't do. She's going to live her dreams."

"Why don't you stop worrying so much about Melody's dreams and think about your own, Willow? Why do you have to have your nose up her ass all the time? Do you just have that miserable of a life that you have to live vicariously through your sister all the time?" I spat.

For a split second, her walls crumbled and she looked wounded. Then they were right back up and she smirked again. "One of my dreams is to see my sister happy. To watch her with a bunch of kids. To know she's living the life she always dreamed of living. And she's going to do that. The guy she went out with is a really nice guy. His daughter is adorable. And he wants more kids, just like Melody. She said she liked him enough to see him again. So maybe my sister will get all the things she wants. A great husband, a big family, and happiness. All the things she didn't have when she was with you because you're a stubborn ass who's too selfish to see what's right in front of him."

Willow didn't give me a chance to respond. She jumped

down off the stool and stalked off into the crowd. I watched her for a second, then felt her words sinking in.

Melody liked the guy. He wanted more kids.

Which meant leaving her wasn't enough to keep her safe. She was still willing to risk her life. She wasn't interested in other ways to grow a family, which meant she wasn't safe.

Anger and fear stirred inside me. If I let them take over, it wouldn't be good. I had to get out of there.

I tossed some bills on the bar and waved at Hudson. He'd add the difference to my tab if I didn't leave him enough. I yanked my coat on and walked out the back door to where the riverwalk lined the cove.

I never considered living anywhere except MacKellar Cove. The small town I grew up in was always home to me, but more than that, it was where Melody wanted to be. Her family life wasn't the best growing up, but she was determined to change that for Amber.

When she found out she was pregnant with Amber, we were so excited. My practice was up and running and starting to do better. Melody was working as a second grade teacher at MacKellar Cove Elementary. She loved it, but the closer she got to Amber's due date, the less she wanted to go back to teaching after she was born. Melody wanted to stay home with our child instead of taking care of other people's children.

I supported her decision, and we made some sacrifices, but we always made it work because we had each other. We were a team.

When she got pregnant with Steven, neither of us considered the possibility that something was wrong. Losing him was a shock to our system, one we hadn't been able to recover from. Melody was in the hospital for almost a week after we lost Steven, and seeing her like that almost killed me. But bringing her home afterward and seeing her start to disappear was even worse. She stopped being my wife and partner. She was a stranger in my house. We snapped at each other all the time, and we struggled to coexist.

And now, she was moving on. She went on a date with another dad from school. She talked to him and told him about herself. She smiled at him. Maybe she even kissed him.

I hated the idea of letting her go. I hated sitting back and doing nothing while I lost my family for good. I thought for sure she would have come around by now and realized I was right. Instead, she was planning a family with someone else.

What the hell was I going to do?

6

MELODY

J loved hearing Amber laugh. Her giggle when she was happy was the best sound in the entire world. Knowing I did something that made her make that sound always made me feel like I could do anything.

"Did you have fun with Gina last night?" I asked her, hoping to get her thoughts on me dating.

She nodded and made another snowball. "Yeah, it was fun. She said her daddy was going to kiss you, though. We fought about that because I told her the only person you kiss is my daddy, not her daddy."

My smile froze on my face. I avoided looking at her while I tried to think about how to explain to my five year old that her daddy didn't want to kiss me anymore.

"Well, I might kiss her daddy sometime. Would that bother you?"

She scrunched up her face and stared at the snow for a minute. When she met my gaze, her eyes were less happy. "I think that would bother Daddy."

I forced a smile for her. "I will always love your daddy, but he doesn't live here anymore."

"That doesn't mean you should be kissing another daddy," she said. Her voice grew louder. Her body was tense.

"In a way it does, honey. Your daddy didn't want to kiss me anymore. He wanted to live somewhere else instead of with me. So, I might kiss another daddy."

"No! You can't. You have to kiss my daddy, not Gina's. I hate Gina. And I hate her daddy!" She ran into the house and slammed the door.

I sighed and followed her, hating that I was having to deal with Amber's anger alone. I loved my daughter, but divorce was something I never thought she'd have to learn about. Especially not as a five year old.

Her coat was on the floor just inside the door. Her boots were next. Then her scarf and hat and gloves. I picked each item up as I followed the trail to Amber's closed bedroom door. I knocked softly, but she didn't answer.

When I opened the door, she was laying facedown on her bed. I called her name and she turned her head away from me.

"I don't like you," she said.

I remembered thinking the same words many times as a child about my own mother. My mother was cold and distant and almost cruel, and I vowed I would never be like her. I would never give my kids a reason to hate me.

But I did.

"I know, Amber. And I'm sorry. I wish I could change things with your daddy, but I can't. He's the one who left. I love him, and I will always love him."

"He doesn't love you?" she asked, turning to look at me. She scrambled up to sit and crossed her legs.

I shrugged. "I don't know. He said he didn't want to be married to me anymore."

Her lip trembled, and her eyes filled with tears. "Does that mean he's going to stop loving me, too?"

I pulled her onto my lap and kissed the top of her head. "No, baby, no. Of course not. Daddy will always love you. He will always put you first. He's not going anywhere and will always be in your life."

"But he left. You said he didn't want to live here anymore. He didn't want to live with me."

I shook my head. "No, Amber. No. That's not true," I said firmly. "Your daddy would live with you if he could. When he moved out, we agreed the best thing for you would be to stay in your room, in your bed, in your house where you've always lived. He was the one who wanted to leave, and since his work schedule makes it hard for him to take you to school and pick you up, we agreed I would stay in the house with you."

"I want both of you to live here," Amber whined softly.

I nodded and pulled her into my arms again. "I know, baby. Me, too."

We sat on her bed for a few more minutes, just holding on to each other. I glanced at her clock and knew I needed to start dinner. I offered her a trade.

"What if I start dinner while you call Daddy? Tell him about your day and let him know you're thinking about him."

She pulled back and nodded, a smile finally back on her face.

Amber settled on the couch with my phone while it rang. Once she grinned and said, "Daddy," I went to the kitchen to start dinner.

One of Amber's favorite meals was tacos with mac and cheese, so I put water on to boil and some ground beef in a pan to brown. I got out the rest of the ingredients and was stirring the ground beef when the doorbell rang.

Amber was still talking to Ramsey when I walked by to see who was at the door. I smiled when I saw my sister through the peephole. "Hey," I said when I opened the door. "I didn't know you were coming over."

She shrugged and stepped inside, closing the door behind herself. "I wanted to see how you were doing and check in on my favorite niece."

"She's talking to Ramsey. We had a little issue earlier."

"Issue?" Willow asked.

I nodded and jerked my head to the kitchen. Willow got the hint and hung up her coat, then followed me out of the room.

"I asked her if she had fun with Gina the other day. I was trying to get a feel for her thoughts about me dating."

"And?"

I shrugged and added the pasta to the boiling water, then stirred the meat and added in taco seasoning. I was avoiding the question, and we both knew it. But Willow was patient.

"She said Gina told her I was going to kiss her daddy, and Amber was mad because I was only supposed to be kissing Ramsey."

Willow shook her head. "I knew they argued about something, but neither of them would tell me what it was. What did you tell her?"

I sighed. "The truth. That Ramsey doesn't want to be married to me and that I might kiss other daddies because hers doesn't want to kiss me."

Willow grinned. "How well did that go over?"

"She asked if Ramsey is going to stop loving her, too."

Willow's face fell. "Poor thing. This is a lot for her to handle."

I nodded. "It is. And I hate it. I always said growing up that I didn't want my kids to have to deal with the stuff we dealt with. The crappy parenting and not being able to be emotional."

"And she's not," Willow argued.

"No, but she doesn't have the childhood I hoped she would have either. Her parents are getting divorced."

"When we were kids, we were so afraid we'd end up like Mom and Dad. People who couldn't say anything. You wanted a big family that would be wild and love each other fiercely and always be there for each other."

"So much for that dream," I said bitterly.

Willow nodded. "That's why you let Ramsey go. Because he wasn't interested in supporting your dream. He wasn't willing to try again."

"He was worried about me," I said.

"He was a chicken shit. He couldn't handle it. Every pregnancy has risks. Every day has risks. He used it as an excuse to get what he wanted."

"But—"

"No, Mel. You and I both know that's what happened. I know you love him, but he's never been right for you. Now you have a chance to find someone who is. Someone who wants the same things you do."

I nodded, knowing she was right but not liking it. She was never team Ramsey, but she knew how much I loved him. She was the first person I told when I realized I loved him. Even though she was five years younger than me, Willow was always the person I talked to. About everything.

"I don't want Amber to be hurt by all this," I admitted.

Willow offered me a kind smile that said I wasn't going to get what I wanted. Not this time. "She's going to get hurt, Mel. Her parents are splitting up. Her world is changing. When he left, it was hard. When she realizes he's not ever coming back and someone else will be sharing your bed, it'll be even harder. But she'll get through it. Kids survive."

I nodded and hoped Willow was right. She usually was, which was why I listened to her. She knew me better than anyone else in the world, and she adored Amber like an aunt should. We were lucky to have her.

"Aunt Willow!" Amber yelled, rushing into the kitchen. Willow scooped her up and spun her around, both of them laughing.

"How is my princess today?" Willow asked.

"Good. Mommy and I played in the snow when we got home. And Daddy said he's always going to love me and Mommy, so Mommy doesn't have to kiss Gina's daddy again."

Willow's eyebrows darted up. She glanced at me.

"Amber, honey, that's not really the truth," I said.

Amber turned to me, her forehead wrinkled in the middle. "But Daddy said he loves you. And he said he loves me."

I nodded and crouched down in front of her. "Yes, honey. And I love Daddy and you. But Daddy and I aren't going to be married anymore."

Her lip trembled and tears filled her eyes again. "But Daddy loves you. Why won't you stay married to him?"

My breath caught in my throat. I wish I had a good answer for her. One that would make sense to her five year old mind. "Sometimes people who love each other aren't actually supposed to be together. Sometimes someone gets sick or dies or—"

"Is Daddy going to die?" she screeched.

"What? No. Amber, no, honey, Daddy is fine."

"Then you are?" she shouted, her eyes wild with fear.

"No, Amber. No one is going to die. No one is sick. It's—"

"Then why can't you and Daddy stay married?"

I sighed. "Because Daddy and I want different things."

"Like when I want mac and cheese for dinner but you tell me I have to eat chicken instead?" she asked.

Willow coughed to cover up a laugh, but I just nodded solemnly. "Exactly like that."

"But you always make me do what you want. Why don't you just do that with Daddy? Make him do what you want so you can stay married and you don't have to kiss Gina's daddy."

I wanted to laugh but it was really just too sad for me to find the humor. I was breaking my daughter's heart. Shredding her childhood. She wanted her parents together. I did, too, but neither of us were going to get what we wanted. And I was sick of feeling like nothing I did mattered.

I flashed Willow a look, and she grinned then scooped up Amber. "Why don't you show me what book you and Mommy are reading right now?"

Willow carried Amber out of the room. Amber chatted constantly about Charlotte's Web and what part of the book we were on. She told Willow the whole story, her voice drifting as they walked down the hall and away from me.

When I couldn't hear them anymore, I finally breathed a sigh of relief. I wanted to throttle my husband. He was the one who asked for the divorce. He was the one who refused to talk about more kids. He was the one who left. And I got to break our daughter's heart and try to explain why over and over again.

It sucked.

I finished dinner while Amber and Willow were gone. When they came back, I had three plates of food on the table and water in three cups.

"Ooh, am I staying for dinner?" Willow asked Amber.

Amber nodded excitedly. "Yeah, yeah. Will you, Aunt Willow?"

Willow grinned. "Of course, princess. Which seat should I sit in?"

"That one," Amber said, pointing to one of the seats. Amber chose hers, then I sat at the last one.

Willow and Amber talked about books and school and everything except Ramsey and me until we finished dinner. I stayed silent, preferring to let joy reign instead of fear and sadness. Amber asked Willow to stay and read to her, so I let Willow give Amber her bath and said goodnight before Willow read to Amber and tucked her in.

I was sitting on the couch when Willow left Amber's room. "Is she out?"

Willow nodded. "Like a light. She barely lasted half the chapter."

"Thank you," I told her.

She sank onto the couch next to me and nodded. "I'm sorry she's not taking this well. She deserves more than this."

"I"m doing my best," I said softly, hating that even my sister, my best friend, thought I wasn't pulling my weight as a mom.

She shook her head. "I mean from her father. Ramsey shouldn't leave all this for you to figure out. He should be explaining himself. He's such an ass."

"Why do you hate him?" I asked her. I'd always known my sister didn't like him, but I never knew why. And I'd never had the guts to ask her.

At my direct question, she froze. "You know I've never liked him."

I nodded. "I do know that. What I don't know is why."

"He's not right for you," Willow said, avoiding my gaze.

"Why does that mean you should hate him? Not liking him, maybe, but hating him?"

She shrugged. "I love you. You're the one I worry about. He doesn't deserve you." She stood and glanced at the door. "Do you need help cleaning up the kitchen?"

I shook my head and stood with her. "I took care of it while you were reading to Amber."

"Okay, then I should probably go."

"You don't have to," I said. I wished I could take back my question. Willow hated Ramsey because she knew he wasn't right for me. I didn't need to know more than that. Maybe there really wasn't more than that.

"No, I need to go. I have some stuff to do tonight. I'll see you in a couple days."

She hugged me and waved as she walked out the door into the cold night. I stood in the middle of the living room wondering why everyone I loved seemed to want to be anywhere but with me.

BEFORE I WENT TO BED, I checked my phone to see if Willow texted me. She usually did after she walked home from being at my house. And she usually did before she went to sleep.

I sent her a quick text saying good night and waited. Nothing popped up immediately, so I opened Book Boyfriends Wanted to see if I had any new matches. Maybe seeing someone who wasn't the dad of Amber's classmate was a better idea.

There were a few guys that matched with me. I read through their profiles quickly, swiping right on each of them. Dating was a numbers game, according to Willow. If I dated a bunch of men, I was more likely to find my new The One.

I hadn't closed the app yet when a message popped up from one of my new matches.

RH214

Hey WebMommy. How are you?

Really? That was his opening line? He sounded like he

had as much experience dating in the last decade or two as I did. But he reached out, so I had to answer.

WEBMOMMY

Hi. Good. How are you?

Wow, yeah, I was so good at this.

RH214

I'm good, thanks. I see you're a mom. Aren't kids awesome?

I clicked back to his profile. He had a daughter, worked in a professional field, and was divorced. His profile picture was a spider, which was funny since mine was a web.

I went back to the chat and replied.

WEBMOMMY

Most of the time. My daughter got upset tonight when I tried to explain why her daddy and I aren't getting back together.

RH214

Mine had a meltdown tonight, too. That's the hardest part. When you want to take their pain away and can't.

WEBMOMMY

I agree. My daughter doesn't understand that two people can love each other and still not want to be together. Of course, I'm not sure I understand it at times either.

RH214

How long have you been divorced?

There was no option for separated, so my profile said divorced. I didn't like lying, so I admitted the truth.

WEBMOMMY

I'm actually not. We've been separated since last summer. But putting married didn't feel right either.

RH214

Same. Sorry. It sucks. I thought I was going to be with her forever.

WEBMOMMY

Agree.

RH214

Can I ask why your name is WebMommy?

I laughed.

WEBMOMMY

My daughter's favorite book is Charlotte's Web. We read it every night before she goes to sleep. It was the only thing I could think of.

RH214

Uh. That's a weird coincidence. Mine does the same.

No. There was no damn way. It couldn't be. No.

RH214

Is this Melody?

"No! Are you kidding me? What the hell?" I groaned.

WEBMOMMY

Ramsey?

RH214

Wow. Well, I guess we do have a lot in common. It would make sense we'd be paired together.

I closed the app without waiting for his reply and ignored it when one popped up. What were the freaking odds?

I opened messages and looked at the text I sent Willow. It was still unread. Which meant she wasn't talking to me. I almost texted her about being paired with Ramsey, but he was the reason Willow left earlier.

I locked my phone and decided the best thing for me was sleep. Everything was always better after a good night's sleep.

7

RAMSEY

J was still reeling the next morning as I sat in my office and tried to think of anything other than Melody. What were the chances Melody and I were paired together on that app? Apparently good, but damn, it was not what I was expecting.

I told myself I was going to reach out to one of the women I matched with and strike up a conversation. I needed to move on. And the one woman I chose, the one whose profile was the most interesting to me, was my freaking wife.

The shittiest part of it was I was enjoying talking to her before I figured out who she was. I felt good, proud of myself for putting myself out there. And then she said they always read Charlotte's Web and it all clicked.

WTF?

It just wasn't fair that the only woman I wanted to reach out to was my wife. And she was definitely not interested.

I seriously considered deleting the app, but I couldn't bring myself to do it. I stared at the conversation again, imagining Melody's smile when she flirted back with me, then her shock when she realized who I was. I had to hold on to the smile.

A knock on my door had me shoving my phone in my pocket before I called out for my new client to come in. I stood and walked around my desk as he opened the door.

Colin Jones pressed his lips into a grin and glanced around the room before he walked the rest of the way inside. I noted his worn work boots paired with his neat and clean suit. The navy jacket and the black pants didn't really match, and the gray shirt underneath looked like it was a tee shirt.

I was wearing one of my best suits. Gray with a navy dress shirt with black shoes and a red tie. It was one of my power suits because I felt good in it, and after flirting with Melody, I needed the extra armor. Except it didn't feel like armor when Colin Jones scanned it.

"You're my grandmother's attorney?" he asked me, his face showing clear surprise.

I nodded and offered him my hand. He stared at it for a long moment before he reached out and shook my hand. "Ramsey Holland. It's nice to meet you, Mr. Jones."

He breathed a laugh and shook his head. His dark hair was cut short and didn't shift with the movement. He was ready to bolt for the door if his dark brown eyes were any indication. He was not impressed with me.

"Why don't we sit and talk, Mr. Jones?" I offered, taking a step back.

He glanced at my chair and looked around the room again. I tried to see my office from his perspective. It wasn't huge, but I did my best to make it impressive. Bookshelves held a combination of textbooks and awards I'd received plus a few decorative items. The walls boasted my degrees. The guest chairs were comfortable, and my desk was impressive. But Mr. Jones clearly didn't see the same things.

"I don't think this is going to work," he said carefully.

"I worked with your grandmother for years. Can I ask why you're not willing to sit and talk to me?"

He looked at me and sighed. "Listen, I'm not a corporate kind of guy. I work outside, and I like it. I picked out the nicest clothes in my closet, and I still look like a bum next to you. I need someone who's a little more real. Someone who'll understand what it's like to struggle a bit."

He turned to walk away and I knew I had to say something. "I'm going through a divorce," I blurted.

He paused and looked back at me over his shoulder. When he saw I wasn't joking, he turned around and crossed his arms over his chest. "And?"

"I'm living in my friend's old apartment because I moved out of the house I shared with my wife and daughter. I don't know how to cook for myself so I eat out almost every night. I finally signed up for online dating and the first woman I reached out to was my actual wife."

A laugh burst out of him. He tried to cover it quickly, but it was already in the open.

I grinned. "I'm not a corporate guy either. I own this firm because I always wanted to help people. If someone wants to have their own business, I want to help them make that happen. Some of my clients prefer a guy who looks like he has his shit together, but none of them know I'm not living with my wife. And I sure as shit am not going to tell them I met her on a dating site six months after I walked out on her."

Colin drew a deep breath and shook his head. "I think you might be just as screwed up as me."

I grinned. "I might have you beat. Why don't you sit down and we can talk a little more about what's going on with the farm?"

Colin finally closed the door behind him and nodded. He sat in one of the guest chairs, and I went back behind my desk. I grabbed the folder I had prepared for him and handed the letter inside over.

"What's this?" he asked.

"Your grandmother left it with me. She wanted you to have it when you decided to take over."

He looked at me carefully, then turned over the sealed letter. I hadn't read it yet, so I didn't know what it said. I waited as Colin opened it and read the page.

"Is this for real?" he asked.

I shook my head. "What do you mean?"

"It says there are two of us who could inherit the property."

"What?" I blurted, grabbing for the letter. I pulled my hand back. "May I see it?"

"You haven't read it?"

I shook my head. "No. She asked me to give this to her grandson when he came here for help, but she didn't say anything about there being two of you."

"I don't have any cousins," Colin said slowly.

I read through the letter quickly. Cleotha didn't name any names, just said she hoped they were good to each other.

"You don't have any cousins?" I repeated, finally realizing what he said.

Colin shook his head. "No. Do you think she was crazy?"

I chuckled. "Not in the least. Cleotha Jones was all there. There must be some explanation. She was your father's mother, right?"

Colin nodded. "Yes. And he didn't have any siblings."

"And neither do you?"

Colin shook his head again. "No. That's why I don't know what she's talking about."

I folded up the paper and set it on top of my keyboard. "I'll dig into this when we're done. For now, let's talk about what you need to do for the business."

"Are you sure I can? If there's someone else, won't that person have a say in things?"

I drew in a breath. "It's possible. But if he doesn't want to be involved, then he won't be. If he does, the two of you will have to work out the details, but you need to get things moving in the right direction. You're within your legal rights to do so."

Colin breathed a relieved sigh and nodded. "If you're sure, then that's what I need to do. Spring will be here before I know it, and I have a lot of work to take care of if we're going to get maple out of these trees when they start to thaw."

"You're going to make a lot of people in this area very happy."

Colin laughed. "As long as I don't screw it all up."

I smiled at him. "You won't. Now, let's make a plan."

WHEN COLIN LEFT MY OFFICE, I pulled up everything I had about his grandmother and her family. Since it wasn't much, it didn't take long for me to realize I had no idea who the other grandson was.

Could it have been wrong? I didn't think so. Cleotha was very clear in her letter that there were two of them. She never named names, even Colin's. Finding him was simple, but there was no trace of this other grandson.

I walked out of my office and went to find Penny. She'd been my assistant for years and was the best person I knew when it came to digging up information. She was in the storage room, sorting files.

"Does Cleotha Jones have a second grandson?" I asked her when she turned and saw me standing in the doorway.

Penny shrugged. "Not that I'm aware of. Why?"

I shook my head and handed her the letter. "This letter says there are two of them."

"Wouldn't Mr. Jones know if he had a cousin?" she asked with a laugh.

I shook my head again. "He said his father was an only child and so is he. He doesn't know of any cousins."

"Ooh, a mystery. Want me to dig into it?"

I nodded. "Yes, please. If anyone can find answers to this, it's definitely you."

She grinned. "Thanks, boss. Hey, how are things with Melody?"

I groaned. Penny wasn't just my assistant, she'd become a friend. She was a little younger than Melody and me, but she was married to her high school sweetheart and had a daughter a little younger than Amber. When Melody and I separated, Penny was almost as upset as I was.

"Not great. I keep screwing up with her."

"What did you do now?"

I laughed. "I got paired with her on a dating app."

"What?" Penny asked, half-laughing.

"I signed up for this online dating app the other day after she went on a date with someone. I was pissed and decided I wanted to move on, so I signed up."

"Even though you still love your wife and don't really want to move on."

I grinned sheepishly. She knew me too well. "Yeah, well, she doesn't want me back."

"But you were paired together, so she had to accept you, right? Isn't that how it works?"

I nodded. "Yeah, but she didn't know it was me. The app doesn't use our pictures. We were talking, and it was…nice. But I figured out who she was and asked her. I don't think she was happy about it."

"She was probably just shocked. Maybe that's a way for you to talk to her. Flirt with her."

"I can't flirt with her."

"Why not? She's your wife still. And you love her."

"Which is exactly why. I don't want her to think I'm…"

"You're what?"

"I don't know," I sighed. "I just…I want my family back. I want her to stop dating other men and planning more kids with them. I want her to want me back."

"Maybe she does, but you are so stuck on her not getting pregnant that you won't listen to everything else."

"I don't even know what that means."

"Have you ever asked her why she's willing to risk her life to have another baby?"

I thought about it for a second, then shook my head. "She just said she always dreamed of a big family."

"Okay, but why?"

"Because her own family wasn't great."

"Lots of people have crappy childhoods. That doesn't mean they have to have big families. There's something else."

"Like what?"

Penny shrugged. "Only Melody knows that answer." Penny patted me on the shoulder and smiled. "You need to talk to your wife. I'll find the missing grandson."

Penny walked out of the room, and I just stood there. There's something else. Another reason Melody wants more kids. Why is she willing to risk her life?

I had nothing. But I needed to understand, so I was going to have to ask the tough questions.

IT WASN'T my night with Amber, so I went home after work.

No, not home. To Ian's apartment. I appreciated him letting me stay there, but I hated every second of being there.

The shop was quiet when I walked in, which wasn't unusual. Ian worked shorter hours through the winter since most people didn't think about their boats until the weather turned nicer and it was an option to get out and enjoy the water.

I was almost to the apartment before I heard any noises. It was quiet, like I could have easily been dreaming, but I was fairly sure there was someone there.

"Hello?" I called out. The space was large and open, but there were still plenty of places to hide.

"Shh," was the almost immediate answer.

"Who's here?" I demanded, not willing to let someone hide out or sneak up on me. I pulled out my phone and unlocked it. "I'm calling the police."

"Relax, Ramsey," Ian said from somewhere in the darkness. "It's just us."

"You gave me damn heart attack," I breathed. My heart throbbed in my chest.

Ian stepped into the light and straightened his shirt. Blake was right behind him trying to smooth her hair down.

"Sorry," Ian said. "Blake came to see me and we got a little carried away."

"Ian!" Blake admonished him.

Ian snickered and shrugged. "Do you really think Ramsey cares?"

Blake gave me an embarrassed grin and her cheeks turned red. "It's not a very polite thing to do."

I shook my head. "It's fine. You guys should be happy. After all the years I heard this guy whining about you being with someone else, I'm happy things are going well."

Blake put her head on Ian's shoulder and looked up at him. Melody used to do the same thing to me, and it made me feel like the luckiest man in the world. She was every-thing I ever wanted or needed, but she wasn't looking at me like that anymore.

"Things are going really well," Ian said. "In fact, we're getting married."

"What? No way. That's awesome. Congratulations," I said, fighting back the gnawing despair in my gut. I was happy for them, and my own failed marriage wasn't their fault.

"Thanks," Ian said happily.

Blake smiled, like she could see the pain I was trying to hard to hide.

"How's Melody?" Blake asked instead.

I forced a smile. "Doing well, I think. She's dating."

"Yeah, Ian told me. Are you okay with that?"

I huffed a laugh and shook my head. "No, not really. My wife is seeing other men and trying to find someone new who'll get her pregnant. I'm not okay with that at all."

"Have you talked to her about it?" Blake asked. She looked up at me with her brown eyes. Hope. That was the emotion in them. A woman at the beginning of a relationship. Someone who hadn't been destroyed by the person she loved. A woman who still believed love could last forever.

I lost that sometime in the last few years.

I drew a breath and shook my head. "I said something to her last weekend and it didn't go well. I was an ass, and she called me on it. She's moving on, and the best thing for me to do is to let her. I will always love her, but I'm not any good for her."

"I don't think that's true," Blake said with a tentative grin. "I think Melody still loves you. I think she'd be happier with you."

"As long as I'm willing to get her pregnant and kill her."

"What?" Blake breathed.

I shook my head. "Her doctor said if she got pregnant

again, she could die. She's not willing to listen and keeps insisting she wants more kids. It's the whole reason I left. I can't sit back and watch it happen."

"Wow," Blake breathed. "I had no idea. I'm so sorry."

I shrugged. "It is what it is. She's going to do what she wants to do."

"I really think—"

"I think we should let Ramsey relax for a little while, honey," Ian said carefully.

"Oh, right. Sorry. I seem to want to fix other people's relationships lately. I'm sorry, Ramsey," Blake said.

I nodded.

She walked over and hugged me, then released me and walked out with Ian.

When the door closed behind them, I headed into the apartment and set my stuff on the table. All my clothes were in the bedroom, but it still didn't feel like my home. I did not want to be there, but going to O'Kelley's again made me feel like a complete loser. I couldn't spend every night in the bar. Which meant I needed to find something to eat and something to do.

I ordered food and flipped through channels to find something to watch. I stopped on Melody's favorite movie, The Notebook. I couldn't help but imagine her sitting there with me as I reached for my phone to tell her it was on.

Instead of sending a text, I opened Book Boyfriends Wanted. I smiled when I read our exchange from the night before, then sent her a new message.

RH214

The Notebook is on TV right now. Thinking of you. Thought you might want to watch.

I didn't expect a reply, but one came through almost immediately.

WEBMOMMY

Thanks. Almost have Amber in bed. I need to relax and forget life for a little while tonight.

RH214

Everything okay?

She didn't text right back and I assumed it was because she was putting Amber to bed. I waited, hoping she would reply, while I watched the movie.

The bell rang and I went to get my food, then headed back to finish watching the movie. There was a message waiting.

WEBMOMMY

Amber is struggling with all this. The guy I went out with the other night was nice, but the daughter seems to think it was serious. I get the feeling he didn't tell her about his other dates so she thinks ours was a big deal. It's been really bothering Amber the last couple days.

RH214

Want me to talk to her again?

WEBMOMMY

Thanks, but no. That only confuses her more. She got off the phone with you convinced we were getting back together, and I had to tell her that wasn't what you wanted. She was really upset with me. Willow had to calm her down.

RH214

I didn't mean to cause problems. Are you sure you don't want me to talk to her?

I waited for her to reply and knew I had to say something else.

I had a message typed out and ready to send, but she beat me to it.

WEBMOMMY

I'm sure. Thanks for letting me know about the movie. I'm going to watch and get some sleep. See you Friday.

She signed off before I could reply. Before I could tell her she was wrong. Before I could say getting our family back together was the only thing I wanted.

8

By the time I got to the house Friday night, I'd decided to talk to Amber again, even though Melody said I didn't need to. Melody didn't have to be the only one who dealt with Amber's confusion over our situation.

I got to the house and rang the bell. I still had keys in my pocket, but I didn't feel right using them when it wasn't really my house anymore. I paid the bills, but I didn't get to walk in like I lived there, so I didn't.

Amber opened the door with a huge smile on her face. Melody was right behind her, making sure it was safe, with a matching grin. Except Melody's grin was only for Amber.

"Daddy!" Amber shouted as she jumped at me.

I caught her and lifted her into my arms, pressing my nose to her hair. The same strawberry scent as usual filled me, making me feel like I was home. Amber always loved the strawberry scented shampoo, and it was nice to know some things hadn't changed.

"Hey, smart girl. How are you?"

"I'm great because you're here now. We can all have dinner together."

I glanced at Melody. She was watching Amber with a sad smile, and when Amber mentioned dinner, she met my gaze. I raised an eyebrow, and she nodded.

"Well, dinner together sounds pretty awesome. Did you help Mommy cook?"

Amber nodded. "I did. I stayed out of the kitchen so Mommy could focus."

I fought a grin as Melody shook her head and smiled, telling me Amber's answer was dead-on. "Well, that was very helpful, I'm sure."

"It was, Daddy. Mommy said so."

"Well, good. Are we ready to eat now?" I looked at Melody for an answer to that one.

"Yeah, everything is done. I wasn't sure exactly when you were going to be here."

It was one of the things we argued about before I left. My hours. What I never admitted to Melody was I was afraid to come home most days toward the end. I didn't know how to help her, and I never said the right thing, so I started working later and later to avoid fighting with her.

She accused me of having an affair once. She thought my late nights were spent in bed with another woman. It hurt that she thought I could even look at someone else when the woman I loved was still alive, but it didn't change the fact that I wasn't being fair to her. I left her with Amber even longer hours, and I wasn't pulling my weight as her husband and rock to lean on.

"I should have called," I told her instead of saying any of the things going through my mind.

She smiled, but it didn't reach her eyes. I was trying to remember the last time I made her smile and all of her lit up. It had been a while.

"Carry me, Daddy," Amber said, breaking whatever tension held Melody and I together.

I turned to her and smiled again, then followed Melody into the kitchen. We sat at the table that was too big for our little family of three and Amber told me all about her week.

Melody bustled around the kitchen, her curvy body hidden by the loose tee and sweatpants she wore. I tried to stay focused on Amber, but knowing Melody wasn't running away from me was drawing my attention. Those were her casual clothes, her hang out at home clothes, and if she was wearing them, it meant she wasn't going to run as soon as dinner was over.

"Daaaaddddy," Amber whined.

I dragged my attention from Melody and smiled at Amber. "Yes, sweetheart."

"You're not listening to me."

"I'm sorry. Tell me again."

"I said I have to make a mailbox for Valentine's Day. Mommy said we can all make it together. Can we do it tonight?"

I looked at Melody for approval, but she hid her eyes from me. "Um, we'll see."

"Are you leaving after dinner?"

Again, I looked at Melody. "I wasn't planning to…"

"I'm going to meet Aunt Willow," Melody said. "I told you that, honey. That's why we can't do it tonight. But we'll find a day."

"You are?" I blurted.

Melody looked at me. A flash of the pain I caused the last time she met Willow lit her gaze then vanished as defiance stepped in and dared me to say something about it.

I forced a smile I didn't feel. My wife was going out again. To meet men and flirt and who knows what else. Willow would only help her do all of it. Maybe even encourage more than flirting.

I wanted to demand she stay home and help Amber and me with her Valentine's Day project. I wanted to tell her until we were divorced, she wasn't allowed to touch another man. I wanted to throw her over my shoulder and carry her to the bed we shared for a decade and show her what she was missing without me.

All I did was smile and keep eating my dinner.

Amber did the rest of the talking for us. When we finished dinner, Melody disappeared into the bedroom with the door closed.

Amber showed me what she learned in dance class that week. I tried to pay attention to her, but half my focus was on Melody and what she was doing behind the closed door. When I lived there, we never closed the door unless we were getting naked together. It was just one more change, one more reminder that I didn't belong there.

When the door opened again, Amber barely had a quarter of my focus. I smelled Melody before she walked into the room, her light flowery scent meeting my nose. I turned to look at her and every fiber of my being rose up and wanted to demand she change. Her jeans hugged her curves in a way that made my mouth water. Her top was loose but low-cut. When she bent over to put on her boots, images of bending her over the couch and the table and the bed and even my desk assaulted me.

A tiny sliver of skin was visible as her top slid up her back while she zippered her boots. I couldn't remember the last time I touched her or kissed her. She hadn't been mine in so long that I was starting to forget the way she smelled and how soft her skin was. I never thought about those things before, but I missed them now. I missed everything there was to know about my wife.

And it fucking killed me.

I wasn't strong enough to walk away from her. I wasn't man enough to tell her to move on. I still loved her and I wanted her and letting her walk out the door was not an option.

"Why don't you stay here and hang out with us?" I suggested when Melody stood and reached for her coat.

She didn't look at me. "I told Willow I was about to leave. But I'll be home tonight."

She delivered the last line with a glare that was almost as painful as the slap she delivered the last time.

I nodded and decided not to push. Pushing her to talk, pushing her to give up her dream of a big family, pushing her to be present…that's what led to me leaving. I could only push so much.

Melody said good night to Amber and gave her a hug and kiss, then waved to me and disappeared into the night. I sat still for a long time, staring at the door and willing her to walk back in.

Amber called my name a few times before I acknowledged her. When I finally did, she asked, "Why doesn't Mommy stay here with us?"

I smiled. "Mommy needs some time to visit with Aunt Willow. They're just having some fun. What do you say we do something for Mommy? Something that will show her how much we missed her being here with us."

Amber's eyes lit up. "Yeah! Mommy will love that."

"What should we do? We can clean up the house so Mommy doesn't have to."

Amber wrinkled her nose. "That's no fun. We should make her something."

"Like what?"

Amber tapped her finger on her chin for a minute, then her eyes widened and she looked up at me with a huge smile.

"We should make Mommy a Valentine! She said she always loved Valentine's Day. It used to be one of her favorite days. We should give her a Valentine so she loves it again."

Leave it to kids to say the most honest thing that completely rips you to shreds. Valentine's Day was our day. A day we celebrated each other. I was burying my head in the sand, ignoring the fact that the day was coming, and coming fast. I wasn't sure I could take it knowing I wouldn't be spending it with Melody, but Amber was right. It wasn't about me. It was about Mel.

"I think that's a great idea," I told Amber.

"Yay! I'll go get all the supplies."

She took off toward the art supplies in the corner of the living room. Melody always wanted Amber to feel free to express herself in whatever way she felt was right, so she kept art supplies and books and plenty of paper and pencils nearby at all times. She also made sure the living room furniture wasn't too close together so Amber had space to dance if that was the mood that struck.

Amber struggled to lift the box, so I hurried over and grabbed it from her. "How about we set things up at the table? That way we can spread it all out and see what we want to use."

Amber nodded. "I have so many ideas for Mommy. She's going to love it."

I grinned and followed her to the table. She climbed up onto a chair and sat on her knees while I unpacked the box. Markers, crayons, and colored pencils were each in individual bins. Sheets of paper filled the bottom of the box. Spilled glitter coated most of the sheets of paper. There was glue, small bags of glitter, stickers, fancy tape, and stamps tossed into the box. We could do a hundred things for Melody and never make a dent in the supplies in that box.

"What do you want to do first?" I asked Amber.

"A card. Mommy should have a card that says we love her."

"Sounds good. Pink?"

Amber shook her head. "Mommy likes the darker pink color."

I dug through until I found the right shade and pulled that one out. The corner had glitter on it, but half of it fell onto the table when Amber tried to fold the paper in half. Two of the corners were close, but the other two were off by over an inch. Her bottom lip wavered.

"I didn't do it right."

"How about I give it a try while you decide what you want to put on the card?"

She handed it over and grabbed stickers and markers while I folded the sheet in half. When I set it back in front of her, she stuck her tongue out and started drawing hearts on the page.

I watched her for a few minutes as she covered the front with hearts. She added a few stickers, then opened the paper up and wrote *Love, Amber* on the inside.

"Are you going to sign it, too?" she asked me, turning to look up at me with her brown eyes.

I nodded and gave her a smile. "I will. If that's okay with you."

She nodded and tossed the marker on the table. It rolled toward me, and I grabbed it before it rolled off the edge and landed on me. I signed my name and handed the marker back to Amber. She happily continued while I sat there and wondered if that was the last Valentine I'd ever give Melody.

My throat tightened with the thought and I told Amber I'd be right back. I walked down the hallway to the bathroom and stopped myself from going into my former bedroom.

When I walked out, I honestly believed Melody would stop me. I thought she'd never let me leave. When she did, I sat in the driveway, waiting for her to run out and tell me she was wrong. When that didn't happen, I drove straight to Ian's and told myself she just needed some time to think it through and I'd be back in a day or two.

It had been six months. Six months of wondering what I was missing. Of wanting to be there. Of hating myself for walking away.

I wasn't willing to give in and try for another baby. I couldn't. Losing Steven was the worst thing I'd ever been through in my life, but almost losing Melody was worse. Knowing if she got pregnant again the same thing was likely to happen told me pregnancy wasn't an option. She couldn't have more kids, not if she wanted to be around for them. Because if the pregnancy didn't kill her, it was highly likely she wouldn't carry to term. And if she lost another baby, I knew she wouldn't come back.

And if I lost her, I'd never forgive myself.

I tried to talk to her about adoption or fostering, but she wasn't interested in either. She said she wanted to be pregnant again. She wasn't interested in hearing about the risks. She just wanted to be pregnant.

I washed my hands and pulled out my phone. I was an asshole, but I couldn't stop myself from sending Hudson a text asking him to make sure Melody didn't leave with another man. Or do anything with another man.

Hudson understood. His wife was gone, and she was never coming back. He knew what loss felt like. And thankfully, he was the kind of friend who was okay with helping me suffer through my misery.

"No men," he texted back. "She's sitting at the bar and I'm glaring at any who get too close."

"You're a damn good friend," I replied.

He answered with a thumb's up.

I tucked my phone away and went back to the kitchen

where Amber had made a massive mess. "Whoa. What happened in here?"

Amber looked around like it was no big deal and shrugged.

"All right, little girl. Now we definitely need to clean up for Mommy."

"After I finish this one."

I nodded and started collecting items and storing them back in the box. As she worked, I got out the broom and the vacuum, knowing Amber wasn't going to be much help with either.

She finally finished her overly glittered masterpiece and picked it up to show me. The glue was still wet, so some of her pieces started to slide.

"Put it down, honey. Let's let that glue dry," I told her.

"But then Mommy will see it. I have to put it in my closet so she won't see it," Amber said.

"How about I take it with me? That way we can keep it a secret until Valentine's Day."

Amber nodded. "Good idea, Daddy. You can give it to her when you and Mommy go on your date."

"Um, what date?"

"The one you always go on for Valentine's Day. Aunt Willow always watches me."

"How do you know that?" I asked her. We never made a big deal out of what day it was when Melody and I went away, but obviously Amber put two and two together anyway.

"It's always when we have our Valentine's party at school. That's why I know Mommy would like the hearts. She told me hearts mean you love someone."

I nodded. "They do mean that. And I'm not sure Mommy and I are going on our date this year."

"Why not?" Amber asked. She tilted her head and yawned.

Her red hair swung gently, her bouncy curls brushing over her shoulders.

"Well, because Mommy and I aren't together right now."

"I know," Amber said. "But Mommy will be home later and you'll be together then."

"That's not what I meant."

Between her eyebrows wrinkled with confusion. "Then what did you mean?"

"I mean Mommy and I aren't going to be married for much longer. And—"

"But you said you still love Mommy," Amber said. "If you love her, why don't you want to be married to her?"

"I do want to be married to her, but things are complicated when you're an adult. Not everything is as simple as yes or no."

"I don't think I want to become an adult," Amber said matter-of-factly. "I think I'm just going to stay a kid forever."

I chuckled. "I wish I had that option. Being an adult isn't always fun."

"And you don't get to do the things you want like stay married to Mommy. Does Mommy not want to be married to you?"

I shook my head. "None of this is Mommy's fault. We just disagreed, and we can't figure out how to agree again."

"So, if I disagree with you or Mommy, will you not want to be my parents anymore?"

I smiled and reached for her, pulling her onto my lap. I kissed her hair and breathed in her strawberry scent. "No, honey. That's never going to happen. I still want to be married to Mommy. And I'm always going to want to be your daddy. And Mommy is always going to want to be your mommy. We both love you, and I will always love Mommy."

Amber drew in a breath and yawned again. "Okay, Daddy."

We sat there for a few minutes before she fell asleep in my arms. I picked her up and carried her to her room. I tucked her in and turned on her nightlight, then closed the door and headed back to the kitchen.

I cleaned up the art supplies, then picked up the kitchen. I didn't step foot in her room, but I made sure the rest of the house was as perfect as possible. And when it was almost midnight and Melody still wasn't home, I sat down on the couch and turned on the TV, hoping my wife would be home before too much longer.

9

MELODY

I wanted to be home earlier, but Willow convinced me to stay out with her. I sent Ramsey a text, but he never answered, which meant he was pissed. I was not looking forward to walking into my house and have him accuse me of being a whore again.

I took a deep breath and bit my lip to keep the guilty look off my face. I didn't owe him anything. If he was pissed, he was going to have to deal with it.

The door opened silently. The TV was on in the living room, but otherwise the house was quiet. I toed off my shoes and hung up my jacket. I sent Willow a text letting her know I was home and locked the front door. Habit.

I walked into the living room and stopped. Ramsey was on the couch, the TV was on, but he was sound asleep. His head rested against the back of the couch, his mouth slightly open.

I stared at him for a minute but couldn't resist the urge to walk over and sit down next to him. He shifted but didn't wake up. I leaned closer, admitting to myself how weak I still was when it came to him. I hated how much I wanted him, how much I still wanted him. After loving him for two decades, walking away wasn't easy. And neither was saying no to him.

In sleep, he looked like the boy I fell in love with. The boy who made me dream of a life together. We had that life, for a little while, but it was all gone. Gone but not forgotten. How cruel was that? I could look at him and still remember all the dreams and plans we had for our life together, but just like my husband, they were out of reach.

But he was sleeping. He wasn't entirely out of reach. I eased closer to him, and he didn't budge. He was always a sound sleeper, the kind of man who never once heard Amber cry in the middle of the night. I wanted to be mad at him at the time, and I was, but I also loved spending those sleepy nights cuddled up with our daughter. She had his nose and eyebrows, and when she slept, it was like looking at him as a child.

I ran my finger down his nose, just barely touching his skin. His breath tickled my finger, and my need to touch him grew. I caressed his cheek softly and drew in a breath. I missed laying with him and hearing his heartbeat under my ear. I missed feeling his arms around me, his entire body tight against mine. I missed everything there was to miss about being one half of a couple, but I missed it with Ramsey.

I moved closer to him and rested my head on his chest. The steady thump of his heartbeat eased some of the tension I'd been feeling lately. Tension I didn't want to think about. Ramsey was there. I wasn't going to remind myself he was there to see Amber. He was there. And I could just carefully, slowly, slide my arm around his waist and pretend nothing had changed.

I sighed and almost cried at how good he felt. I let myself indulge for another minute, but I knew I needed to move away from him before he woke up.

I started to shift, and his arm slid to my back. He held me in place. I thought he was still asleep, but he whispered, "Don't go."

I looked up at him and the desire in his eyes stole my breath. He hadn't looked at me like that in years.

"Don't go, Mel. Please."

I froze, stuck between the past and the present. He walked out on me, he left me, but he was looking at me the way he did before. Before we lost Steven. Before we lost each other.

"Mel," he groaned, leaning toward me.

My hesitation was acceptance, and the moment his lips touched mine, I knew it wasn't hesitation. No, it was fear and desire and need and pain, all rolled into one. Every emotion I'd ever felt in my life, I'd felt with the man who was snaking his arms around my back and urging me to crawl onto his lap.

I didn't resist and let him pull me over him. My thighs parted and I sank down, feeling the familiar ridge of his hardening cock between my legs. Sex was something that went out the window after Steven, but I still missed it. A vibrator was good, but a man who knew how to use what he was blessed with was even better.

Ramsey tilted my head to the side and pressed his tongue between my lips. I couldn't stop him, and I didn't want to. I wanted him. I needed him.

I wrapped my arms around his neck and slid closer. Every inch of his body felt like coming home. Relief. He was comfortable. The man I'd loved forever. The person who showed me what love really meant. Sure, I loved my sister, and in a way, I loved my parents, but Ramsey was the person who showed me love was supposed to be messy and wild and fun. It wasn't an obligation. It was amazing and beautiful and something that didn't come with rules.

His hands cupped my ass and drew me closer. He groaned when I rocked against him. He pulled away from our kiss to trail his lips down my throat.

"Fuck, I've missed you. I knew you'd get over everything eventually."

The Polar Bear Plunge couldn't have made me turn to ice faster. I pulled back and glared at him, sure I heard him wrong. "What did you just say?"

He looked up at me like he'd almost forgotten I was there. His eyes were glassy with desire, his cock still hard between my legs. It wouldn't take much for me to get off, but I was no longer anywhere close to the mood.

I started to climb off him, but he held me tight, refusing to let go. "Now you want to hold on?"

"What the hell does that mean?" he blurted.

I sighed and crawled off. He let me go, and I felt just as alone as the first time he walked away from me.

He sighed and stood. His cock was at attention, but we both ignored the elephant in the room. "I guess I should go."

I crossed my arms and nodded.

He stared at me for a long moment, but I didn't back down. I couldn't. Not if he thought I was going to agree to anything he wanted just because he was damn good in bed. Sex had never been our problem until we stopped having it. I knew I was the reason for that. Losing Steven scared the hell out of me, and I wouldn't let Ramsey touch me.

He said he understood, but the longer we went, the more tense he became. And the more tense he became, the harder it was for me to be interested in sex. And on and on until we fumbled through an encounter more awkward than our first time.

No, sex definitely wasn't the answer to our problems. And letting sex take over wasn't going to fix anything, and it definitely wasn't going to convince me to get over everything.

The door closed behind him, but I could feel how badly he wanted to slam the door. I locked it again and turned off the lights once I heard his SUV pull out of the driveway.

I needed a shower and a few hours of sleep, but first, I needed to clean up the kitchen. I didn't do it before I left because spending time with Ramsey and Amber was too hard. I almost started to imagine we were a family again, and that was dangerous.

I walked into the kitchen and gasped. It was clean. Spotless. The sink was empty, the table clear, even the floor looked like it had been washed.

I looked around like there would be some magical answer as to how it happened. I turned off the lights and went back to the living room, surprised to realize it had been cleaned, too.

Ramsey didn't clean the house when he lived there. He hated doing it. When I wanted to clean, he always offered to take Amber out so I could get the cleaning done faster. We both knew it was just because he didn't want to help, but I did get it done faster when they weren't there.

But he cleaned the house without being asked and with Amber home. He did it for me.

I pulled out my phone to send him a text, but a text didn't feel right. We texted about Amber, about when he was coming over. I saw his face when I sent him a text. But through Book Boyfriends Wanted, he was a nice guy that I enjoyed talking to.

WEBMOMMY

Thank you for cleaning up. You really didn't have to do that.

I wasn't sure if he'd answer, but almost immediately a message came through.

RH214

Amber and I wanted to do something for you.

WEBMOMMY

Thank you. It means a lot.

RH214

You deserve more. You deserve everything.

WEBMOMMY

I had everything I wanted once.

RH214

Me, too. I hope I'll have it all again one day. If I can keep my foot out of my mouth.

I didn't know how to reply to that, so I didn't. I closed the app and went to my room. I was still keyed up, and I knew I wouldn't sleep until I released some of the energy coursing through me.

I stared at my bed and bit my lip. I looked back at the door and decided to close it. I flipped the lock, too. Then I stripped off my clothes and turned on my shower. I waited until the water ran hot, then stepped inside and took a deep breath. I closed my eyes and replayed my favorite fantasy. One that wasn't really a fantasy but a great memory, the best memory.

Amber was sleeping, so I decided to take a shower. I'd gained a lot of weight when I was pregnant with her and wasn't feeling confident about my body. I slid my hands over my belly and was depressed that it hadn't flattened out more after she was born. Even now, I still carried the extra weight around my belly, but I'd grown used to it and no longer felt so upset by it.

But that was the first time I let myself cry. I didn't realize

Ramsey was even home until he opened the shower door and wrapped his arms around me from behind. I didn't want him to see me. The only time we'd had sex since Amber was born was with the lights off, and with the glaring brightness of the bathroom lights, I was ashamed of the way I looked.

"I'll be out in a minute," I told him, not turning around.

He kissed my neck and asked, "Why are you crying?"

I could hold it together as long as I didn't think about it, but him asking was impossible. I shuddered and tried to stifle my tears again, but he pressed tighter to my back and held me.

"I'm not beautiful," I whispered, then and now. A part of me still held that pain. I couldn't help but wonder if I'd gotten my body back if my husband wouldn't have walked out the door, but that was a thought for another time.

I slid my hand between my thighs and let Ramsey's words from years ago and the look in his eye from hours ago fill my mind. He wanted me. He'd always wanted me. In the shower that day, he kissed every inch of my body and told me how much he loved all of them. And when I finally came, he promised to love me forever.

My fingers were slick with my come. I teased my clit and told myself it was Ramsey's hand between my legs instead of my own. Ramsey was the one turning me on. I pumped a finger inside and drew the wetness up to my clit once more, then stroked quickly over the nub until I was panting and barely able to stand.

It didn't take long for me to come, my entire body shuddering with my release. My knees weakened, and I wished my husband was there to hold me up. He always made sure I was safe.

I drew in a shaky breath and finished my shower, not feeling as much relief as I'd hoped. I wished we could have finished what Ramsey and I started on the couch, but I was alone, and lonely.

I pushed the thoughts away and wrapped in a towel then dressed for bed. It wouldn't be long before I was awake again and starting a new day. We were going ice skating with Willow, which meant we were going to get out of the house for a while.

I unlocked my door and opened it again, then slid into bed. Ramsey's side no longer smelled like him. I hid one of his shirts in his pillowcase right after he left, but Willow found it and took it out. She said it wasn't good for me to hold on to him.

It wasn't good for me to let go of him either.

Sleep didn't come easy, but eventually I drifted off to dreams of a life with Ramsey. But it was just a dream.

AN HOUR of ice skating was all I could handle. I grabbed a hot chocolate and sat on the side, watching Amber and Willow glide over the ice. Families skated around the ice. It was easy to pick out the kids who played hockey or took skating lessons. There were plenty of them. And plenty of parents who'd been skating their entire lives.

The rink would get busier at night when the teenagers would fill the ice, flirting and playing around. One of my first dates with Ramsey was ice skating. I tried to be cool and didn't wear gloves. My hands were freezing by the end of the night, but he warmed them up, then kissed me and heated the rest of me.

"I want to know what put that look on your face," Blake said, taking a seat next to me. She smiled, her brown eyes kind like always.

I still wasn't sure if Blake and I were actually friends or

not. She was nice enough, but Ramsey was definitely going to get Ian in our divorce, and I figured Blake would go with him. Which meant getting closer to Blake was futile.

"Just thinking."

"About Ramsey?" she asked softly.

I smiled sadly in answer.

"I'm sorry. I shouldn't have said anything."

I shook my head. "No, it's fine. How are things with Ian?"

She grinned and probably looked just like I did when I was thinking about Ramsey a minute ago.

"Things are good. Really good. We're...um...we're engaged."

I smiled through the pain and told her I was happy for her.

"Thanks. I kind of feel guilty telling you."

I shook my head. "You shouldn't. At all. Sometimes things work out, and sometimes they don't. The good thing for you is if half of marriages end in divorce, you're on the good half."

"Ah, Melody. I'm so sorry."

I shrugged. "It's fine."

"I still just can't believe you guys haven't gotten back together. Ian was sure you two would talk before now."

"Talking isn't our strong suit," I muttered.

Blake gasped, then chuckled. "Well, it sounds like maybe you shouldn't talk."

I huffed a laugh. "Been there, failed at that."

"Recently?"

I looked at my phone. "Twelve hours ago?"

"No! Seriously? Why did it fail?"

I drew in a cold breath and checked that Amber was still skating and wouldn't overhear me. "I lost my mind and cuddled up to him when he was sleeping on my couch. He woke up and kissed me. Then he said he knew I would get over everything eventually."

"No he didn't."

I pressed my lips together in a smile.

"What is wrong with him?"

"With who?" Elise asked, sitting on Blake's other side. She was in her socks, brown rental skates next to her feet. She shoved one foot in the skate and tightened the laces.

I clamped my lips shut. I didn't know Elise at all. She was a year younger than Willow and someone I only knew from living in the same town. She was everything I wanted to be, though. Young and beautiful and confident. She picked up men and didn't care about anything other than having fun.

I wished I could be so carefree, even for just a day.

"Ramsey told Melody he knew she'd get over everything eventually while they were making out on the couch last night," Blake answered.

Elise's eyebrows went up as she met my gaze. She slid the other skate on as she talked. "First, good for you because your husband is hot as fuck. Second, I'm guessing you were involved in the make out?"

I nodded reluctantly.

"Then who cares? If he's going to be an ass, he's going to be an ass. But can he be an ass who makes it so your orgasms are a doubles match instead of singles?"

"Elise!" Blake gasped. She turned to me. "I'm so sorry for her."

"Don't apologize for me," Elise said. "She married the guy. She clearly still loves him, and everyone knows he's pining for her and waiting for the day she lets him back in the house. Either put him out of his misery and make up or cut him loose. Stringing him along isn't good for either of you."

"I'm not stringing him along," I protested.

Elise shrugged. "I'm not judging. Trust me, I've made

plenty of crap decisions about men in my life. If whatever happened can be fixed, then fix it. If not, move on." Elise stood in her skates and looked between Blake and I. "I'm going to skate. You two can figure out what's going on, but I'm a believer in shooting straight. It isn't worth it to play games."

With that, she walked away. I wanted to tell her I wasn't playing games with Ramsey, but was I? I didn't mean to. Dammit.

"I think relationships are always complicated. I spent five years with William, and I never once felt even a little bit of the love I feel for Ian. But Ian scares the hell out of me. Even now, with a ring from him on my finger, I'm scared he's going to get bored with me and leave."

"Why?"

She laughed. "Because if you and Ramsey can't make it work, I'm not sure anyone can."

I shook my head. "Ramsey and I weren't meant to be."

"Do you believe that? Really, honestly, with all your heart believe that?"

10

$\mathcal{I}$ had to smile while I shook my head because she was right. I didn't. "I fell in love with him before I knew what love was."

Blake smiled. "I think that's how you know it's meant to be. You don't need to define it. It doesn't have to have a name. Love is a feeling, a desire to make the other person happy at any cost."

I sighed and nodded. "Which is why Ramsey and I are over. I've always wanted a big family. My family...it wasn't always good growing up. Willow and I talked about getting married and having a lot of kids. About having a big family with lots of love and laughs and joy instead of what we grew up with." I shrugged. "I still have that dream. She doesn't, but I do."

Blake nodded and bent to pull on one of her skates. She finished tying the first one before she said, "When I was a kid, I dreamed of having a father. A man in my life who would keep my mom sober and watch out for me and take care of things so I could be a kid."

"Shit, Blake. I had no idea."

She shook her head. "It's okay. But what I'm saying is we all have dreams when we're kids. We all want things. Only you know if the dream you had as a kid is still a good dream, or if your dream should change to have something else you want even more. Because we sat here and you talked about Ramsey, but you didn't say anything about wanting more kids."

"I…" She was right.

"Mommy! Did you see my spin?" Amber asked, racing over to me in her skates. Willow ambled slowly after her.

"Great job, baby," I said even though I wasn't paying attention. I was too busy talking about Ramsey to even watch the kid I already had.

"It was just like dance class but with ice. Aunt Willow said I did really good," Amber said, half shouting as she plopped onto the bench next to me.

"You did really good, honey."

Blake touched my arm. I looked at her and she smiled. "I'm going to go skate. It was good talking to you."

I nodded. "You, too. Congratulations, by the way. You two deserve happiness."

She smiled. "So do you."

I smiled and watched her walk away. Willow took Blake's seat and asked, "What was that all about?"

"I'll tell you later."

Willow understood and didn't ask again. I helped Amber get her skates off and we all decided it was time for lunch when we left. I tried to talk them into going home for lunch so we didn't have to spend money, but they were set on hot dogs and French fries.

Just Frank's was busy, even for a Saturday afternoon. We stood in line with everyone else and waited for our turn. Amber sat on the metal bars separating us from the people on the other side. As we moved, she slid, complaining her feet hurt from skating.

When it was our turn, we all ordered hot dogs, fries, and drinks. Amber asked for ice cream, but I told her no since she needed to eat first. Willow ordered a milkshake and promised to share with Amber if she ate her lunch.

Amber smiled after that.

We sat and ate lunch with Amber filling Willow in on her week. She ended with Ramsey joining us for dinner the night before.

"And Daddy said he still loves Mommy," Amber declared.

My heart jumped at her words. Blake said the same thing. And Elise.

"And Mommy will always love Daddy because he gave her you," Willow said, tapping Amber on the nose.

Amber giggled and kept eating. Her hot dog was gone, and her fries were disappearing. Her eyes kept wandering to the milkshake that sat untouched in front of her.

"Daddy and I made a present for Mommy, too," Amber said. "But Daddy took it with him so Mommy doesn't see it."

"Really?" I asked.

Amber nodded. "Yeah, but I'm not going to tell you what it is."

"Will you tell me?" Willow asked.

Amber looked at her then looked back at me. She narrowed her eyes and said, "Are you going to tell Mommy?"

Willow gasped and jerked back. "Why would I do that?"

Amber's glare got harder, and I had to fight not to laugh. "Because you tell Mommy everything. I heard her and Daddy fighting about that. She tells you everything and not him. That's why he moved out. And I don't want to tell you if you're going to tell Mommy and make Daddy mad again."

All thoughts of laughter vanished. Willow's smile disappeared, too. We exchanged a look before I pasted on a smile and drew Amber's attention.

"Aunt Willow is not why Daddy moved out, honey. Aunt Willow wants Mommy and Daddy to get back together, but Mommy and Daddy have some things to work through."

"Daddy goes to work everyday. He should work faster."

I exhaled a laugh and nodded. "He should. And he's working hard. But I don't know if Daddy and I will ever fix everything."

"Why not?"

"Because sometimes people don't fix everything."

Amber narrowed her eyes again. "Like when I was dancing and broke your picture frame?"

I nodded. "Yeah, kind of like that."

"I'm really sorry, though, Mommy. You said I was forgiven." Her lip trembled.

I smiled and hugged her close. "You are, sweetie."

"So, why can't you and Daddy forgive each other?"

"I hope we can one day."

WILLOW CAME BACK to the house with us after lunch. Amber went to her room to play, and Willow asked what Blake said at the rink.

"We were talking about Ramsey."

"What about my soon-to-be ex-brother-in-law?"

I glanced down the hall, and Willow's face pinched. It was quick enough that most people would have missed it, but I knew my sister and that look meant she was worried about what I was going to say.

"It's not that big of a deal."

"Yet you won't say what it was."

"He kissed me."

"What?" she asked, eyes wide and not happy.

"When I got home last night, he was sleeping on the couch. He looked like the boy I fell in love with, and I couldn't resist laying with him. For just a minute. But he woke up and started kissing me."

"Okay?"

"Then he said he knew I'd get over everything eventually."

"He's such an ass."

"He's still my husband," I said.

"Not for long. Listen, Mel, I love you. And I love Amber. And I would love for your little family not to get blown up, but you and I both know Ramsey isn't right for you."

"You've always said that."

She nodded. "Yep, and I was right. He hurt you, Mel. Not just once. The first time he hurt you was in high school. Then again, worse, when he went to college and ended things with you. Then he decided he had to be with you, but it wasn't always easy. How many times did you tell me he flirted with someone else or checked out another girl in front of you? How many times did you think about ending things with him? And worse than all that, how many times did you give up what you wanted because he wanted something else?"

"He's my husband," I said softly.

Willow nodded. "I know. But you act like Dad half the time."

I recoiled instantly.

Willow shook her head. "Mom is in charge. We both know it. She always has been. She never believed in showing affection. She wanted us to be tough. And Dad let it happen. He went along with everything she wanted and never once pushed back. We grew up not knowing if our parents actually loved us because he couldn't stand up to her."

"Amber knows she's loved," I argued.

"She does," Willow agreed. "She also knows her parents are fighting and thinks it's my fault. Maybe she blames herself. You both tell her you still love each other—"

"That doesn't go away," I said fiercely.

Willow shook her head. "No, it doesn't. Love lingers and slaps you in the face just when you think it's gone. It reaches into your chest and squeezes your heart when you convince yourself it's over. It burns through your veins and kills you from the inside out when you realize it's not returned."

"Will?" I didn't know she loved someone. She never talked about it.

She laughed. "I watch too many movies. And I don't want to be like those women. You shouldn't be either. Ramsey has hurt you over and over again. He's the father of your child, but he's not for you anymore. He left, Melody. He walked out that door and the only time he's back is for Amber. He hasn't come back and asked you to let him move back in, has he?"

I shook my head.

"Has he told you he still loves you and wants to try again?"

I shook my head again.

"Has he said he'll try for another child?"

"No."

"Or that you mean everything to him and he can't live without you?"

"No, Willow, no. You know he hasn't said any of those things. Why are you doing this?"

She patted my hand and smiled sadly at me. "Because I want you to remember that all the things you want aren't coming from him."

I swallowed over the immobile lump in my throat and nodded. She was right. Ramsey was waiting for me to give in, like I always did. I was so desperate for him to notice me in high school that I gave up myself piece by piece until I was

Ramsey's wife. I was no longer Melody. I was Ramsey's wife and Amber's mom and Willow's sister. I wasn't Melody. Not anymore.

EVERYTHING WILLOW SAID STUCK in my mind through the weekend. If nothing else, it made me realize I couldn't sit around and wait for things with Ramsey to get better. I needed to start living my life without him. He wasn't coming back, and if he did, it was clearly going to be on his terms.

After I dropped Amber off at school Monday morning, I headed straight to O'Kelley's. Because when you're feeling bad for yourself, you don't want to go home and you don't want to go see the happy woman who just got engaged. Nope, you want to go to the local bar and drink at ten am.

It was a good place to think, and Hudson always knew everything going on. Maybe he could help me find a job. If nothing else, it would give me something to do besides drink all day.

There were a few people inside, but mostly it was quiet. Hudson was behind the bar and gave me a funny look when I took a stool in front of him.

"Um, hey?"

"Morning. Can I have a lemon drop?"

His confused look didn't fade. "Do you know what time it is?"

I glanced back at the door and pointed to the Open sign lit up next to it. "Is the sign on?"

He nodded.

"So, you're open?"

He nodded again.

"What am I missing?"

"What do you mean?"

"If you're open, why am I not allowed to have a drink?"

He sighed and walked away. I watched him grab the vodka and a lemon wedge. He set a martini glass on the bar top and popped the top off a shaker. He poured in the vodka then added a scoop of ice. He squeezed the lemon wedge in and tossed in a spoonful of sugar. Then he put the top on and shook the drink. He poured it into the martini glass, added a slice of lemon, and set it in front of me.

"Thank you," I said, lifting the glass in cheers to him. I took a drink, the sour flavor making my lips pucker as the vodka burned down my throat. I'd never been a big drinker, but I definitely enjoyed a drink now and then. Wine was my go-to at home because it was easy, but when I went out, I liked to try different things.

"What are you doing here?" Hudson asked after a minute.

I shrugged. "I was in the mood for a drink, and I didn't want to be alone right now."

His face softened ever so slightly. His beard hid most of his face, and most of his emotions, but his eyes exposed what he was feeling. Usually the bar was dark and busy and I didn't notice, but with lights on and very few people, I had more of a chance to study Hudson.

"You get it, don't you?" I asked.

He hesitated a moment then nodded. He looked around and shrugged. "That's why I'm always here."

I smiled and sipped my drink.

The front door opened and Hudson looked up from washing the shaker. He nodded toward the back and walked around the bar.

"I'll be in the back for a few minutes with the delivery," he told me. "It won't take long."

I wasn't sure why he was telling me, but I nodded. He followed the guy with the dolly through the swinging door, his face once again a mask of emotions.

The guy came back a minute later with an empty dolly and went outside. It wasn't long before he was back, rolling the boxes through the door again.

"Where's Hudson?" someone asked me.

I turned and smiled at the man. "He's dealing with the delivery."

"Crap. I need to go and wanted to pay my tab."

I slid off my stool and went around the end of the bar. I'd worked enough as a teenager and college student that I could handle just about any register. I typed in a few things on the screen and reached out for the man's card. I found his tab and turned the screen for him to make sure it was right.

"That's me. Are you allowed to be doing this?"

I smiled at the guy and had a lightbulb moment. "I am, because I'm going to start working here soon."

"Really?"

I nodded. "Yep. Hudson doesn't know it yet, but I am."

The guy laughed and signed his receipt. He handed it back to me and nodded. "Good luck."

"Thanks. Have a good day."

He waved as he walked out the door. The delivery guy was right behind him. I filed the receipt and turned to go back to my seat and found Hudson watching me with his arms crossed. He did not look happy.

"What are you doing behind the bar?"

"Helping," I said. "That guy wanted to pay his tab, and you weren't here, so I took care of it."

"How do you know how to use this?"

"I used to bartend in college. One of my many jobs."

"You know how to make drinks?"

I nodded.

"And you can run the register?"

I nodded again. "Which means you should hire me."

Hudson barked a laugh.

"I'm serious," I told him, closing the distance between us. "I need a job. I can't sit around the house all day every day. I'm losing my mind. And Ramsey isn't coming back, which means I'm going to need to find a job. Please, Hudson. I need this."

He sighed and grabbed the bill of his baseball hat. He tugged it off and scratched his shaved head. Then he shoved the hat back on and shook his head. "No. It's not a good idea."

"It's a perfect idea," I argued as he brushed past me. "You won't have to train me. I already know how to do everything. I can help out during the day while Amber is at school and some weekends when Ramsey will take her. It'll be great."

"I don't need a new person."

"Really?" I asked, crossing my arms and staring him down.

"Yeah, really."

"What about when you get deliveries?"

"Those come three times per week, and they don't take long."

"What about restocking the bar?"

"Bartenders do it during their shift."

"What about paperwork?"

He froze. I knew he spent the majority of his time out front, which meant either he took his paperwork home or it didn't get done.

"I've been running my household for years. And when I was growing up, I helped my dad with his accounting."

"How much help?"

"I used to do his taxes."

"Dammit," Hudson breathed.

"I told you I'm perfect for the job. When you need me out front, I'll help out. And when you don't, I can help get the paperwork done and make sure everything is handled. Come on, Hudson, give me a job."

He groaned. "Ramsey will kill me."

I shook my head and forced a smile. "Ramsey won't be my husband much longer. He doesn't care what I do."

Something flashed in Hudson's eyes, but he looked away before I could figure out what it was. When he met my gaze again, it was gone. "Fine. You're hired."

I grinned. "You won't regret this, Hudson. Thank you."

He mumbled something as he walked away. I didn't really care what. I had a job, something that was just for me outside of Ramsey. I wasn't going to be Ramsey's wife or Amber's mom in O'Kelley's. I was just going to be Melody.

RAMSEY

Penny walked into my office with a smile on her face. "I think I found what you're looking for."

"And what is that?" I asked her.

"Another chance with Melody."

I sighed and looked up at her. "We've been over this, Penny."

"I know," she said, lowering herself onto the chair opposite my desk. She pulled her brown hair behind her neck and swooped it over her shoulder. "But I really think this is good."

I sighed again and raised my eyebrows, letting her continue.

"Okay, so you guys have always had a thing for Valentine's Day, right?"

I nodded.

"You should totally surprise her with a date." Penny grinned, her eyes wide and bright.

I didn't want to crush her, but I had no idea what a date would help.

"Before you say no, hear me out," she added, some of her excitement fading.

I nodded and threaded my fingers together on the desk. At least that way I wouldn't clench them into a fist thinking about all the times and all the ways I'd ruined my marriage.

"You should start with a dinner out. Someplace nice, maybe go down to Syracuse or…well, I don't know where you should go, but definitely dinner. Then after dinner, go for a walk. Somewhere you can talk. Get some fresh air and tell her what's going on lately. And then you should go dancing. Wrap her in your arms and hold her close and tell her how much you love her. Then you can go to a hotel for some hot sex."

A laugh bubbled out of me. It was always shocking in a horrified kind of way when Penny talked about sex. She worked for me for years before we had a conversation about anything other than work. She was quiet and shy and highly introverted. She still was, but she'd definitely come out of her shell around me.

I took it as a compliment, but it still threw me.

"I don't think that's going to work," I said carefully.

"Why not?"

I smiled. "Because it doesn't fix the main issue we have."

"Which is?"

"She wants to get pregnant again, and I'm not willing to risk losing her."

"Having sex doesn't guarantee she'll get pregnant. I mean, you still want her, don't you?"

Our make out session from the other night flashed through my mind. I nodded. "Definitely."

"What was that?"

"What?"

"That look," she said. "What was that look for?"

I shook my head. "Nothing."

"Don't lie to me. I know you're lying to me. What happened?"

"I kissed her."

"Melody?"

I rolled my eyes.

"Seriously?" Penny squealed. She bounced on her seat and clapped her hands. "Why didn't you tell me?"

I waved a hand in her direction.

She huffed and sat still. "Fine, I won't get excited. Now, tell me everything."

I sighed again.

"I'm waiting," she said after a minute.

"I spent time with Amber Friday night. Melody went out again. When she came back, I was asleep on the couch. She sat next to me and started touching me."

Penny's eyebrows shot up.

"Not like that. Just put her hand on my waist and rested her head on my chest. Anyway, it woke me up, and when she went to move away, I asked her not to, then I kissed her."

"Did she kiss you back?"

"Not at first, but yeah."

"That's good, right? Isn't that good? Why don't you look like that's good?"

"Because I stuck my foot in my mouth and acted like an ass."

Penny dropped her hands into her lap and glared at me. "Are you kidding me?"

"I didn't mean to. I thought it was a step in the right direction, but she got pissed and threw me out."

"You have got to stop doing stupid shit with your wife. Like walking out on her in the first place."

"But she's—"

"No," Penny said. "You don't get to defend your actions by

accusing her of something. She wants kids. If you want her, you might have to get over your fears."

"I—"

"I said no. You don't get to talk right now. You get to listen. Melody has always done everything for you. She's always been there. She is perfect for you. She's an amazing person and you don't deserve her—"

"Gee, thanks."

She shook her head. "You know it's true."

I nodded.

"I have no idea what you two really went through when you lost Steven. All I know is if Melody wants another child, she's not going to change her mind because you say so. Women put their lives at risk all the time because they think they won't be in the majority that has a problem. We're blind when it comes to having a family, especially if that's all we've ever wanted. I don't know what the answer is, but you're not going to find someone better for you than Melody. I don't care how many dating apps you try."

"How did you…?"

"Know you're trying online dating? I know everything, boss. And you're screwing up. You need to figure out how you're going to make things right with her. And you need to do it now."

"I don't think I can back down from this. It isn't a matter of wanting kids or not. I'd love to have more kids. But after Steven, her doctor said it's not a good idea for her to get pregnant."

"If she's out there dating other men who want kids, then you leaving her isn't solving this. You need to find a way to fix things with her and make sure she's safe," Penny said gently.

"Penny, this…" I sighed. "Is there anything else? Have you

found anything out about Mr. Jones and his unknown cousin?"

Penny sighed and stared at me for a long moment, then passed me a sheet of paper. "It looks like Ms. Jones got pregnant as a teenager. She never told anyone and gave the baby up for adoption."

"Seriously?" I asked.

Penny nodded. "I never would have found it except I was looking."

"Where were you looking?"

"One of those home DNA tests. Ms. Jones did one, but there was no record of a match anywhere. She did it so early on that not many people had done them, but now, there's a match."

"Wow," I breathed, settling back in my chair. "I never would have thought to look in those databases."

Penny smiled. "Thank you."

"Do we know anything about the other grandson? Wait, you said she had a child? Who is her child?"

"Cleotha had a girl. Her daughter grew up in a nice home south of Syracuse. It looks like she had a great upbringing with a wonderful family. She got married right after college and settled in the same town where she grew up. They had one son. Cleotha's daughter died a few years ago, and it looks like the son-in-law did also, leaving the grandson on his own. Of course, he's not a child. He's married and working and independent, but—"

"He's still an heir. We need to reach out to him. Ask him to come here."

Penny nodded. "I already did. You have an appointment with him on Thursday."

I nodded and accepted the file Penny prepared on the new heir.

"I've also called Mr. Jones and set up an appointment with

him for Wednesday. I figured you'd want to let him know and maybe give him the option of being around for the meeting with his cousin."

"Good idea. Thank you, Penny."

Penny nodded, but she stayed in place like she was waiting for something else.

"Yes?" I said.

"About Melody…"

"Penny, please. Not now."

She sighed and walked away.

No one understood how hard it was to talk about Melody like there was something I could do. The only thing I wanted was to keep her safe. To make sure she was still around. I thought leaving would do that, but nothing was working out the way I'd hoped.

I spent the rest of the day doing work in my office. I didn't want to talk to Penny about Melody anymore, and I had plenty of paperwork to catch up on for my clients.

When I was finally ready to leave for the day, Penny was dancing outside my office door.

"What are you doing?" I asked her.

She took my question as an invitation and walked in. "I need to tell you something, but I think it's going to make you mad, so I'm not sure if I should actually tell you."

"Is it more advice about how to make things work with Melody?"

Penny hesitated, then shook her head.

"Is it more wisdom about how I screwed up my marriage?"

She shook her head again.

"Then what is it?"

"Melody got a job."

"What? Why? Where?"

"At O'Kelley's?"

"Are you asking me or telling me?"

"Um, telling. Maxwell saw her there at lunch today. She said she just started working there."

My blood burned. Hudson was my fucking friend, and he hired my wife without telling me. Without asking me.

"He said she was really excited about the job and said she felt like a burden to you."

My heart ached with those words. Melody had never been a burden. When we decided she would stay home with Amber, I was happy. I never expected her to stop doing that, even with Amber in school.

"I, um, just thought you might want to know. Before you heard it from someone else. I'm sorry, Ramsey," Penny said with a grimace, then she ran off before I could say anything.

I growled, the sound loud in the silent, vacant office. Of all the places for her to work, she had to work there. Hudson would look out for her, but he had a job to do, too. He wouldn't be able to keep everyone's hands off her.

Why did he give her a job? I didn't even realize he was thinking of hiring someone. And why didn't he mention it to me?

I was pissed at Melody for thinking I would ever consider her a burden, but I was more pissed at Hudson for giving her a job without letting me know. I needed to talk to both of them, but Hudson would let me take a swing at him if I needed to. Melody, I'd never even consider laying a hand on.

Instead of going to Ian's to change, I went straight to O'Kelley's. I parked a block away from the bar and tried to use the short walk to get rid of some of my anger. It didn't help much.

Hudson saw me walk in and nodded to the end of the bar. I followed his lead, relieved he was willing to face this head on.

He set a beer on the counter in front of me and waited

while I took a swig. I wanted to believe it helped me calm down, but it really didn't.

"Why?" I asked.

He chuckled softly. "She's persistent."

"What the hell does that mean?"

"It means when Melody walked in here this morning and asked me for a drink, we started talking. When I was dealing with a delivery, she closed out a tab for me. And when I told her I wasn't hiring, she made it impossible for me to say no."

"So, you just hired her? Without saying anything to me at all?"

Hudson shook his head and slid his hat off. He rubbed his shaved head. It was a stall tactic, one I'd seen him do many times with difficult customers. He was trying to come up with a way to say something he knew I wasn't going to want to hear.

"Melody said she needed a job. She said she was going to need to make her own money. She's worried you're not going to keep paying for her to be home. And she's bored. She wants something to do."

"She has things to do," I growled.

"Like what?" Hudson asked.

"Like be there for our daughter if she needs her mother. She can't very well do that if she's getting felt up by every drunk mother fucker here."

Hudson glared at me and leaned on the bar. Both his hands turned white from his death grip, and his eyes blazed with fury. He got close enough to me that I could see his eyes weren't just dark, but had a little silver in them. I didn't like being that close to my friend, but I refused to back up.

"First of all, if she's feeling like she needs more in her life, I'm not going to tell her she's wrong. Secondly, you never bothered to ask what her job is. And third, fuck you for thinking I'd ever let anything like that happen here."

"You know it does," I countered. "You've stopped it before."

He nodded. "Exactly. I've stopped it. And one or two baseball bats shows everyone they can't touch. I haven't had a problem in over a year."

"But you have no way of guaranteeing her safety."

He glared at me again. "Nope, because she married your dumb ass. She's going to get hurt again."

I sat back in my seat, hurt and angry that he would go there.

"Pull your head out of your ass and act like a fucking grown up."

"Fuck you, Hudson."

"Is that all you got? Because if you weren't being such a worthless piece of shit, I could tell you she's working in the office and only during the day when Amber's at school. That I know her schedule is not her own and that I have no problem letting her off any time she needs to be for Amber. And that she's only doing this because she wants to protect herself. She's lonely. And that doesn't do anyone any good. So I gave my friend's wife a job in the hope that I can help her out. This has nothing to do with you."

I sighed and let his words sink in. Instead of even thinking about Melody, I was focused on myself. I was pissed off because I wanted to control everything. I didn't want her to have to think about working because if she was reliant on me, she wouldn't think about leaving me. I didn't want her to worry about anything other than Amber because then she wouldn't think about leaving me. I was being selfish, because I was the one who left her. I was the one who did this to us.

"I'm as asshole," I admitted.

Hudson nodded and crossed his arms over his chest.

"I'm a selfish asshole."

He nodded again.

"And I'm sorry."

"Better," Hudson said. "Listen, I get it. You want to protect her. If you two didn't still love each other, this would all be a lot easier. If she was a horrible person, you could write her off without a second thought. The problem is you love her, and she loves you, and neither of you really wants to walk away."

"She doesn't want me back, though."

"Maybe not, but she doesn't want you gone either. And I think Amber going to school was a harder transition than she expected. She told me this morning she didn't want to be alone."

"Did she tell you I kissed her?"

Hudson's brows disappeared under the edge of his hat.

"It was one more thing I messed up. I shouldn't have kissed her. I said I thought she was finally over the baby thing."

Hudson snorted. "It sounds like the kiss wasn't what you messed up. It was the talking."

I rolled my eyes. "Either way, I messed up. I don't know what to say to her anymore. It's like I don't even know her."

"Then get to know her again. Start over. Try something different."

"Like what?"

Hudson nodded to where Melody walked out from the back. "Like saying you're sorry."

12

MELODY

I knew Ramsey was going to find out I was working at O'Kelley's, but I hoped to have a chance to say something to him before he did. He wasn't going to understand, and he was probably going to be mad, but he couldn't tell me I couldn't work there.

I froze when I saw him talking to Hudson. I went out to ask Hudson a question about an invoice I found, but when I saw Ramsey sitting across the bar, I couldn't move. Hudson glanced around and saw me standing there and nodded to me, and Ramsey looked up.

His eyes met mine, and I panicked. I took off, back to the relative safety of the office where only employees were allowed. Yeah, I knew Hudson could give him permission, but it was nice to think I could escape for a minute.

If nothing else, it was a chance to breathe before Ramsey walked into the tiny space I was hiding in.

I seriously considered hiding under the desk, but we were going to have to have it out eventually about my new job. No time like the present.

Ramsey knocked on the door frame and I looked up from

the invoice like I was surprised to see him. "Hey. What are you doing here?"

He walked inside and closed the door behind him. Probably so no one would hear him yell. Ramsey didn't get emotional often, but when he did, fear came out as anger. Then again, so did anger, so I never counted on his emotions being what I expected.

The day he walked out, we had a fight about Steven. It started our day and put us both in a bad mood for the rest of it. I mentioned wanting to try again since it had been months since we lost our son, and Ramsey got mad at me. He said he was putting his foot down and we were no longer going to discuss having more kids. I was pissed off and laughed at him. I actually told him I would get pregnant again whether he participated or not.

I guess I shouldn't have been surprised when he said we should get divorced, but it still hurt. Even six months later, it hurt.

"Penny mentioned you got a new job. I came to talk to Hudson about it."

"Ramsey, please don't take this from me. I know you and Hudson are friends, and you like to spend time here. I'm only here tonight because Amber has dance class. Usually, I'll be here during the day when you're at work, so I won't interfere with your life. You can hang out with Hudson and do whatever else you want to do."

"Like what?" he asked, his voice low and deadly.

I shrugged. "I'm not judging you. You said you wanted a divorce, so you're free to do what you want."

He took a breath and walked farther into the room. He sat in the chair on the other side of the desk and leaned back. He linked his fingers and rested them on the back of his head.

My eyes drifted to his arms. He had great arms. The kind

of arms that made a woman feel safe and protected. He never struggled to lift me, even as I gained weight and felt huge. He made me feel small and delicate, all because of those arms.

They were hidden beneath the dress shirt he wore. I remembered when he got that one. It was Valentine's Day two years ago. We were trying to get pregnant, so we went away for the entire weekend. We spent time in Syracuse and went shopping. I told him it wasn't romantic for me to get him dress shirts, but he said he needed some and sometimes the romantic part was spending time together, not what we got for each other.

That was the weekend we got pregnant with Steven.

"I have a new client," Ramsey said instead of addressing my comment. "He's the new owner of Jones Family Maple Farm. He's a really good guy. He didn't grow up in the area, so he's not too familiar with what he needs to do, but he's smart and he's capable, and he loves working outside."

"Ah, so exactly like you," I teased.

Ramsey chuckled, his eyes squinting at the edges. Ramsey was not a fan of the great outdoors.

"When he came in to see me for the first time, Ms. Jones had left him a letter. She told me to give it to her grandson when he came to run the farm. The letter said she had two grandsons."

My eyebrows went up.

"That was pretty much how I felt, too. I didn't know. She always talked about her son, so I followed that lead instead of searching for another child. Her grandson was blind-sided by the news."

"I guess that's better than his father having another kid."

Ramsey laughed. "You always saw the bright side of things."

"It's part of my charm."

He grinned. "There are a lot of parts to your charm."

I smiled back at him. "Thank you."

He nodded.

"So, do you know who the other grandson is?"

He nodded again. "Penny found him through an online DNA testing site."

I chuckled. "Only Penny would think to look there. Good catch."

"That's what I told her. He's coming to my office Thursday."

"And you're nervous about it?" I asked. Ramsey didn't like giving people bad news. He was always a glass half full kind of man. He said I saw the bright side of things, but that was because I had no choice. If I didn't see life that way, I would have crumbled a long time ago. But Ramsey was someone who always made it easy to find a silver lining because he was looking for them, too.

"I like Colin, the grandson I know. He's a good guy. Down to earth and relatable. He's someone I could see having a beer with after work." His jaw clenched, remembering where we were and why. Then he forced the frustration away and smiled again. "But the other grandson is an unknown. He has a job, but that can always change. If he has an interest in running the farm, they are obligated to do it together."

"It isn't so one gets all of it?" I asked.

Ramsey shook his head. "Cleotha was clear that she didn't want either of them cut out of the farm if they wanted to be involved. Her preference would be that they would do it together."

"As strangers."

Ramsey nodded. "As strangers and cousins."

"Wow. That's a big ask."

"Yeah, it is. Colin already gave up everything, but he knew about the farm. He wasn't living in the area, but he's a single guy who loved being outside. His cousin is married with a family and a desk job."

"What do you think is going to happen?" I asked.

He sighed and leaned back, looking up at the ceiling. I took a minute to appreciate the man I loved. His dark hair was getting long enough that he needed it cut. I wondered who was taking care of that, but I never asked. The scruff on his chin said he didn't shave that morning. His suit was a good one, but not his power suit. Still, it was one of my favorites. His tie was gone with his shirt opened a bit at his throat. His skin was just slightly exposed. I wanted to run my tongue over his collarbone and taste him again.

After kissing him a few days earlier, I hadn't been able to think about much besides kissing him again. For months, I didn't miss sex. It was a relief when Ramsey didn't push at night. But now that sex wasn't an option, I missed it. I missed the feel of his hands all over my body. The press of his skin against mine. The taste of his lips. The ache of desire that filled me as he ramped up my need until I came hard for him. Then the completeness I felt when he slid inside me.

Ramsey was talking again when I looked up from his collarbone. He wasn't watching me so he had no idea I wasn't paying attention.

"...sad, you know? I mean, how did she go her whole life without telling anyone?"

"People keep secrets to protect themselves and others. Usually it's because they don't think the people they're keeping things from would understand," I said.

Ramsey looked at me, his eyes sad and hurt. "Is that why you never talked to me about Steven?"

Just hearing his name sucked all the air from my lungs. My eyes watered instantly, and I worried I wouldn't be able to take another breath.

Ramsey just sat and watched me. He didn't try to comfort me, which hurt. When I was upset, I liked to be held.

I reached out for him, closing my eyes in case he wasn't willing to touch me. I couldn't take the pain alone, and I couldn't watch my husband refuse me. Waiting for him to come to me felt like it took forever, but it was probably only a few seconds before Ramsey lifted me out of the chair and sat down, then lowered me onto his lap.

He held me close while I gained control of my emotions. One tear slid down my face, and Ramsey wiped it away. I looked up at him and the same pain I felt was in his eyes.

"Losing him almost killed me. After all the hopes we had, to hold him and say goodbye was the hardest thing I'd ever faced in my life. But losing you after that...I would have rather died," he said softly.

"Me, too," I admitted. "I wanted to die. I couldn't protect our son while he was inside my body. My body turned on me and didn't keep him safe. I'm the reason—"

"No," Ramsey said firmly. "It is not your fault. Sharon has told you that, all the doctors said the same thing. You're the only one who believes it was your fault."

"I don't know how you don't blame me."

Ramsey brushed the hair back from my face and tilted my chin up until our gazes collided. His smile was tentative and sad, but it was there. The same smile he had on his face the first time he asked me out. The smile he gave me before we slept together the first time. The same smile from the night he proposed.

"I love you," he said simply. "You're the best mother in the world. There's no way you would have ever done anything to hurt Steven, or anyone, if you could control it. I would never blame you, Melody. Never."

"Oh, um, sorry," Hudson said, walking in without knocking. "I, um..."

"Wanted to make sure we weren't killing each other," Ramsey provided.

I scrambled off his lap and avoided eye contact with both man. "I need to go pick Amber up. I'll, um…Bye."

I raced out of the office, past a confused looking Hudson and through the bar that ignored me even more as an employee. I jumped in my car and rushed over to the dance studio, barely making it on time.

My phone buzzed in my purse, but I ignored it while I got Amber from class and took her home. She helped me fix dinner and was barely able to stay awake long enough to eat it. Dance nights were always the toughest ones because she burned off the last little bit of energy she had left.

Once she took her bath and went to bed, I checked my phone. I had an alert from Book Boyfriends Wanted.

RH214

Sorry I upset you. It wasn't my intention.

WEBMOMMY

It's fine. It's just hard to talk about.

I put my phone down and cleaned up the kitchen quickly. I went back to the living room and admitted I was tired, too. It had been a long time since I spent a day on my feet, and I was exhausted. I was also sweaty and a little smelly.

I made sure the house was locked and turned off all the lights, then took a quick shower and slid into bed. I thought about reading a book, but even that felt like it would take too much energy. I plugged in my phone and realized I had another message from Ramsey.

RH214

Steven is hard for me to talk about, too. Even harder because I always knew it hurt you so much.

WEBMOMMY

Losing a child is one of the hardest things a couple can go through.

RH214

True. It frequently leads to divorce.

WEBMOMMY

I don't like being average.

RH214

I hate it.

I laughed. Ramsey hadn't been average his entire life. He was always better looking and smarter and better at sports than everyone else. It was a part of who he was, and a part that made him humble in many ways. He recognized that those were God-given things that he had no say in, and at times, he felt guilty. He never came out and said that, but I knew that was how he felt.

WEBMOMMY

Average isn't always a bad thing.

RH214

No, it's not. I wish I'd been more average growing up.

WEBMOMMY

You were perfect.

RH214

You still are.

I smiled. Ramsey and I hadn't spoken to each other like that in almost two years. Since the day we found out I lost Steven. The day before, life was normal and we were happy. But when I lost him, everything changed. We changed, and we hadn't been able to find our way back to each other.

But now, through Book Boyfriends Wanted, we were talking again. Flirting even.

RH214

> I should get some sleep. I have a lot going on this week to get ready to meet the mysterious cousin on Thursday. Thanks for talking to me today.

WEBMOMMY

> Thanks for not being mad about the job.

RH214

> I just want you to know I will never, and I mean never, ask you to leave the house or pay for anything or do anything different. We agreed you would stay home with Amber, and if you want to work, I'm not going to stop you, but I'm not going to stop supporting you and Amber. Ever.

I smiled and choked back the fears in my heart. He could say that, but when he found someone new, and he would, she might not feel the same. She might want more money, or she might want the house, so I needed to be prepared. I needed to protect myself.

WEBMOMMY

> Thanks.

But that was all I could tell Ramsey.

O'KELLEY'S DIDN'T OPEN until a little later on Wednesday, so my third day on the job was a short one. Instead of going home after I dropped Amber off, I decided to get some breakfast at Cracked.

Blake was working and smiled when I walked in. She

nodded toward a table as she was taking an order, then walked over while I was looking at the menu.

"Good morning. I don't usually see you in here. How are you?"

I nodded. "I'm good. Figured I'd grab some breakfast here instead of going home."

"Working a little later today?"

"Yeah, O'Kelley's opens at noon instead of ten, so I have time to kill."

Blake grinned. "I hope this doesn't come off wrong, but I was shocked when Ian said you were working there."

I shrugged. I didn't know how much I wanted to share with her. She was nice, but we were only barely scratching the surface as acquaintances. Friends would kind of be pushing it. "Yeah, I don't do much."

Blake's smile fell and she shook her head. "No, I'm sorry. I didn't mean it like that. I just meant Hudson doesn't really let anyone in. He's been closed off since Hillary died. Piper and everyone else who works there make it sound like he barely tolerates them. But you're in his office and running things after only two days. That was all I meant. I'm sorry. Um, what can I get you for breakfast since I'm full of my foot?"

"It's fine," I told her. I didn't like making people feel bad, or feel uncomfortable, so I pasted on a smile and ordered breakfast.

Blake rushed away and put in my order. When she came back with the coffee pot, she didn't stop to talk. Sure, it was a little busy, but I knew it was because I made her feel awkward.

When she brought my food over and asked if I needed anything else, I said, "I was bored."

"Um, excuse me?"

I smiled at her, hoping she wouldn't judge me. "I was bored at home. I worked before Amber, but Ramsey and I decided I would stay home once she was born. With her in school, I don't know what to do all day. I went to O'Kelley's to ask Hudson if he knew of anyone hiring, but ended up talking him into hiring me. I was bored and I was scared that Ramsey is going to stop supporting me once we're actually divorced."

Blake sighed and sank onto the seat across from me. Her chest rested on the edge of the table when she leaned forward. Her brown eyes screamed pity, which was exactly what I didn't want.

"I have no idea what you're going through. I'm not going to sit here and pretend to understand. And I don't say that to make it sound like I'm better than you, just that I'm not trying to say I get it. I would love to tell you that's never going to happen, but we can't predict that either. What I do want to tell you is I'm sorry. I'm sorry you feel this way. And I'm sorry I haven't been there for you."

I waved my hand. "You don't need to worry about that."

She smiled. "I wanted to be friends. I still do. I don't reach out to people very easily because I always feel like I'm intruding on their lives. You and Willow are so close that I feel like you don't really need someone else, but we all need people."

"It's okay. I figured Ramsey will get Ian, and by extension you, in the divorce, so it doesn't make sense for us to become close."

Blake breathed a laugh. "That's probably true, but Ian has never told me what to do. Not when it comes to who I'm friends with."

"Yeah, but you never know…"

She smiled. "He knows better. I'd withhold sex if he tried to control me like that."

I surprised laugh burst out of me. Blake Dewitt and I definitely weren't close enough to talk about sex.

She grinned. "See? Now we have to be friends because I told you I withhold sex from my fiancé if he's an idiot."

I chuckled.

"Come to girls' night out on Sunday. We meet at Book Boyfriends Unlimited at seven," Blake said.

I shook my head. Finley really didn't like me, and going to her bookstore was not a great idea. "I don't think I can."

"Why not?" Blake pushed.

"Um, well, I have Amber."

"Ask Ramsey to watch her."

"And Finley hates me."

Blake shrugged. "She'll get over it."

I huffed a laugh. "I'm not so sure about that."

"She will if you show up. She'll have to. Come on, Melody. We're friends, so you have to come."

I sighed and said, "I'll think about it."

Blake stood and grinned. "Good. And I'll keep bugging you until you say yes, so I'll count on it being a yes."

I shook my head knowing she was right.

"Is there anything else you need right now?" she asked.

"No, I'm good."

"Enjoy."

"Hey, Blake," I said as she started to walk away.

"Yeah?"

I met her gaze. "Thank you."

She smiled and squeezed my shoulder.

13

RAMSEY

*A*ll Colin knew was we found his cousin. He didn't know anything about how he had a cousin or who the cousin was. I was not looking forward to telling him.

Penny and I were both on edge all day. Instead of pacing my office and feeling off base, I sent Melody a message.

RH214

> Meeting with Colin today. Think I might throw up.

I set my phone on my desk and told myself I wasn't waiting for her to reply, but when she did, I snatched the phone up so fast I almost dropped it.

WEBMOMMY

> That would probably go over like a fart in church. Drink something and breathe. The worst is over. He already knows what news you're giving him. It's unlikely he knows his cousin. You're going to do great.

Thanks. You always know what to say to make me feel better.

WEBMOMMY

Just trying to help. I gotta run. At work.

I tucked my phone away and took a deep breath. Then another. Melody was right. Colin handled the news of an unknown cousin well. The meeting was only to talk to him about who the cousin was and tell him what I knew. And to ask him if he had an interest in meeting his cousin.

When Colin knocked on my door thirty minutes later, I was feeling more in control. We shook hands and he sat across from me, holding my gaze with his own dark one.

"Just rip the band-aid off and tell me," he said.

"Your cousin's name is Carter Sinclair. He lives closer to Albany. He grew up south of Syracuse. He's an only child, and his mother was your father's sister."

"Was?" Colin asked.

I nodded. "She and her husband both died a few years ago. Carter is married, he has two kids, and he has a good job from what I can tell. He's connected to his community."

"So, he's not going to want to move here, right?"

I shook my head. "Not necessarily. I have a meeting with him tomorrow to tell him everything."

"He doesn't know yet?"

I shook my head again. "I've reached out to the attorney for your grandmother's estate. Since her will explicitly said the farm was to go to her grandson, they need to be there to notify him. We can't tell him over the phone. We'd also like you to be there."

Colin sat back in his chair with a huff. He ran a hand over his dark hair and down his face. He leaned forward with an exhale and looked up at me. "What the hell am I supposed to do?"

I took a breath and laid it all out for him. "You never withheld information. You had no idea you had a cousin, or an aunt, so you're not in trouble with any of this. The worst case scenario for you is you have a partner who knows nothing about working outside."

Colin's eyebrows went up and his mouth curled into a wry smile. "He's a desk jockey?"

I nodded. "He is. If I were to guess, he's not going to want to leave his life. But I can't make that decision for him, so legally we have to let him know. If he does want to move here, he'll only own half the farm. There are rules in a situation like this, and if you decide to run it together, it will operate as a partnership."

"And if he doesn't? If he wants to stay? Do I just get the whole farm?"

I exhaled slowly and smoothed my tie. I knew he was going to ask, because Colin was a smart guy, but planning my response and actually telling him were two different things. "That's where things get tricky. There are basically two things that could happen. If he doesn't want the property, he can waive his rights to it and sign something saying you own the farm free and clear and he has no claim to it."

"And if he doesn't?" Colin asked with fear in his voice.

"If he doesn't, he could ask you to buy him out."

"Fuck," Colin breathed. Then he winced. "Sorry."

I shook my head. "Not a word I've never said before. And pretty much my thoughts."

He huffed a laugh but didn't smile. "I'll be honest. I don't have the money to buy him out."

I nodded. "I'm not surprised. The farm isn't cheap. Most people don't have cash like that lying around. If Carter insists that he wants to be bought out, you can take out a loan against the property or you can sell it."

Colin laughed. "You're kidding, right?"

I shook my head. "I know it doesn't make any sense. To sell it when you're trying to save it. The problem right now is we have no idea who your cousin is. If he's a ruthless businessman, he might say if it's half his birthright, then he owns half of it. It'll get dragged through court while you continue to work and try to make a profit, not knowing if your work will be worthwhile. If he's a reasonable person, and I'm hoping he is, then hopefully this entire conversation ends when you walk out the door."

Colin rested back in his chair again and stared out the window behind me. He could see the water if it was a clear day. In January, the water froze over at times, but some of the big ships still came through and broke up the ice. I chose the office I did because it was far enough from the middle of town to feel like I could focus but close enough that I could still be nearby if Melody needed me. And now that Amber was in school, it was only a block to the elementary school, which was really nice.

Colin cleared his throat and lifted his eyes to mine again. "When I was a boy, my dad brought my up here one summer. The syrup was flowing and I remember wanting pancakes the entire time we visited with his mom. She was nice to me, and she said she hoped I would take over one day. My dad was never all that interested in the maple farm, and by the time I finished college and got a job, my grandmother and father weren't in touch very often. I considered calling her about a job, but I didn't think she would hire me fresh out of college, so I never did."

"She mentioned you to me once. She said she wanted you to work for her, but she knew you loved your job and she didn't feel right asking you to leave," I told him.

Colin linked his fingers together and smiled. "I wished she had. I did love my job, but I was only there until I felt like I was good enough to come up here. When the lawyers called me, I thought it was a joke. Then my dad said she died, and I couldn't believe it." He sighed. "I love that place. My mom said she and my dad fell in love there, and I think that's part of why my dad stayed away. When my mom died, he couldn't face it. But for me, it feels like home. Losing it…it's not an option."

I nodded and felt the weight of his pain on me. This place was his home, like Melody was mine. I could save his home, keep it with him so he never lost it. And I would. I couldn't coerce his cousin into walking away, but I hoped he was a reasonable person who would see that holding onto the farm and harming his cousin, who did nothing wrong, wouldn't solve anything.

And hopefully, it would be enough to have Carter play nice.

WEBMOMMY

How did the meeting go?

I SMILED when I saw her message. I resisted the urge to reach out to her, but she messaged me first. It felt like a huge win.

RH214

He's worried. The cousin is an unknown. I hate it for him because he loves the place. He'll do it justice and bring it back to what it was before Ms. Jones got sick.

WEBMOMMY

That sucks. Do you think the cousin is going to want it?

RH214

I have no idea.

WEBMOMMY

What time is the meeting with the unknown cousin tomorrow?

RH214

Ten.

WEBMOMMY

Good. Get it over with early so you don't have to stress about it all day. Make sure you eat a good breakfast.

I chuckled out loud.

RH214

I will. And you're right. Thanks.

WEBMOMMY

Good luck. Let me know how it goes. Talk tomorrow?

RH214

Definitely.

I smiled as I put my phone down on the nightstand. It felt damn good to have Melody ask about my day. I wasn't sure the last time that happened.

Definitely before Steven. Before I lost my wife. I thought she was coming back a few months after the miscarriage, but the only thing she was interested in was getting pregnant again as quickly as possible.

I resisted her and it became an issue. An issue that grew because I loved my wife and wanted to make love to her every chance I had but I couldn't because she refused to take her birth control.

It was only after her doctor told her she needed to start

birth control that she did and we managed to have sex for the first time since Steven. But it didn't go well.

We were awkward and stiff, and not the good kind of stiff. Not the kind I was at the moment.

I closed my eyes and let my mind wander. Melody on our wedding day. Melody's eyes wide with pleasure the first time we slept together. Melody reaching for my hand when she found out she was pregnant with Amber.

I tugged my shorts down and wrapped my hand around my cock. Melody was as good as I was at making me come, and I kept my eyes closed and let my mind believe it was her hand wrapped around me.

I squeezed as I stroked to the tip and groaned. "Fuck, Melody," I moaned. It felt too good.

I pictured her smiling face. Her seductive face. Her O face. I groaned again and stroked harder.

"Melody," I moaned, jerking faster. My fist pumped up and down my shaft, bringing me closer and closer. My throat tingled and my balls pulled up tight. I kept going, seeing Melody in my mind.

Then everything released. I grunted through the orgasm, letting my come squirt over my hand onto my shorts. The whole time, I played the highlight reel of Melody behind my eyelids. Always Melody.

I cleaned myself up and changed the sheets, thankful Ian kept more than one set of sheets in the apartment. The relief was temporary, though, because just as quickly as the relief happened, the loneliness sank in and I missed my wife.

I just fucking missed my wife.

PENNY WALKED the estate lawyers into my office. They were out of Alexandria Bay so I didn't know either of them well.

When Cleotha died, I worked with them enough to hand over the information I had, but they took over most of the information dealing with Cleotha's estate.

We exchanged greetings and Penny brought everyone coffee, smiling even though she was just as tense as everyone else. Kim and Roger, the A-Bay lawyers, were still trying to figure out how they missed another grandson.

"I never would have caught it either," I assured them. "Cleotha never mentioned another child. If she hadn't mentioned something in her letter, we never would have looked."

"I just wish she'd have mentioned the other grandson before we read her will," Kim said with an eye roll.

I nodded. "I agree, but she clearly didn't know how to tell her family about this. I imagine she wasn't very proud of it, even though she clearly never stopped caring about her daughter and her daughter's family. For her to have known she had another grandson, and only one grandson, she obviously kept up with the other side of her family."

Roger raised his eyebrows and nodded. "I guess I can see that, but how shitty is the first one going to feel if some cousin he never knew existed swoops in and demands half of everything? Wouldn't it have been easier to just tell the truth about it all along so he was prepared?"

"Do either of you have kids?" I asked them.

They exchanged a glance and shook their heads.

"Telling your child something difficult is painful. It's something that you never want to have to do. It's worse when it's your kid because kids look at their parents like they are heroes, like they can do no wrong. But when you have to tell your child something that will make them look at you differently…it's impossible. I'm guessing she wanted to protect her son."

Kim and Roger both looked chagrined and embarrassed.

Good. They had no right to judge Cleotha, or anyone else. Until they'd walked in her shoes and knew what she'd been through, they couldn't judge. No one could.

Penny broke the ice with a question about things to do in A-Bay, and everyone settled into a surface conversation while we waited for Carter Sinclair to show up.

When the front door opened, Penny walked out to welcome Mr. Sinclair. We were silent as they talked quietly. Penny laughed softly as their voices grew louder.

Penny walked in first. She was looking over her shoulder at Mr. Sinclair. He was a few steps behind her and his step faltered when he saw all of us waiting to talk to him.

"Um, hello," he said with a confused smile.

"Mr. Sinclair. Thank you for coming up here to meet with us. We know it was a bit of a trip for you. I'm Ramsey Holland," I told him. I extended my hand.

He shook it without hesitation despite the weariness in his eyes. "Of course. It sounded important."

Kim and Roger stood and introduced themselves. Mr. Sinclair shook their hands and said it was nice to meet them. We all sat and Penny offered Mr. Sinclair coffee, and the tension in the room continued to climb.

When everyone was good, Penny excused herself and left Mr. Sinclair alone with us lawyers.

We'd all agreed I would tell him what happened. When Kim and Roger looked at me, Mr. Sinclair followed their gaze.

"Mr. Sinclair," I said with what I hoped was a compassionate smile. "We know this is a strange situation. We also know you don't really know what is going on."

He smiled. "Is anyone going to tell me?"

I chuckled. "Yes, sir. From what we understand, your mother was adopted. Is that true?"

He nodded, his eyebrows pulling together above his dark brown eyes, the same color as Colin's. "She was, but I'm not sure what that has to do with anything. My mother died years ago."

"We know, and I'm sorry for your loss, Mr. Sinclair," I said.

He nodded again. "You can call me Carter."

I nodded. "Okay, so, Carter, your mom's birth mother was a woman named Cleotha Jones. Cleotha got pregnant with your mother when she was a teenager. She hid her pregnancy from everyone, so no one, we believe including her husband and son, ever knew about your mother. Unfortunately, we don't know anything about her birth father, but we do know she was your grandmother."

Carter leaned forward. "Cleotha Jones was my grandmother?"

I nodded again. "I'm sorry, but she died recently."

Carter shook his head and huffed a laugh. "Um…okay… huh…why the hell am I here?"

"Your grandmother, Ms. Jones, she had a son. And her son had a son. He's your cousin," I said.

Carter looked at the faces in the room and quickly dismissed the two white men as decidedly not his cousin.

I grinned. "Not one of us. Sorry. No, um, her grandson, her other grandson, he's not here. He wanted us to talk to you alone. Colin grew up not too far from here, but he moved back after your grandmother died."

Carter was still confused. I was screwing the whole thing up. I needed to just get to the point.

"Okay, Carter, here's the deal. Your grandmother…she owned a farm. Jones Family Maple Farm. It's a huge farm of maple trees that makes the best maple syrup in the area. When your grandmother was sick, she wrote a letter to her grandsons, a letter saying she wants you to know each other and she wants you to be there for each other. And you've both inherited her maple farm, if you're interested."

Carter breathed a laugh and shook his head. "You're joking right? I mean, this can't be real. A grandmother I never knew existed died and left me a farm?"

I nodded, not smiling at all.

Carter's grin fell. "You're…you're serious?"

I nodded again.

"Holy fucking shit," he breathed.

14

I kept watching Carter, trying to get a read on what he was thinking or feeling. He stared at the wall for a minute, then finally looked at me again.

"I...I don't even know what to ask."

"Well, Mr. Sinclair," Kim began, "the first thing you need to know is that you don't have to say anything right now. You can sit with this information and make a decision later."

He looked at me. "Is that true?"

I nodded, even though I was hoping he would decide quickly. "Yes. You can have time."

He relaxed a little after that. "That's good. It's a...it's a lot to process. Right now I feel like I'm a little overwhelmed."

"Why don't you tell us a little about yourself, Carter," I suggested. "You're married, right?"

A smile curled his lips up. His eyes went far away. He was definitely a man in love. "I am. Amanda's the best thing that's ever happened to me. We met at my first job out of college. From the first time I saw her, I knew she was the person I was going to spend my life with. She's kind and beautiful and smart and the most wonderful mother. We have two kids,

Caroline and Adam. Caroline is into dance, and Adam likes soccer."

"How old are they?" I asked.

"Caroline is twelve, and Adam is nine."

I nodded. "My daughter is into dance, too, but she's only five."

"Kindergarten?"

I nodded again. "Yep. She's exhausted every day. It's wearing my wife out."

Carter grinned. "I remember those days. They were tough, but they were a lot of fun. Before they learn how cruel life can be or how cruel people can be. I hope you're good to your wife. Especially if she's the one home most often."

I nodded but didn't say anything else about Melody. It didn't feel right to lie, but I couldn't tell him the truth either.

"Amanda stayed home until Adam went into kindergarten. She lasted a few months, then she decided she needed to go back to work. She was too bored all day without the kids home. She only works part time, but it's been enough so she can get out some and still be around if the kids need her."

I smiled. "Mine just started working this week. She was feeling the same way."

Carter chuckled. "I guess it's good to know things aren't that different up here." He looked around, spotting the River out the window. "It's a beautiful area. What would the work be like if I decided to work on this farm? I'm assuming I'd have to work it if I wanted to accept it, right? I'd have a job?"

I nodded, but Roger was the first one to answer. "You'd have a job. Your grandmother's will only states that her grandson, or grandsons we now know, have to agree to work on the farm if they get any ownership. You wouldn't have to live there, but you could. It's a maple farm, so it's probably quiet through most of the winter but busy in the spring through fall. I don't know much about it, though. Ramsey might be able to tell us."

"Roger is right. Things are quiet now, but it won't be long until taps are being put in trees and sap is being collected. It's a lot of manual labor, not that I'm trying to scare you off. The farm hasn't been fully operational for a few years. When your grandmother got sick, she didn't keep up with it. Her workers were seasonal mostly, and the caretaker of the property became a caretaker for her. This year will be the first in a few years that anything is happening."

"And you said I have a cousin?"

I nodded. "Colin Jones. He's already said he wants to work on the farm. He moved onto the property a month ago and has been learning everything he can and getting things ready for this year."

"Does he know about me?" Carter asked.

I nodded slowly. "He does. Cleotha left a letter for her grandson, for me to give him when he came to get information about the property. That was the first any of us knew about you. She mentioned in the letter that there were two of you."

"Damn," Carter breathed. "That had to be a shock."

I smiled. "It definitely was."

"Do you, uh, do you think he'd be willing to meet me?" Carter asked.

"I do," I told him. "Colin wanted you to have a chance to process all this without him here, but I think he'd be willing to get together. How long are you in town?"

Carter shrugged. "I was planning to go home this after-noon. I really didn't expect all this. I could come back…next weekend, I think. I'd have to check with Amanda and see what works for us. Is that too long? Do you need to know sooner than that?"

I shook my head. "It's fine. I do need to let you know that

Colin is working there. He's setting things up and getting ready to run the farm. Whatever you decide to do, you need to know he's staying. He's in it."

Carter nodded. "That's good. I think that's really good."

I could tell Carter was about done and needed time to process everything. I ended the meeting, thanking him for driving up to meet with us and asking him to let me know what he decided. I also suggested I meet him and his family at Jones Family Maple Farm when they came and promised to let him know if Colin was okay with the idea.

Kim and Roger weren't far behind Carter, thankfully. When everyone was gone, I went back to my office and sank down into my chair.

"How did it go?" Penny asked.

I scrubbed my hands over my face and shook my head. "I have no idea. He was definitely surprised."

"What do you think he's going to do?"

I sighed. "A part of me really thought he was going to walk away and say no, but he asked if he can meet Colin and visit the farm. He sounds like he might be interested."

"Did you get the feeling he's after the money?"

I shrugged. "I don't know. I told him it hasn't run in a few years because I want him to understand it's not something he can walk into and expect much from the start, but it's still a huge farm."

Penny screwed her lips to the side. She sighed and pushed her ponytail behind her shoulder. "What are you going to tell Colin?"

"The truth. That's all I can do. I wish I had more for him, but for right now, his life isn't settled."

Penny stood and smoothed down the front of her dress. "Do you want me to call him? Get it over with?"

I nodded. "Thanks, Penny."

My conversation with Colin went about as well as

expected. He had no problem meeting Carter or showing him the farm, but he was worried. Not that he wasn't willing to work with Carter if that was what Carter really wanted, but because he didn't know Carter at all. He could be great for the farm, or he could be a complete drain on it. Colin had more questions than I had answers, and I hated that.

After I talked to Colin, I messaged Melody and told her the meeting was over and no decision had been made. She said she hoped it all worked out. I had another meeting, so I didn't have much time to chat with her and said we could talk later.

LATER BECAME the next day when Melody was busy with Amber. Willow had dinner with them and since we did not get along, I didn't try to get in touch after Melody told me Willow was there.

I didn't hear from Colin or Carter and was driving myself crazy wondering what they were thinking. Colin loved Jones Family Maple Farm, and he was the one doing the work to make it operational again. He had a good plan to start small, and he made the right decision to invite the former caretaker back to help him learn and get started.

It all sounded easy, but I knew nothing in life was ever really easy. Especially not anything that was worthwhile.

I left work Friday night and went to Ian's. He was already gone for the day, so I changed and headed back out. Instead of going to O'Kelley's, I drove straight past town to my former home.

I'd never dropped in on Melody. Not since I moved out. I always called or texted her to let her know I was coming over, but I needed to see her and didn't think about warning her until I was in the driveway.

I sat in my SUV and stared at our house. Her house. I decided if things progressed to us actually getting a divorce, I was going to make sure she got the house. I wasn't willing to change anything else on either of them.

The purple door was what drew Melody to the home in the first place. She said it was quirky and unique while still being welcoming. I only cared that she loved it. She dreamed of filling all the bedrooms with kids and showering them with the kind of love she didn't have growing up. Everything in her life centered around kids.

It always came back to kids. Not having them, having them, working with them. It was always about kids.

I was still sitting in my SUV when the front door opened. Melody looked out and waved hello tentatively. I waved back. She waved like she was inviting me in, and I finally turned off the vehicle and got out.

"I didn't know you were coming over tonight."

"Sorry. I can go."

She shook her head, her brown hair cascading over her shoulders. She wore a pair of sweatpants and a loose tee that used to be mine in college. She stole it a long time ago, but I couldn't help the primal urge to have her when she was in my clothes.

"You don't have to go. Why are you sitting out here?"

I shrugged. "I didn't want to intrude on your night."

She smirked. "So you decided to sit in the driveway like a creeper?"

I chuckled. "I didn't really decide anything."

She stepped back. "Come in. We haven't eaten yet, but there's plenty for you if you're hungry."

I smiled. "Thanks."

Melody closed the door behind me and took my coat and hung it up. Amber plowed into me from behind, surprising me. She wrapped her little arms around my legs.

"Daddy!"

"Hey, big girl. How was your day?"

"Great! We got to color today at school. With markers."

"Wow, really?" I asked as I scooped her up.

She nodded and showed me her marker covered hands. "Yep, and now I'm all different colors. Isn't it pretty, Daddy?"

I grinned. "It sure is. I love it."

"Me, too. Mommy said I need to wash it off when I take a bath."

"Well, you need to listen to Mommy. She wants to make sure you don't get sick when you lick your fingers and eat marker."

"I don't eat them, Daddy. I just color with them."

"Are you sure? Because it looks like you might have eaten one, too." I pointed to the smear of pink on her cheek.

She giggled and shook her head. "No, I just wanted a line on my cheek like Noah. He fell out of a tree and cut his face and people said he looked weird, so I drew a line on my face, too."

I met Melody's eyes over Amber's head, and she nodded. My throat swelled tight and I swallowed around it and hugged Amber tight. "You're a very sweet girl. Don't ever change, okay?"

"Okay, Daddy," she choked out.

I let her go and she pushed away to get down. She scrambled back to the table where she was coloring some more. Melody nodded toward the kitchen, and I followed her.

"Are you okay?" she asked quietly when we were alone.

I shrugged. "I don't know. This case with the farm is tougher than I expected. I thought it was going to be an easy one where I could hand over the letter, Colin would go about his business, and I could enjoy the fruits of his labor. Instead, I'm mediating between two men who don't know each other, one of whom doesn't know what he wants to do. It's wearing on me."

Melody's hand went out to reach for me, but she closed her fist and pulled it back. She smiled, avoiding my gaze, and said, "I'm sorry, Ramsey."

I shrugged. "It's part of the job, I guess."

"Yeah, but that's never been your favorite part. You like building things up, not tearing them down."

I chuckled mirthlessly. "Except for us. I tore that down."

Melody's eyes snapped to mine, hers sad and hurt. Her gaze drifted from my eyes down my body and something deeper, darker lit her gaze. Almost as quickly, it disappeared, but every cell in my body reacted to it. My cock twitched in my pants, begging me to press her against the wall and build everything we used to have back up. Starting with her desire.

Melody gasped. Her eyes widened. A flush rose up her neck. She knew what I was thinking, and if I knew her at all, which I did, she was on board.

Well, fucking hell.

"Um, I need to check on dinner," she said and quickly left the room.

I stood there and stared after her, wondering if I could get away with following her and finishing what she started with that slow perusal of my body. The answer was a definitive no when Amber called me over to show me her latest masterpiece.

"How's school going?" I asked her.

"Good. Mommy said I can have Makayla over this weekend."

"That will be fun."

"Yep. And Aunt Willow might come over Sunday night. Mommy is going out and said she needs Aunt Willow to stay with me. So, I'll see Makayla on Saturday and Aunt Willow on Sunday."

"And me on Friday," I added, trying not to be hurt that her exciting weekend didn't involve me.

"I know, Daddy," she said. "But I always see you on Fridays."

I smiled and ruffled her hair. Her curls tumbled into her face and she pushed me off with an exasperated sigh.

"Daddy."

"What?" I asked innocently, then did it again.

"Daddy! I'm trying to color a picture for Mommy. It makes her happy when I color. She's sad a lot."

I sucked in a breath and closed my eyes. I wanted Melody to be happy. I was causing her pain, and I hoped she would be happier if I wasn't around hurting her. But if she was sad enough that Amber picked up on it, that wasn't good.

"Why is Mommy sad?"

Amber shrugged. "I don't know. But I hear her in her room at night sometimes. Sometimes she's in the shower so I won't hear her make noise, but I still hear her."

"In the shower?"

Amber nodded. "Yeah. She cries and makes mad noises. Sometimes she says your name, but she said you weren't there."

It all clicked. Amber wasn't hearing her cry. She was hearing Melody masturbate. In the damn shower. Thinking about me.

"Are you guys ready for dinner?" Melody asked, smiling as she walked into the room.

I looked up at her and met her gaze. Her smile fell when she saw the look in my eyes. The flush came back and the panting lifted her breasts. My eyes went to them, her nipples hard beneath her clothes. She crossed her legs, something she did when she needed relief. I lifted an eyebrow and she bit her lip.

The woman was definitely going to kill me.

"I'm almost done, Mommy. I told Daddy I color pictures so you're not sad anymore. Maybe he can stay tonight so you're not alone if you want to cry tonight," Amber said. She was matter-of-fact and innocent in her suggestion, but nothing about her suggestion was innocent.

Melody's eyes went wide. She knew I knew exactly what Amber was talking about. The pulse in her throat fluttered, speeding up with each breath she took.

I grew harder just sitting there, next to our daughter, watching my wife get turned on just thinking about getting off later. Fuck me, I wasn't going to survive dinner and bedtime with Amber. Not when there was a chance Melody might be dessert.

God, let there be a chance.

15

MELODY

Jesus, I was hot. Dying. I checked the stove to make sure I turned it off. I even wondered if I bumped the thermostat. But no, none of it was the reason I was practically sweating through my clothes. That honor rested squarely on the broad, sexy shoulders of my husband.

The man was a fucking heat-seeking missile, and he was not going to miss.

His gaze flickered from my lip clenched between my teeth to my aching nipples begging to be let free from my bra to the throbbing pulse between my legs. By the time he met my eyes again, I was almost sure I could come just from the look in his eyes.

When Amber asked me the one morning if Daddy was there at night, I thought she had a dream. When she said she heard me crying again and that I said Daddy's name, she thought I was mad at him. I realized exactly what she heard and did my best to play it off, but it obviously didn't work as well as I'd hoped.

She told Ramsey I was thinking about him while I got

myself off. And he put the pieces together like I did and drew the right conclusion.

I still wanted my husband.

"Should we eat?" Ramsey asked, his eyes drifting down and settling between my legs.

I shifted and wished I could run to my room and take a shower. I was too damn close.

"What's for dinner, Mommy?" Amber asked.

"Um, baked spaghetti," I told her, forcing a smile as I died inside.

Ramsey walked over while I was talking to Amber and not paying attention to him. He brushed past me, his arm grazing my sensitive nipples. I gasped and pulled back. My core clenched, readying for him.

"Sorry," he mumbled. "I didn't realize you were sticking out like that."

I glared up at him, but the only heat in it was the kind reflected back at me from him. I was definitely going to burn alive.

Ramsey moved around the kitchen like he still lived there. He got water for all of us and sat down across from me. He asked Amber about school and what she was going to do with Makayla the next day.

And tortured me with every second.

I thought he'd push. I half expected him to kiss me. Hell, even an accidental brush of our feet under the table. But I got nothing from him. He was keeping his distance and staying focused on Amber.

He was being a good dad, which was awesome, but it meant I couldn't be mad at him, even though I was mad at him.

The first time we slept together was the summer before he went to college. We knew we were going to break up, but we loved each other and said we wanted to have sex. He wasn't a virgin, but I was. We drove up the river a little until we found a quiet area and parked in a field that was overgrown enough that his truck was hidden. He had a blanket in the back and enough condoms to last us a few months, but the fact that he thought about any of it made me love him that much more.

Condoms and a blanket weren't the only things he thought of. He thought of me. He touched and teased me until I was screaming into the night and begging him to fill me up. He knew it would hurt for me, but he did everything he possibly could to make it a good experience.

And holy shit, did he ever.

For the next few weeks, I attacked him every chance I had. I couldn't control myself around him. Being even a little bit turned on had me crawling on top of him and getting off every chance I got.

Not that he minded at all. He reaped all the same benefits. But when he went to college, my need went with him. He was the one I wanted. It wasn't sex, it was Ramsey, and once he left, I no longer cared as much about sex.

But Ramsey was the one sitting in my kitchen, ignoring me. He turned me on and left me to sit, and he knew exactly what he was doing.

But two could play that game.

I finished my dinner quietly while Amber and Ramsey talked about school and he told her about work. He asked if it was okay if she went with him to Jones Family Maple Farm the following weekend and I said yes. Amber was excited and asked him a ton of questions about the farm and what they would see and do. Ramsey patiently answered all of them, but when I stood with my plate, he stopped talking.

"You two finish up," I said. "I'm already done, so I'm going to take a shower."

"What?" he asked.

"A shower. I really need a shower, and since you're here with Amber, I'm going to go take care of that."

"Melody, you should just wait."

"Why, Daddy?" Amber asked.

I raised an eyebrow and looked at him.

Ramsey clenched his jaw and forced a smile for Amber. "I just thought Mommy might enjoy her shower more if she waits until after you're in bed for the night."

Amber looked at me. "Are you going to cry, Mommy?"

I smiled. "I promise you, honey, I'm not going to cry."

Ramsey choked on his water.

Amber stood and slapped him on the back. I walked over and leaned on him, helping her to clear the liquid from his lungs. He choked again when my breasts rubbed his arm.

"Daddy, are you okay?" Amber asked, sounding worried.

Ramsey coughed once more, then nodded. "I'm good, honey. Just got a little choked up."

Amber took her seat again and continued eating.

"Don't go," Ramsey said. He grabbed my wrist and met my eyes. "Please."

"Why not?" I asked softly.

"Please, Mel. Let me be there for you."

Ever since Ramsey and I started talking again, I'd been dreaming of him saying something similar. Of him wanting me. And he was sitting in my kitchen, his thumb sliding across my sensitive skin, asking me to let him take care of me.

"Okay," I finally said.

His eyes went wide and his grip tightened. "Yes?"

I nodded.

A seductive grin curled his lips up, and damn if I didn't want to just crawl on his lap right then and there.

I went back to my seat and watched them as they talked and ate. When they were done, I cleaned up the kitchen, but

Ramsey stayed and helped. He carried plates to the sink and put everything on the table away. He even wiped the table clean when it was clear.

Amber wanted to watch a movie before bed, so the three of us piled onto the couch with Amber in the middle. She was enraptured by the movie, even though she'd seen it before, which meant she wasn't paying attention to Ramsey and me.

His hand started on the back of the couch, behind my right shoulder. Then it moved closer and brushed the hair back from my cheek. Then he stroked one finger down my throat. Then the same finger glided over my racing pulse point.

I drew in a breath and told myself to move away from him, but instead I leaned closer. His hand slid to the back of my neck and he rubbed to ease my tension. Then he ratcheted my tension right back up when he used my collarbone as a preview for what he was going to do to my clit. Slow circles, then a fast thump, then wider circles and a pinch in the middle. Then his thumb hard and fast while his fingers slid over my shoulder in a rhythm that made me squirm.

I had to bite my lip to keep from moaning.

Amber yawned and Ramsey and I both jumped to get her ready for bed. Amber protested that she wasn't really that tired, but she yawned again, ruining her defense.

Amber wanted Ramsey to put her to bed, so I sat on the couch and waited for him to be done with her. They laughed and talked while she took a quick bath, then his low, soft tones were the only sound I heard as he read her book.

I started to calm down until he closed her bedroom door. Then every inch of me tightened and demanded attention.

Ramsey walked into the living room quietly, like he wasn't sure what he was going to get from me. He sat down on the other end of the couch and clasped his hands together, leaning over his knees.

"What are we doing?" he asked after a minute.

"What do you mean?"

He turned his head to look at me. "I love you, Melody. That's never changed. And if this is just scratching an itch or getting off, then fine. But I need to know so I don't get my hopes up that you thinking about me while you finger-fuck yourself in the shower isn't more than just that."

I sucked in a breath at his honest and vulgar words. Instead of making me second guess the teasing we were doing, his words made me want him even more.

"I don't know what it is, Ramsey. All I know is I'm horny, and the only man who's ever made me feel good is you. When I close my eyes and get wet, your face is the one I see. Your hands are the ones I imagine. Your cock is the one I want fucking me."

"Jesus, Melody," he breathed. "I can't...I need you."

I don't know which one of us moved first, but it wasn't long before we were in each other's arms. His lips crashed into mine, both of us starving for what only the other could give. He nipped at my lip, then sucked hard to draw it into his mouth. I whimpered, imagining him doing the same to my clit.

He tugged me on top of him, his hands rough on my thighs as he pulled my body tight to his. His cock pulsed against me, the thin sweatpants I wore doing nothing to hide how hard he was. His hands went to my ass, kneading and messaging as his fingers drifted closer and closer to where I was already wet and ready for him.

"Melody, are you sure about this?" he breathed against my lips.

"Please, Ramsey. I need to come," I begged.

He yanked my sweatpants down and shoved a hand

between us. I loved feeling his cock, but one brush of his fingers on my sensitive skin and I was backing away to give him access.

He groaned when his finger slid into me. "Fuck, Mel. You're so damn wet. Have you been thinking about me a lot, baby?"

"Yes," I answered honestly. "All the time."

"What do you think about? Tell me what you wish I was doing to you."

"Touching me. Your fingers inside me. Playing with my clit. And your cock stretching me out."

"Do you get out your vibrator?" he asked.

I shook my head. My hips rocked with his gentle strokes. I needed more, but Ramsey never let me down. I wasn't sure how long I could be patient. "After Amber heard me, I've been afraid to make too much noise."

"Oh, babe, I'm sorry. I wish I was here to help you."

"You are now," I breathed.

"Yes," he groaned.

He pulsed a finger into me, and I almost screamed. I let my head fall forward and bit into his shoulder to stifle the shout. He thrust in again, swiping his thumb over my clit, and I swear, I saw fucking stars.

"More," I begged, not ashamed at all that I was whimpering.

He listened, adding another finger and pressing my thighs wider with his free hand. "I can smell you, Mel. You're close, beautiful. Tell me you're close. I can feel it."

"So close," I murmured. I rode his hand, needing to let go. I threw my head back and cried out when he cupped my breast and plucked my nipple. He met my body's strokes, pulsing in and out of me in the same rhythm. His thumb on my clit, his fingers inside me, his hand on my breast. All of it was too much. Not enough. Just right.

"Yes, babe, yes," he groaned as my orgasm hit me. "Fuck, Mel, you're so fucking gorgeous. Don't stop, baby. Take another one. Come again for me, sweetheart."

I couldn't say no as his fingers fucked me harder. He added a third and sent me flying just that quickly. I bit my lip so Amber didn't hear us and pumped my hips up and down, needing more and more and more from him.

"Jesus, Mel, I love you so much."

"I love you," I breathed, relieved to say the words I'd been fighting for so long.

I collapsed onto him, exhausted from the orgasms. I hadn't been able to make myself do what he did, and it was amazing and beautiful and exhausting.

Ramsey held me, one hand stroking up and down my back while the other stayed locked between us, his fingers still buried deep inside me. Every twitch made my body jump, but I was too worn out to come again.

As the fog lifted, I heard Ramsey whispering to me. Nothing profound, just words of love over and over. "I love you. I miss you. You're so beautiful. Sexy as hell."

"Thank you," I whispered back. The simple words weren't enough to convey how much I appreciated him. Not just for the orgasms, but for everything. For being there. For letting me in. For giving us another chance.

I finally sat up and took stock of us. His face was a mask of desire with a smirk for good measure. I smiled at him and shook my head.

"What?" he asked.

"You look so pleased with yourself."

He chuckled and wiggled his fingers. "I'm pretty pleased with you."

I moaned. My eyes slid closed and my body clenched his fingers.

"More?"

I shook my head. "I think I'll die if I have more."

He chuckled. "What a way to go."

He meant it as a joke, something we said to each other all the time, but it was a reminder of Steven for me. A reminder of the one person we shared who left us.

I pulled back and moved to crawl off him. His hand got stuck in my sweatpants. I met his gaze, and whatever he saw in mine had him sighing and extracting himself from me.

I stood and fixed my pants. He watched me, his eyes never leaving me. I took a breath and chewed on my lip.

"I didn't mean it that way," he said softly.

I nodded. "I know. It's just that he's the reason we're here. He's why we're not together. He's the reason you're going to walk out that door instead of hold my hand and follow me to bed. He's why we just did…that…on the couch instead of in our bedroom. Because we lost him."

Ramsey shook his head and stood. He was still erect, his cock poking at his zipper. The greedy, horny side of me wanted to ignore everything and drop to my knees in front of my husband, but the grown up adult side said we needed to talk.

"Losing him isn't why I left. It's why you did."

"I didn't leave," I said. "You were the one who walked out."

"After you left. You checked out, Mel. Losing him destroyed you, and—"

"He was our son, Ramsey. He was our child, a part of us that we brought into the world, and instead of keeping him safe, I lost him. I let him down. He died inside of me."

"And again, that was not your fault. I know losing him almost killed you. It almost killed me, too. But losing you was so much harder. Losing you…I can't handle that."

"Then why did you walk away?"

"Because you weren't willing to change your dream, Melody. You weren't willing to accept that our family was perfect. And if it wasn't, it wasn't going to be perfect if we lost you."

"You're not going to lose me," I said.

"We did, Mel. We did. You were gone. For six months, you didn't exist. Amber and I tiptoed around you. And when you finally came back to us, all you cared about was getting pregnant again. You would attack me when you thought you were ovulating. You didn't want me, you wanted a baby. Do you know how it felt to know the only reason my wife was interested was because she hoped I'd get her pregnant?"

"Why is that wrong?"

"Because keeping my hands off you is almost impossible for me. Because when you walk into a room, I get hard. Because when I think about you, I want to strip you down and make you scream my name. But you only saw a sperm bank. A sperm bank that could either kill you for real or destroy you when you lost another baby."

I stared at my husband and wondered who he was. How he could possibly think I didn't want him, especially after what just happened. It wasn't about sex or getting pregnant. It was about sharing something with him. It was about relief, but it was also about Ramsey.

"Ramsey…"

"Tell me one thing, Mel. Do you still want a baby? Is that still something you will do anything to have? Or are you ready to find a new dream together?"

I froze. A voice inside whispered to answer him, but I couldn't. I couldn't.

And after a minute, he nodded and left. The soft click of acceptance louder than a slam would have been.

16

———

I cried myself to sleep after Ramsey left. I felt like shit when I got up Saturday. Makayla and Casey showed up for lunch and I barely had the energy to make food for us.

"Are you sick?" Casey asked when Amber rushed Makayla to her room.

I shook my head. "No, I'm fine. Just upset."

"Did Robin call you?"

"Robin? From class? No, why would she call me?"

"She asked me about you helping her with Andrea's party. I figured that's why you were upset."

I sighed. "Nope. I'm upset because of my husband."

"Got any wine?"

I cocked my head to the side in question.

"Don't you know 'playdate' is really code for letting our kids entertain each other while we drink?" Casey asked.

A laugh bubbled out. I shook my head. "I have been doing playdates all wrong."

Casey looped her arm through mine. We chuckled and headed for the kitchen.

Once we had glasses of wine and took a seat at the table, Casey asked, "So, what's wrong?"

I chuckled and shook my head. "Trust me, you don't want to know."

Casey grinned and leaned in. Her dark hair slid over her shoulder and her eyes sparkled. "Now I really want to know."

I groaned and looked up at the ceiling, hoping it would give me some answers. Unfortunately it didn't, but I had a friend sitting there who might have some.

"Ramsey came over last night," I began.

Casey put her hand on mine. "Was that a good thing?"

I breathed a laugh. "It was a very, very good thing. Three times."

"You slept with him three times? Damn. You were making up for lost time."

I shook my head. "We didn't have sex."

Casey smirked. "Even better. Good for you taking what you want from him."

I grinned. "It wasn't like that. Well, it was, but I didn't really mean it to be."

Casey's grin fell. "Okay, back up and tell me exactly what happened."

I sighed and told her the whole story from Ramsey showing up to Ramsey walking out the door. She reacted the way anyone would have going from delight to shock when I admitted what happened that led to him leaving.

"Are you okay?" she asked.

I shrugged. "I don't know."

"Can I ask you a question?"

I nodded.

"How good were the orgasms?"

I snorted a laugh. "Really, really good, but I don't know what that has to do with anything."

"If the orgasms were that good, I'm jealous, first of all.

Secondly, you still have chemistry. That means there's a chance for you two."

I shook my head. "I don't know. He asked if I was ready to give up wanting to get pregnant again. He said nothing had changed if I wasn't. And he's right."

Casey gave me a sad smile. "When Kyle and I decided to start counseling, I wasn't sure it was going to work. He hadn't looked at me in far too long. I was half convinced he was having an affair. Our spark was gone. I still love him, but he felt more like a roommate than my husband. Even now, there are days when I'm annoyed when he comes home. Maybe I shouldn't admit that, but it's true because at the end of the day, we still don't have that chemistry. He doesn't look at me and make me wet. I wish he did, but he just doesn't."

"God, Casey, I'm so sorry. How do you live like that?"

She shrugged and took another sip of her wine. "I pretend to be asleep when he comes to bed. I avoid eye contact when we're awake. I don't rock the boat and I schedule playdates when I know he's off work."

I laughed with her but neither of us found it very funny.

"What I'm saying is I wish I had what you have. I know your husband moved out and I know things suck right now, but he still wants you. You still want him. And sex doesn't fix everything, but it sure does help."

I sighed. The wine was helping me relax. I leaned back in my seat. "I think it's almost the opposite for us. I want more kids. I've always wanted a big family. I lost our son, and my doctor said getting pregnant again was a risk. I could...I could die, and if I survived, I might not be able to carry the baby."

Casey flinched. "Seriously?"

I nodded.

"I'm sorry, but I have to ask why in the hell you would even consider getting pregnant again."

"I've always wanted a lot of kids. We bought a four bedroom house, and I pictured the kids sharing rooms. I love kids. It's why I became a teacher."

Casey nodded, her lips pursed and her brows pulled together. "I still don't get it. If you get pregnant again and something happens, you still won't have another child, but you could also die, which means you wouldn't be around to see those kids. With how many kids out there who need homes, why wouldn't you adopt if you want more kids?"

I shrugged again. "I loved being pregnant. I love everything about it. And the doctors...well, it's not a guarantee. I could have a perfectly normal pregnancy with no complications."

"They told you that?" Casey asked.

I shook my head. "Well, no, but I know that's how it works. None of this stuff is a hundred percent. And I had Amber without any issues."

"Um, sometimes that isn't how it works, though," Casey said carefully. "There are medical conditions where you can't get pregnant."

"My mom was told she couldn't get pregnant again, then she had my sister," I argued.

Casey nodded. "Sure, but a lot has changed since then. We learn more every day than we used to learn in a year it seems. And medicine...everything is different now than when we were born. I don't think the doctors were telling you not to get pregnant because they don't want you to have children. I think they were telling you because they don't want you to die."

I took a breath and tried to hear her, really hear her, but my brain blocked the words I didn't want to process. So I smiled and nodded and sipped my wine and asked her about Makayla.

Sunday wasn't much better than Saturday. Amber and I spent the day together, playing outside and being silly. I tried to let it boost my mood, but I couldn't shake it.

Willow came over late in the afternoon looking like she'd been up all night.

"Well, not all night," she said with a wink.

I just shook my head. I adored my sister and was jealous of how easily she let her guard down.

"How are you? You look all mopey and weird," Willow said, taking stock of me.

I shook my head again and avoided meeting her gaze. Willow could always read me. When we were kids, it came in handy to warn the other one about Mom's moods, but as adults, it was just annoying. Especially when I wanted to hide my thoughts from her.

"I'm fine. Just anxious about this."

"Then don't go," Willow said quickly. She and Finley had never gotten along either, so it didn't surprise me she wasn't in favor of me hanging out there. The rest of the women seemed nice enough, but we weren't friends. It wouldn't take much for Willow to talk me out of it.

"I told Blake I'd come."

"You told Blake you'd think about it."

I sighed. "I don't feel right blowing her off. She's been nice to me."

"I'm always nice to you, and you're fine blowing me off."

"That's because you're my pesky little sister," I said with a smile.

Willow stuck her tongue out at me. "How late are you going to be? Do I need to get Amber into bed?"

I shrugged. "I have no idea. Hopefully not, but who knows."

"Maybe I should call you thirty minutes in and say you need to come home."

I snorted. "That's what you do on a bad date."

Willow blinked. "And?"

"This isn't a date. It's just a night out with some new friends."

"Mmm hmm."

After we ate dinner, I brushed my hair and swiped on some lipgloss. I hated how women always felt the need to impress each other, but I still fell victim to the trap. It was cold out, so I wore fleece lined leggings and a long sweatshirt. I added a pair of boots and my winter coat and decided it was going to have to be good enough.

"Are you coming back?" Amber asked before I left.

I nodded. "Of course. I don't know how late, though. If I'm not back before bedtime, Aunt Willow will help you."

"Can I stay up until you get home?"

"Um, no. You need some sleep. But I'll be here in the morning."

Amber nodded and hugged me tight. I'd already warned Willow she'd been extra clingy all weekend. I loved it, but it wasn't like Amber, which concerned me.

I was still trying to figure out what could be bothering her when I knocked on the door to Book Boyfriends Unlimited. The closed sign was flipped, but lights were on in the back so I hoped Blake wasn't joking when she said they met there.

After a long moment, Finley appeared. She narrowed her eyes when she saw I was the one on the other side of the door. I pressed my lips into a smile and waved.

Finley unlocked the door and said, "We're closed. You're going to need to come back tomorrow."

"Actually," I said as she closed the door in my face, "Blake invited me."

Finley's eyebrows jerked up. Her lips flattened into a line. She finally stepped back and let me walk in.

It was warm inside her store. I'd never been there before since she was the owner, but it was a cute place. A display near the front proudly displayed book recommended by locals. I recognized some of the covers, but a lot of them were books I didn't know.

"We're in the back," Finley said flatly, leaving me to follow her.

"Who's here?" her friends asked before I walked into view.

Finley didn't reply, but I could feel the tension when I turned the corner and saw all of them sitting in a circle. There was a cake plate with a chocolate cake on a coffee table between them. Finley took a seat in an oversized red chair. The others just sat and stared at me.

Except Blake. Thank God for Blake. She jumped up and hugged me like we were the best of friends. She dragged me over to sit with her on the loveseat she'd claimed and smiled.

"I wasn't sure you were going to come," Blake said.

I shrugged and looked around. I still had my coat on and held my purse on my lap. Uncomfortable didn't even begin to describe how I was feeling.

"Take off your coat," Blake said. "We're really casual here. And we're talking about this book. It just came out."

I nodded and struggled to remove my coat while I was sitting on it. I felt like an animal at the zoo. Or maybe a fish. They all just stared at me, waiting to see what I was going to do next.

"Guys," Blake hissed, and finally broke their spell.

"You totally should have told us," Elise said, not bothering to hide her irritation.

"Why?" Blake demanded. "Melody is my friend. And she needs friends. I invited her here because she's going through some shit, and we're always going through shit. We all know what it's like to feel alone. So, I invited her here so for a couple hours, she didn't feel quite so alone."

My cheeks burned. I pressed my lips together to keep from saying I was going to just go. Blake stared down her friends, begging each of them to challenge her. I appreciated the show of solidarity, but I wasn't sure it mattered to a group of people I didn't know.

"Well, I don't know what the problem with you being here is, so I'm going to say hi and pretend it's not all awkward. I'm Trinity," she said. She waved from her seat across the room. She was beautiful with naturally curly hair and perfect curves.

I said hi and thanked her.

Elise spoke up next. "Did you kiss your husband again?"

I gasped and wondered how in the hell she knew that. "What?"

Elise snorted when she saw my face. Then she smirked and cut a piece of cake. She handed it to me, got one for herself and sat back. "We need details."

"There are no details," I said softly.

"Ah, no. That's not how this works. If we're going to be friends, you need to spill." She turned to everyone else and said, "She and Ramsey kissed a couple weeks ago. She was all upset about it because he said something stupid, but she still wants him. And it looks like maybe she got her way."

"My sister is home with Amber right now, not Ramsey, so I definitely didn't get my way," I said.

"You got something," Elise said, raising an eyebrow in challenge.

I held out as long as I could then sighed. "Fine, yes. We... fooled around the other night. But he left when I couldn't tell him I don't want more kids."

"You don't?" Blake breathed.

"No, that's not what I meant. He asked me if I was ready to give up on getting pregnant again, but I didn't answer him because I'm not."

Again, the room was quiet.

After a minute, Elise leaned forward. "Can we go back to the 'fooled around' part?"

And just like that, the tension in the room broke. Everyone laughed, and I managed to relax just a little bit.

I filled them in on what happened with Ramsey, feeling guilty that I was sharing it with people I barely knew and kept it from my sister. But I knew Willow would be mad. Blake and her friends were excited about it.

"I gotta tell you," Laura said. "If I had a man I loved as much as you love Ramsey, I would give up anything to be with him."

The others groaned.

"You have to hold your ground. You can't let him walk all over you and make demands. A relationship should be a partnership," Elise said. "Trust me, if it's not and one person has all the power, it gets ugly."

I was clearly the only one who didn't understand all the nuances of what she was saying, but I agreed with her. "My entire relationship with Ramsey has felt like letting him decide everything. I've always given in to him."

"About what?" Blake asked.

I shrugged. "Everything, it seems. From little things, like that we named our daughter, to big things, like where we live, Ramsey's always been the one in charge."

"I like it when a man takes charge," Karissa said. "I spend too many hours a day making decisions, and once in a while, I want someone else to do something."

"I get that, but if he's making demands, that's not healthy," Elise countered.

"Was it like that?" Blake asked.

I shook my head. "He never made demands, not like that. He just never gave up until I saw things his way. After a few years, I think I stopped forming an opinion and waited for him to tell me what to do."

"You're making me really not like your husband, and I don't even know him," Trinity said.

"Yes, you do. Ian's best friend, Ramsey," Blake said.

Trinity's eyes went wide, and she flashed me a guilty smile. "Sorry. I kind of hit on him a few weeks ago."

I shrugged and waved it off, but knowing another woman was flirting with my husband stung. Not because she admitted it, but because he never told me. He didn't tell me a lot of things. How many other women flirted with him? Did any of them do more than flirt?

We were technically still married, but we were separated, so he could sleep with someone else if he wanted. He could do anything he wanted. And I wouldn't be able to say a thing about it because if I'd been able to keep my husband happy, he'd still be at home instead of living like a bachelor.

"She's spiraling," Finley said.

"No, I'm not. I'm just…"

"Spiraling," Finley repeated. "It's okay. We all have our moments. You're just now realizing that your husband might have slept with someone else. And you're worried about it. Because you still love him and have hope that you'll be able to figure it out. You want him back."

"Well, of course I do! He's my husband. I've loved him almost my entire life. For twenty years, he's been the man I wanted to grow old with. He's it for me." I looked at Karissa. "Even your app paired us together. I know he's the one for me, but we can't get over this. I won't give in again, and he won't either."

"You used my app?" Karissa asked.

I nodded.

"And it paired you with Ramsey?"

I nodded again and chewed on my nail.

Karissa grinned. "Nice. I like it."

"But if we're supposed to be together, why aren't we?"

Everyone looked around and avoided me. I felt just as alone as when I walked in until Laura leaned forward and put her hand on mine. "I wonder the same thing all the time."

"Yeah, but you're in love with your boss," Finley said. "She wants to get back together with her husband. It's a little different."

"It is," Laura agreed. "But she's the kind of person who can give me hope. If it's meant to be, it'll be. Like Romeo and Juliet."

The others groaned.

"Romeo and Juliet is Laura's favorite romance, even though it's not really a romance," Blake said.

"It's a tragic love story," I said. "The Notebook is so much better. They fell in love, but lost each other. Then years later they were able to find each other again and build a life together. It's still a little tragic, but everyone dies eventually. No love story truly lasts forever. That's what makes love so perfect. It's fragile and delicate but life changing when it's right."

"And when it's wrong," Finley said. "Falling in love with the wrong someone can change you, too. It's not a good change, but not all change is good."

"True," Elise said. "If I'd never met Andy, my life would be very different than it is today."

Again, I was the only one who didn't understand. The others nodded, and Karissa grabbed Elise's hand.

And I realized going there was the best decision I'd made in a long time. I prejudged most of them, but they were amazing people. They cared about each other, and they wanted to find what Ramsey and I had. They loved and lost people, but they were still standing, fighting, striving for the kind of love I shared with my husband.

Which made me wonder if they were right. If there was a way to keep Ramsey in my life, why wouldn't I do it? Why did having another baby matter more to me than having my husband in my life? Because at the end of the day, did anything really matter if the people we love aren't there to share our lives?

RAMSEY

Blake refilled my coffee mug and asked if I was ready to order.

"Yeah, I'll have the special. And keep the coffee coming. I need it today."

"Everything okay?" Blake asked. She tucked her pad into her apron and tilted her head.

I didn't like people knowing what was going on in my world, but Blake wasn't just anyone. She was going to marry my best friend. "Just Melody."

"Aw, okay. Sorry. I shouldn't have asked." Her cheeks turned pink before she had a chance to get away.

"Do you know?" I asked.

She shook her head, but the flush darkened. "Know what?"

"Since when are you and Melody friends?"

Blake sighed. "Since she came to girls' night out last night."

I groaned. "She told everyone."

"Well, we kind of dragged it out of her."

I closed my eyes and took a deep breath. It didn't help. I

didn't know if I should be more angry or embarrassed. At the moment, embarrassed seemed to be winning the fight.

"Look, it's fine. We were all talking about relationships and stuff, and it's no big deal. We're not gossips," Blake said.

"Elise?"

Blake snorted. "Well, Elise kind of is, but never with anything we talk about there. It's like Fight Club. Or Vegas."

"What?"

Blake shook her head. She looked even more uncomfortable than I felt. "You know, the first rule of Fight Club?"

"Okay, but Vegas?"

"What happens in Vegas…"

A laugh broke free. I shook my head. "I hope you're right because I don't want the whole town talking about…that."

"Don't worry, it'll be…um…it'll be fine. Uh, Ramsey?"

I looked up at her and narrowed my eyes when I saw her staring past me. I turned in time to see Melody grin and walk toward me.

I was locked in place, watching her move around the tables, her curves brushing the edges of the tables and the backs of chairs as she wound through the crowd. Just seeing her move like that turned me on. Fuck me, everything about her turned me on.

She walked over and said hi, then stripped off her coat and hung it on the other chair at my table. "Hey, Blake. Can I get a coffee. And a scrambler?"

"Uh, sure. Yes, of course. Coffee? Wait, you already asked for coffee. I'll be right back."

Blake scurried away. I just kept staring at Melody.

"Hey. How are you?" she asked me.

Did I have a brain tumor? Or was I dreaming? I looked down. I wasn't naked, so at least it wasn't that dream. But Melody was sitting at a table with me about to have breakfast. It sure as hell wasn't reality.

"Ramsey? Are you okay?"

"Um, I don't know. Are you real?"

She laughed and shook her head. Blake set a mug down in front of Melody and filled it up with coffee. "Thanks, Blake."

"You're welcome."

Blake started to walk away, but I grabbed her arm. She looked at me with an eyebrow raised.

"Do you see her, too?"

Blake chuckled. "Yes, I do. She's really sitting there."

I let go of Blake's arm and picked up my coffee mug. I swallowed too much and it burned my throat going down. I coughed and gulped water to help the burn. "What are you doing here, Melody?"

She shrugged. "I wanted to have breakfast with you."

"Okay, but why?"

She sighed. "I think maybe we should start over. Try again. I know we have history, lots of it, but somewhere along the way, I think we lost why we're together."

"I know why I'm with you. Because I love you."

"Tell me five things you love about me," Melody said.

"Your smile, the way you are with Amber, how much you make me laugh, the way you look when you come, and waking up to you in the mornings when you're all sleepy and ruffled and don't want to get up but you do because you take care of everyone."

Her cocky grin faltered.

I leaned forward and linked my fingers before resting my hands on the table. "I'm guessing you can't tell me five things you love about me." I lifted an eyebrow in a challenge.

"I can actually. I love how you always make sure I'm happy before you ever think of yourself, the goofy side you only show me, how patient you are with Amber, the lengths you go to help your clients get their dreams, and the look in your eyes when you're turned on."

My cock pressed against my zipper. I drew in a breath and tried to figure out what was going on.

"I went out with Blake's friends last night," Melody began.

"I heard."

She looked up at me, then her eyes widened and her neck flushed. "I didn't mean to tell them what happened. We were just talking and it sort of came out."

"It's fine," I told her. "Blake said they don't talk. Even Elise."

"I know, but I don't want you to think I'm going around telling everyone intimate details of our relationship."

"Aside from them and Willow, who did you talk to?"

"I didn't tell Willow," Melody said.

"Really?" I shook my head. "It doesn't matter. I know you told Blake's friends. It's fine."

"Good, but um, they said something that made me think. I don't want to lose you. I know we still have stuff to figure out, but I don't want to lose you."

"Um, okay."

"I love our family, and I love you, and I know we can figure this out, okay? Just, let's try, okay?"

Her lip wobbled, and I had to nod. I hated when she cried. I'd spent more than half my life trying to make sure she was happy, and when I failed to do that, I couldn't handle it.

"We'll try, Mel. We'll try."

She reached across the table and grabbed my hand. I held on to hers until Blake brought our food out.

Melody talked through the rest of breakfast like nothing had ever happened between us. When we were done, she kissed me on the cheek before she went down the street to work, leaving me next to my car to figure out what in the world was going on.

THE REST OF THE DAY, Melody sent me messages in Book Boyfriends Wanted with things she loved about me. She never said exactly what Blake and her friends said that made her want to work things out, but I was cautiously optimistic.

Colin showed up Wednesday after lunch while I was reading the latest message from Melody.

"You look happy about something," he said when he walked into my office.

I locked my phone and set it face down so I didn't get distracted by any other messages from her. "Hey. I didn't realize we were meeting today."

Colin shook his head. "We're not. I just wanted to check in."

"I still haven't heard from Carter," I told him as he sat.

He sighed. "Any idea how long he's going to take to make a decision? I have stuff that needs to get done, but if I have to buy him out, I don't want to spend too much money."

Colin looked more like I expected was normal for him. His jean coat had a thick lining. Beneath his coat was a brown zip-up hoodie the exact color of his skin and a gray tee. His jeans were well-worn and his boots had clumps of dirt on them.

He was the kind of person I went into business to help. An everyday kind of guy who just wanted to do something he enjoyed. Someone who had a dream and wanted to live out that dream.

"I'll reach out to him today. We didn't give him a deadline, but you shouldn't be waiting around forever either. What kind of time frame are you looking at to make some decisions?"

Colin shrugged and crossed one boot over the other knee. He grabbed his ankle and met my gaze. "A couple of weeks? Sooner would be better, but according to Nicky, two to three weeks is all I have to start spending some money if I want to open up this year."

"You don't think you will?"

"I want to. I plan to. But what if Carter says he wants his half and he has some opinions on how the place should be run?"

"He might not," I said.

Colin nodded. "I can't go to the bank with might. I need to know one way or another. I want to open the farm. I want to tap all the trees, not just a few acres. I want to make this place what it used to be. I know it's going to take time, and I know it's not going to be easy. But it'll be a hell of a lot easier if the money I'm going to sink into this place is going to turn a profit instead of get sucked into the bank account of some guy who's never set foot on the land."

I took a deep breath, hoping if I remained calm, Colin would relax. He had every right to be pissed off and worried. I thought Carter would have called by now. It had been almost a week since he was in my office and I told him he was a partial heir to a maple farm. It was a big deal, but a week was a long time to think about it and start to come up with a plan.

"Do you want me to call him right now? While you're here?"

Colin shook his head. "No. I don't think I can handle that." He stood. "Are you still going to bring your daughter out to the farm this weekend?"

I nodded and stood with him. "If that's okay."

"Yeah, of course. I'm trying to think of some activities I can set up for kids. Maybe talk to the local schools about doing field trips once we're up and running full time. I want the Farm to be what it used to be. A place where people felt comfortable and wanted to spend time."

"That's a great idea, Colin. My wife used to be a teacher

and still knows some of the teachers at the elementary school. I'm sure she can put you in touch with someone."

Colin's brows went up. "Your wife? Does that mean you've reconciled?"

I chuckled and shook my head. "I don't know what it means."

"Well, I guess it means that look you had on your face earlier was because of her."

I smirked.

He clapped me on the back. "Good for you."

I shook my head again. "It's not all fixed."

"But you're trying?"

I shrugged. "She wants to try again. To start over and figure things out together. I haven't moved back in yet, but we're talking more in the last couple days than we have in almost two years, so I'll take it."

"Good," he said. "Good. It's all going to work out. Hey, why don't you bring her to the Farm this weekend with your daughter?"

"I'll ask her. See what she has going on."

"Sounds good. Hey, let me know as soon as you know something, okay?"

I nodded. "I will, Colin."

He shook my hand and left with a smile on his face. I just hoped it would stay there after I talked to Carter.

SINCE CARTER WORKED A NINE-TO-FIVE JOB, I waited until the end of the day to call him. He answered on the second ring.

"Hello?"

"Carter. This is Ramsey Holland. We met last week. I'm the lawyer for Cleotha Jones."

"Hey, Ramsey. Um, this isn't really a great time. Do you think I can give you a call tomorrow?"

"Um, sure. We're just anxious to hear if you've had a chance to think—"

"Yeah, sorry. I'm running out the door. I'll give you a call in the morning. Thanks. Bye."

He hung up before I could say another word. I stared at my phone until a new message popped up from Melody.

WEBMOMMY

I love your voice in the morning right after you wake up when it's all scratchy and sexy.

I smiled and shook my head. If nothing else, sharing all the things we loved about each other was doing wonders for my imagination. I could picture Melody getting off in any number of ways because of all the dirty things she said she loved about me.

And the not so dirty.

RH214

I love the way you look in the shower…with bubbles running in rivers over your body, catching on your nipples and your curves and your pussy. I can't wait to watch you shower again.

She texted me a winky face as Penny walked in with her coat on.

"I'm heading home for the day unless you need anything else."

I shook my head. "No, I'm good. I'll walk out with you if you give me a second."

"You're ready to leave?" she asked.

I rolled my eyes. "Haha. Yes, I'm leaving. I'm making an

effort to be a normal person and get out of the office at a reasonable hour."

"Are you going to see Melody?"

"No, I'm going to Ian's."

"Ian and Blake's or Ian's where you live?"

"Ian and Blake's. They invited me over for dinner. I think Blake feels bad that she told me Melody was talking about us."

"What about?"

My cheeks heated. I ducked my head to collect my things, hoping she wouldn't notice. "Just some things going on."

"Ramsey Holland! Are you messing around with your wife?"

"She is my wife. It's not like I'm messing around on her."

"Ramsey, that's great news."

I shook my head. "I don't know if it is. She stopped it when I made another stupid comment. She said she still wants more kids. But then Monday, she met me for breakfast and since then has been sending me messages about all the things she loves about me."

"Aw, that's so sweet."

I chuckled. "Yes, but a few weeks ago, we were barely speaking. Now, she's jumping me when I come into her house and telling me all the dirty things she wants to do to me and with me. Something changed, and I don't know what."

"Why do you need to?" Penny asked. "She knows you aren't willing to have more kids. If she's doing all this, she's doing it because she's ready for things to go back to how they were. She wants you back."

I nodded and tried to smile.

"You don't think that's what's going on?" Penny asked.

We locked the office and stepped out into the cold. There was something going on with Melody that I couldn't put my finger on. I didn't know what it was, but something about the whole thing wasn't sitting right.

"I'm sure that's all. I think I'm just trying not to get my hopes up. It's been a long time."

Penny patted my arm. "It's almost over now."

I smiled and thanked her. Maybe she was right. Maybe I was being paranoid.

I was working on being hopeful on my drive to Blake and Ian's. They were all happy and shiny and perfect, and I couldn't let my failing, hanging-by-a-thread marriage taint theirs.

Ian opened the door when I knocked and immediately handed me a beer.

"Uh, thanks. That bad of a day?"

Ian shook his head. "Blake's on a mission to make you like her. She asked me what your favorites foods were and tried to cook."

"Tried?"

"She doesn't cook," Ian said quietly. "And there's a reason for it. I love her, but she's not a chef."

"What did she make?"

"Pulled pork and mashed potatoes."

"Really?"

Ian nodded and pursed his lips. He handed me a twenty. "Pick up dinner on your way home."

I pushed his money back at him and laughed. "It can't be that bad."

Ian's brows went up and he grinned. "Oh, just wait."

I followed Ian to the kitchen where Blake was waving her hand in front of the open stove. Smoke was billowing out of the oven.

"Hey, babe. How's it going?"

"Fuck. Fuckity fuck fuck. How long until Ramsey is here?"

"Hey, Blake," I said.

"Dammit. I burned dinner. I'm so sorry, Ramsey."

"No worries, Blake. We can just order a pizza or something."

"But we invited you over so you could have a home cooked meal. I'm sure some of it is still good." She grabbed pot holders and pulled the smoking meat out of the oven. She set the pan on the stovetop and grabbed a set of tongs. She started picking apart the sizzling pork. With each pull, smokey meat flaked off like charcoal.

Ian and I exchanged a look. Ian stepped forward. "Babe, it's fine. Let's call something in."

"No, Ian. I wanted this to be good. I'm sure it's okay. We can just put some sauce on it. It'll be fine. I wanted to do something nice for Ramsey."

"When Melody and I first got married, we were both working, and neither of us had lived on our own much. Neither of us cooked a lot, so we ate a lot of burnt meals."

"Is it that bad?" Blake asked, her watery eyes going back to the pile of smoke.

"No, Blake, it's fine. Let's try it. Plates?" I asked.

She pointed to a cabinet and wiped the tears running over her cheeks. I searched for what I needed while Ian pulled her into his arms and whispered something to her.

Seeing them together reminded me of Melody and I before everything went to shit. Blake laughed, and Ian kissed her. My chest fucking hurt. I wanted that again.

Did it matter if something else was going on with Melody? Did I really care? Or was I ready to stop fighting with her and have my family back?

I was pretty sure it was the second option.

I never heard back from Carter. All week I waited for him to call me back like he said, but he never did. I tried him a few more times, but each call went unanswered. I did not have a good feeling about that.

By the time I left work Friday afternoon, I was frustrated. I didn't know what it meant that he wasn't answering my calls, and without a clear deadline for when he needed to accept or reject the farm, I was just sitting on my hands, waiting for Carter to do something.

The only good news I had for the week was Melody invited me over for dinner. She said she wanted the three of us to spend some time together.

I still couldn't figure out why she'd changed so quickly, but I was trying hard not to fight it. I wanted things to get better with Melody, so I was being open to whatever she wanted.

As long as it wasn't a kid.

I drove home and changed quickly, then went back to the house. I rang the bell and waited.

Melody opened the door looking like the best fantasy in

the world. Her hair was pulled up in a messy ponytail with pieces falling out everywhere. She was in another of my old tees. She had leggings on and bare feet. No makeup and a streak of something that look like flour on her cheek.

"Why didn't you just come in?" she asked.

I took a minute to keep staring at her.

"What?"

I shook my head. "Nothing. Just thinking about how beautiful you are."

She scoffed. "Not even a little. I'm a mess. I wanted to make a good dinner, but the day got away from me."

"You're gorgeous, Melody. The most beautiful woman I've ever seen." My voice hitched with emotion I could barely hold back. She was definitely my home. She was everything I'd ever wanted in life. And she was willing to try again.

"Thank you," she finally said softly. "Come in. Get out of the cold."

I nodded and stepped inside. She closed the door behind me and rubbed her hands together.

"It's getting colder. All the parents are worried school is going to be closed a few days next week."

"It's possible. We're at the end of January, so plenty more winter to come."

She grinned. "I know. I love it."

Melody always said winter was her favorite season. Between Thanksgiving, Christmas, New Year's, and Valentine's Day, winter had all her favorite holidays. She said even more than that, she liked the cozy nights in front of a fire, the hot chocolate after a day of sledding, and ice skating.

Of course, my mind just picked up on the cozy nights in front of the fire. We had more than a few of those.

"What are you thinking about?" she asked.

I grinned. "I was just wondering if I should start a fire in the fireplace."

A blush crept up Melody's cheeks. She bit her lip and nodded. "That sounds like a really good idea."

"Daddy!" Amber shouted, racing into my arms.

I grabbed her and held her close. One day, I promised her silently, we'll all be under the same roof again for good.

"How was your day, big girl?" I asked, carrying her to the living room.

"Good. My teacher said I'm a great reader," she told me with a grin.

"I bet it's because you and Mommy read all the time."

Amber nodded. "That's what my teacher said, too."

"Reading is a great thing to do. Hopefully you keep reading."

"I will, Daddy. Are you staying here tonight?"

I shook my head. "No, honey. But I am going to build a fire. Do you want to help me?"

"Really? A fire? Mommy said we can't when I ask because we're almost out of wood."

I glanced at the small pile next to the fireplace. "Is this all you have?" I asked Melody.

She nodded. "I can't carry the packs by myself to get them into my car."

"I'll get some for you. Especially with the storm coming next week. Just in case."

She smiled. I winked at her, then went back to building a fire with Amber. Melody went to the kitchen while we worked on getting the fire going.

We decided to eat in front of the fireplace so we could enjoy it. Melody cooked pot roast, one of my favorite cold weather meals, and baked fresh bread, which explained the flour I finally told her was on her cheek.

"Are you going out with Aunt Willow later, Mommy?" Amber asked as she reached for a slice of warm bread.

Melody glanced at me, then shook her head. "No, honey. I'm staying home tonight."

"Good. I like it better when you're home."

"Me, too," Melody said.

We finished eating dinner and I put another log on the fire. Amber was extra cuddly, so we all sat on the couch and watched a movie. She held my hand and rested her head on Melody's chest until she fell asleep partway through the movie.

"This week took a lot out of her."

"Do you think she's getting sick?"

Melody shook her head. "No, but they've been playing outside all week at school. Sledding down the hill behind the school. She's been coming home more exhausted than usual. Hopefully she can rest a little extra this weekend."

"Is it still okay for her to come to Jones Farm with me tomorrow?"

Melody nodded. "Absolutely. She's so excited about that."

"You should come, too," I said casually, hoping I didn't sound as excited about spending more time with her as I was.

Melody smiled. "I would, but I have a meeting. One of the other moms in her class wanted to talk to me about helping plan her daughter's party."

"Oh, okay. I should have asked earlier."

"It's fine. You and Amber haven't been spending as much time together lately. I feel like I'm intruding on your nights with her."

I reached across Amber with my free hand and cupped Melody's jaw. She looked up at me from beneath her dark lashes.

"I miss both of you. I want to spend as much time with both of you as I can. So, no, you're not intruding. I'd rather have you here."

Melody smiled and nodded, gently dislodging her cheek from my hand.

"Should I put her to bed?" I asked.

Melody looked down at Amber, softly snoring against her shoulder, and nodded. "Probably. She's not going to wake up. She can brush her teeth in the morning."

I lifted Amber into my arms and carried her down the hall to her room. Melody followed us, pulling Amber's blanket back so I could lay her in her bed. We tucked her in and both whispered goodnight, then closed her door and went back to the living room.

The cartoon movie Amber picked was still on the screen. Transitioning from daddy to husband was as easy as stopping the movie and tossing a pillow on the floor in front of the fireplace.

Melody looked at me with those eyes that said she was just as ready for the rest of our night as I was.

She moved around the coffee table and stood in front of me. My fingers ached to reach out to her, but I was still trying to follow her lead. If she said no, I was done. If she begged me to touch her, I'd gladly do it. But she was the one calling the shots.

She tilted her head and threaded her arms around my neck. I slipped my hands onto her waist and eased her closer, resisting the urge to yank her body tight against mine. She pulled me down to her until our lips brushed.

I still held back, dying inside, but letting her lead. She pressed her tongue to my lips and moaned softly when I opened for her. I swept my tongue through her mouth, needing to take just a little from her. She moved closer, her perfect breasts flattening against my chest.

I tightened my hold on her, wrapping my arms farther around her body. Her curves tortured me. All the softness of her cradling my hardness. I ached to sink into her, to forget about anything keeping us apart and just have her again. I wanted to move back in and never let her go again. But I committed to letting her call the shots. To letting her decide how things were going to go. I was the one who messed up and walked out. I wasn't going to mess up again.

Melody pulled back just a little and wiggled for me to loosen my hold on her. She kissed my jaw and nibbled on my neck. She pulled my shirt up and pushed at my jeans.

"Mel," I groaned.

She lowered to her knees in front of me and unzipped my jeans. She guided them to the floor then slid my briefs down. My cock was hard and ready for her, but I still jumped when she wrapped her little hand around it.

"Fuck, Melody."

"I've missed this," she said softly. "I've missed being able to make you lose your mind."

"It's already fucking gone, baby. Every time I see you I lose my mind."

She smiled up at me as she stroked my cock. I yanked my shirt up and off so I didn't miss a thing. Her hand squeezed and stroked. Her thumb swiped at the drops of pre-cum that leaked out.

Then she leaned forward and slicked her tongue along the underside of my cock.

"Oh, God, Mel," I groaned. I grabbed her hair, pulling it back from her face to watch my cock disappear into her pretty pink lips.

She slid her tongue to my head and licked around my crown, then opened her mouth and sucked me inside. My hand had nothing on her mouth. It had been so long since I'd been inside her, I'd almost forgotten how good she felt, but one suck and I was ready to blow.

"So perfect, Mel. You're so fucking beautiful. I love watching you."

She hummed her agreement and looked up at me. She held my gaze as she pumped her head and hand together. I didn't have to guide her at all. She knew exactly how to squeeze and stroke and suck to bring me right to the edge.

"You need to stop, Mel," I groaned, dying to come but knowing she needed to first.

She bit down gently on me, and I saw fucking stars. I couldn't control myself anymore. I fucked her mouth, needing to come more than I needed anything else in life. Except her.

She cupped my balls and tugged gently, and I fucking lost it. I thrust deep into her throat and held her there as I emptied myself. The entire time, she watched me, her eyes on mine as I lost my damn mind.

I loosened my grip on her hair and she eased back. She sucked me back in once more, and my whole body jerked, then she released me and swallowed.

Her lips were red and swollen. I dropped to my knees in front of her and kissed her hard. She responded immediately, opening her lips and tangling her tongue with mine. I could taste the last bit of my come in her mouth and wanted more. I needed more. Of her. Of us.

"That was…"

"Yeah," she said. "I've missed that. A lot."

"Thank you."

She smiled and hugged me, holding me tight. We stayed like that, on our knees in front of the fire, for a long moment. When we finally pulled back, she looked up at me with a smile. "Thank you for giving us another chance."

"Thank you," I said honestly. "I never thought you'd be willing to even talk about something else. I know we have a lot to figure out, but I'm just happy we're going to try."

"Me, too," she said against my chest. "Do you want to stay

for a little while? We can watch a movie and just be here together."

"What about you?" I asked her. "You didn't get to come yet."

She shook her head and pulled back to look at me. "I just wanted to taste you tonight. Is that okay?"

Normally, I would have said no, but the look in her eyes said she got all she needed from giving me a blow job. I felt like a cocky ass for even thinking it, but I knew how amazing it felt to be able to make the person you love feel good. So I nodded and got dressed, then held her on the couch while we watched a movie. Together.

THE LAST TIME I was at Jones Family Maple Farm was before Amber was born. Melody loved their maple candy, and the syrup was the best around. We always planned a visit around the beginning of the season.

I'd never been there when there was snow on the ground. Colin was doing what he could to get the farm ready to open, but it was early. In two months, he'd be almost finished collecting sap from the trees. After that, he could open the place up and start to accept visitors.

Amber whispered, "Wow," from the backseat as we drove up the long road toward the barn. Massive maple trees lined the road, showcasing exactly why the farm was there.

"Pretty awesome, right?" I said.

She nodded. "Can we get some syrup while we're here?"

I chuckled. "I'm not sure if they have any yet. It's a little early in the year."

"They have some at the grocery store," Amber said, clearly not impressed.

I nodded. "True. But this is special syrup. We'll ask Mr. Jones."

Amber nodded again and kept looking out the window. When we made it to the barn, she scrambled out of the back-seat and stared up at the trees far above her head.

"Hello!" Colin greeted us. The door slammed closed behind him. He walked toward us, grinning from ear to ear. "I see she's a tree lover."

I nodded. "She is. She loves being outside. Amber, this is Mr. Jones. Colin, my daughter, Amber."

"Hi," Amber said shyly, holding onto my leg. Growing up in a town like MacKellar Cove where everyone knew every-one, Amber hadn't met many strangers. Even her teachers were people she'd seen around town before she started school. But Colin hadn't been in MacKellar Cove long, so Amber didn't know him.

"It's nice to meet you, Amber," Colin said, crouching in front of her. "Do you want to see my favorite tree?"

"You have a favorite tree?" Amber asked.

Colin nodded. "I do."

"How did you pick just one with all these trees?"

"It was the first tree I ever tapped myself."

"What does that mean?" Amber asked. She pushed her hat back with a gloved hand.

Colin pulled a spile out of his back pocket. "This is a spile. We drill a small hole in each tree, more than one if it's a big tree, and we put this in. A bucket hangs right here and collects the sap."

"Can we eat some?" Amber asked, her eyes bright with excitement. She reached for Colin's hand and let him lead her toward the barn.

Colin looked back at me and winked then nodded for Amber. "We can, but only the syrup. Some people drink the sap, but I don't have any trees tapped yet. Maybe you can help me with that today."

"Really? Can I, Daddy?"

I nodded. "If Mr. Jones says it's okay, it's fine with me."

"Let's go, Mr. Jones," Amber said, pulling him forward.

Colin laughed and hurried to keep up with her.

Inside the barn, Colin grabbed a small bag of tools and a bucket then led us out the back. Amber asked him questions about all the trees while we trudged through the snow.

The trees filtered out the sunlight, making it colder than it felt before we got to the farm. I pulled gloves on and tugged my collar up, wondering how Melody's meeting was going. She was nervous when I got there to pick up Amber and said the meeting was with one of the moms she didn't like that much.

I'd never been as deep into the farm as we were walking. Cleotha invited me out a few times a year, but we didn't go too far from the barn. I looked back and couldn't see it anymore.

"This is it," Colin said, stopping in front of a gigantic tree. "This is a black maple tree. We don't have that many of these because they're a little more common west of here, but this is one of our biggest. The first year we tapped this tree was when I was about your age. It had just gotten big enough to tap, and my grandmother let me do it."

"Really?" Amber asked.

Colin nodded. "Really. It's always the first tree I tap, and it's a little early, but I think you might bring us some luck this year. What do you think? Do you want to try?"

Amber nodded rapidly. "What do I do?"

Colin brushed off a spot and moved around the tree. He stopped and nodded. "Well, I think this is the right spot for the tap."

"I can't reach," Amber whined.

"Don't worry. We'll take care of that. If your daddy is willing to help us, we'll be good."

They both turned to look at me, and I stepped forward. "What do we need to do?"

Colin pulled a drill out of his bag and handed it to me. "The tape tells you where to stop. We're going to drill right here," he pointed to a spot on the tree just a tiny bit above Amber's head, "so that's where the drill is going to go."

"What do I get to do?" Amber asked.

Colin grinned and pulled out three pairs of safety glasses. He gave Amber and I each a pair and put on his own, then he lowered to one knee in front of the tree. "You're going to help your daddy drill that hole." He patted his thigh. "Step up here so you can reach."

Amber moved to climb on his leg, but I stopped her. "Her boots are muddy."

Colin shrugged. "I get muddier than this every day. Come on, Amber."

Amber grabbed his hand and let him help her climb up on his leg. Colin held her steady with both hands on her waist and nodded up at me.

"You need to drill at an upward angle, not a drastic one, but enough so the sap can flow down. You won't have to go far."

I moved closer and bent to put the bit on the spot Colin pointed to before. "Okay, Amber, hold on to this. We're going to do this together. It's going to be loud."

Amber nodded and focused on the spot where the bit rested on the tree, both of us leaned forward so we could see what we were doing. Then we pulled the trigger together.

Amber's tongue stuck out the side of her mouth while she concentrated. I tried to pay attention to where the tape was so we didn't drill too far into the tree. Amber and I let go at the same time and pulled the drill out.

"That was awesome," Amber gushed. "Now what?"

Colin took one of her hands and reached into his bag with the other. "Now, you two need to put in the spile."

He handed me a hammer and the spile, then held Amber with both hands again.

"Clean out any wood shaving from around the hole, then insert the spile. The hook needs to face out so we can hang the bucket on it."

The spile went in cleanly. Amber and I tapped gently on it to make it seat fully against the tree.

"Great job," Colin said. "I think I need to hire you two."

Amber grinned and jumped down off Colin's knee. I clapped him on the back and thanked him.

"All right, Amber. Last step. You need to hang the bucket. Right there on the hook."

She took the bucket from him and put it up on the hook. We all stared at it for a minute, and a drop of sap ran into the bucket.

"Great job," Colin said. "Our first tree."

"The first of many," I told him.

Colin nodded. "I hope so."

MELODY

I was nervous. Maybe a little terrified. Robin was an intimidating person, and meeting with her at her house was overwhelming.

I parked in the driveway and took a breath. She asked me to bring some ideas for a party so she could see what I was capable of. It was like interviewing for a job instead of just helping a mom in class decorate for a party.

I brought two of my party bins with me to give her a few ideas. She didn't tell me much about what her daughter, Andrea, liked.

Robin opened the door almost as soon as I rang the bell. She offered a tight lipped smile and stood back so I could walk inside.

"You can leave your shoes right here. We'll go into the dining room." She nodded to the room behind me.

She looked almost as uncomfortable as I felt. I toed off my boots and followed her into the dining room, doing my best to set the bins down without dropping them. Why didn't she offer to help me?

I mentally rolled my eyes and decided it wasn't worth it to worry about why Robin did what she did.

"What did you bring?" she asked after a minute.

I forced a smile and tried not to be insulted that she didn't even offer to hang up my coat. It was big and bulky, but I'd talk her through everything wearing it.

"The first bin is what I call a party in a bin. It's basically everything you need to set up a party. Games and decorations and favors are all coordinated. It's something that's really easy for your daughter to help you set up. It takes the guess work out of planning a party because it's basically done. There are a lot of games online, and since Amber is an only child, we've tried out a lot of ideas. Being a stay at home mom gave me a lot of time to entertain her, so I have a pretty good handle on what five year olds enjoy."

Robin gave me a tight lipped smile. "What is the other one?"

I sighed and pressed on. "The other one is more of a party option kit. You can mix and match things, maybe do an extra game instead of an extra thing in the goodie bag. Or there's props if you want to do a photo shoot or something like that. It's basically themed or un-themed."

Robin looked through both bins with her nose up. She acted like I left a bag of dog shit in the bottom.

"And you do the set up, right? Like you did for Makayla's party?"

"Oh, well, I was just helping Casey out. But, um, I don't see where that would be a problem."

Robin nodded. "That would be helpful. The party is in a week. Invitations went home this week. I tried to find your website, but I wasn't sure the name of your company."

"I don't have a website."

"That's why I couldn't find it. You only work word-of-mouth. That's smart because it means you're in demand, but

I think you could really make some decent money if you started a website."

"What?"

"Well, these kits that you have. I assume you could package them in a box to send out, right?"

"Um, yeah, I guess," I said. I had no idea what she was talking about.

"If you did some nice packaging and offered themed kits and the mix-and-match kits, you could list all of them on your website. I don't know if you have space in your house, but if you did, I imagine you could sell at least a few a week. As word spreads, you'll be selling even more. It might be something other moms could help you do. I'm sure it's something the teachers would get on board with also. Classroom parties, or at least ideas. There's a lot you could do with this."

"Yeah, there really is," I agreed, trying to keep up.

"Anyway, for Andrea's party, if you come and set up, I'm also hoping you're willing to clean up, and I know you'll be here since you've already said Amber is coming, then that's about four hours. I'll still pay for the time during the party just in case you need to help out with something, if that's okay."

"Pay?"

Robin nodded. "Yes, I don't know how much your kits cost, but I'll take two of them, themed, and four hours of your time. Does five hundred sound reasonable?"

"Dollars?" I blurted.

Robin looked at me like I'd grown an extra head. She nodded slowly. "Yes, for your time and supplies. If you usually charge more, that's fine."

"I...um, I don't usually charge at all," I admitted.

Robin flinched. "Why not? This is a genius idea. As a mother, I love having a party all planned out, having it all coordinated and organized. If you offered this as a service, you'd make a decent amount of money."

"But I…I never thought of this being something I'd make money doing. I just love it. I was a teacher, and I think that side of me wants to get out again."

"Then teach the rest of us how to throw a party that has our kids talking for weeks about how much fun they had, because that's what Andrea's been doing since Makayla's party. She begged me to ask you to help with her party, and I don't believe in asking someone to do something without paying them what they're worth."

I highly underestimated Robin. She was still a control freak and a bit odd, but she wasn't willing to take advantage of me. For Casey, we were friends, so helping her was natural. For Robin, I was dreading the thought. But her paying me…my mind was definitely spinning with her ideas.

"Thank you, Robin. I really appreciate that."

She nodded. "So, you'll do it?"

"I will, but not for that price. How about half that price and you help me figure out how to make this into a business?"

Robin grinned. "Deal."

AMBER HAD fun helping me create a party kit for Andrea. Once we pulled it all together on Sunday, I made us lunch and we had a dance party. Her clothes were still wet from playing outside the day before with Ramsey. He didn't stay long after they got home from the farm, but he did give me a toe-curling kiss when Amber wasn't looking.

A part of me felt guilty for not telling him about my party planning business idea. Or, Robin's idea. I needed to sit with it for a little while before I shared it, especially with him.

Things were still tentative between us, and I didn't want to do anything that would jeopardize that.

He messaged me Sunday afternoon asking if I would be home that night. Blake asked me to come to girls' night out again, so I told him Willow was going to be home with Amber.

RH214

I'll bring some wood tomorrow after work.

WEBMOMMY

Thanks. I appreciate the help.

RH214

Sorry I haven't been there when you needed me.

WEBMOMMY

We're working on it. We've both made mistakes.

RH214

I love you.

WEBMOMMY

I love you.

We'd gotten in the habit of saying *I love you* again. It felt good. Everything felt good. Which just made me feel that much more guilty for keeping my potential business idea from him.

I mentioned Ramsey to Willow when she came over to watch Amber that night. She was not happy with the subject.

"You need to just move on. I don't know why you're giving him another chance. He's not worth it," Willow said with a huff.

"He's my husband, Will. And we've already talked about this. If we work things out, you're going to need to find a way to get along with him."

"So, what? You've given up on having more kids? You're just going to stop wanting what you've wanted your entire life? I don't understand that," Willow pushed.

"I'm not giving up on anything," I argued. "I want a family, but I want a family with Ramsey."

"So, what? You're going to get pregnant without him knowing?"

I shook my head. "I didn't say that. And I don't know what my family is going to look like. It might just be the three of us."

"But forever, Mel, forever, you've wanted a big family. You said you wanted at least four kids. He walked out six months ago because you weren't willing to give that up. What's changed?"

I shrugged. "In some ways, nothing, and in some ways, everything."

"Melody, you want a family. You want kids. That one date you went on was with a guy because he wanted more kids. I think you're making a mistake."

I bit my tongue and changed the subject before I said something she couldn't forgive.

I left not long after that, heading to girls' night out. Elise was walking down the street the same time I was and waved.

"Hey," I said.

"I wasn't sure if you would come back," she said.

"Um, is it okay that I did? Blake texted me."

Elise chuckled. "Yeah, it's good. It's good to have a project."

"I'm a project?" I asked.

Elise knocked on the door to Book Boyfriends Unlimited and nodded. "Yep, but in a good way. Blake's happy, and the rest of us are so single we're planning a party with no couples allowed for Valentine's Day. You're kind of in between, which means you're good as a project. Something to give the ones who want to find someone hope."

"I…thanks, I guess," I said, unsure if I should feel better or worse.

Elise laughed as Finley opened the door and let us in. She gave me a tight smile and stepped back for Elise and I to walk in.

I followed them to the back where the others were already eating their cake. It was a marble cake with bright yellow frosting. My mouth watered at the sugary scent that filled the air.

"This is so good," Karissa said with a mouthful. "You guys need a piece before I eat it all."

Elise jumped in and grabbed a plate. She tucked her chin-length hair behind her ear only to have it fall forward again. She ignored it as she cut a piece of cake and slid it onto her plate. Then she turned and handed it to me.

"Uh, thanks," I said.

She nodded. "Trust me, you don't want to miss out on this. Trinity's cake is amazing."

I smiled at Trinity and took a seat next to Karissa. I took a bite while Elise cut another piece of cake for herself. Karissa groaned next to me, and as soon as the cake hit my tongue, I did, too.

"Oh, my God, this is good," I said with my mouth full.

"Told you," Karissa and Elise both said.

I laughed and nodded, taking another bite. I was too busy groaning over my cake to realize they were all watching me. "What?"

"We're all wondering if you're going to tell us what's going on with Ramsey," Blake said.

"Yeah, everyone in town has seen the two of you together," Elise added.

"And we're all talking about if he's moving back in," Karissa said.

"Or if he already has," Laura said.

"Seriously?" I asked, chewing slowly and swallowing the cake. All of a sudden, the cake felt more like a bribe than a treat.

"I told you…project," Elise said.

"She is not a project," Blake argued. "She's a friend, and we don't make friends into a project."

"We made you into a project and got you to realize you were in love with Ian," Elise said with a smirk.

"I was not a project," Blake said firmly.

The others chuckled. "You totally were," Finley said.

"And a tough one. You didn't want to admit how much you liked Ian," Karissa said. "It was not easy getting Buttercup to accept love. Melody should be easier, though. She likes The Notebook. She believes in second chances and love that defies all logic and happily ever after."

"What's wrong with that?" I asked softly.

"Nothing," Laura said. "It's a great thing. We should all believe in love like that."

"And that's why we want to know what's going on," Elise said. "Because the rest of them think love is something that can conquer all."

"You don't?" I asked her.

She shook her head and gave me a sad smile. "I did once, but not anymore. Not for me, at least. For everyone else, I hope it exists."

I wondered what happened to Elise to make her not believe in love, but I didn't know her well enough to ask yet. Maybe one day.

"So, are you going to tell us what's going on with your sexy husband? Any more good nights?" Trinity asked.

I opened my mouth to say no, but my heated cheeks revealed the truth.

They all laughed and grinned. "Spill," Blake said.

I told them about our truce and about the week we had trading messages. And I told them about Friday night.

"Good for you," Elise said.

"I never understood the whole reciprocal sex thing," Laura said. "I mean, it shouldn't be a one-for-one kind of thing. Sex should be because you care about each other."

"That's how I feel, too," Blake said. "There are plenty of times Ian gets off and I don't, but it's not like it was with William. With William, he didn't care enough to make sure I enjoyed myself. With Ian, we're partners in every way. Sometimes I get everything I need from pleasuring him."

"That was how I felt," I admitted. "I just wanted to make him feel good. To see him lose control. I didn't really care if I got off or not, as long as he was satisfied."

"I'm hoping the reverse is also true," Karissa said.

Blake and I nodded. "Absolutely," I said with a satisfied grin.

"I need a boyfriend," Finley said.

"Just hook up with a guy from Karissa's app," Elise said.

"What?" Karissa barked.

"Oh, please, you know that's why most people join a dating app," Elise said with an eye roll.

"I did not create Book Boyfriends Wanted so people could have sex," Karissa cried.

Elise shrugged. "Sorry, Rissa. People like sex, and dating apps are a good way for people to meet someone else who's willing."

"Please don't use it to meet someone to have sex," Karissa begged. "I don't want it to become like all the other dating apps. It's better."

"It is better," Elise said soothingly. "It's so much better. And I'm sorry I suggested Fin use it to hook up."

Behind her hand, Elise winked at Finley. Karissa rolled her eyes as everyone else laughed.

"It's okay," Finley said. "I'd rather have someone for more than just sex. I have a few vibrators that are much more effective than a one night stand with a guy who isn't interested in finding out more than where to stick his junk."

"I'm with Fin. I've talked to a few of the guys I've been matched with, but I'm not interested in hooking up with someone random," Laura said.

"You guys are depressing me," Elise said. "It's time for more cake. Cake makes everything better."

The conversation changed to who was making cake next week and I found myself volunteering.

"What kind of cake do you know how to make?" Blake asked.

"I can bake fairly well, but my caramel cake is always a favorite," I said.

"Caramel cake? That sounds good," Karissa said.

"Hey, did you guys hear Jones Family Maple Farm might be opening back up?" Finley asked. "I loved it there."

"Ramsey is working with the grandson. He's the new owner and is hoping to be open this spring," I told them.

"Oh, so you have a connection?" Elise said.

I chuckled and shook my head. "I don't know about that. Ramsey and Amber were out there yesterday. Amber helped tap the first tree. She said sap started coming out."

"I'm so jealous of your kid right now," Elise said. "I loved going out there as a kid. Ms. Cleotha was always so sweet. And she'd sneak me candies when I was there."

"Me, too," the others said.

"It sounds like her grandson is a good guy, but I don't know if he'll be sneaking anyone candy," I said.

"I bet he'll sneak your daughter some candy. I might need to borrow her sometime," Elise said.

I grinned. "Free babysitting is always good for me."

"Free candy is always good for me," Elise said.

"Ooh, can you make a maple cake instead of caramel?" Laura asked. "You guys have me wanting maple sugar and maple syrup."

"I can definitely try," I said.

We started talking about different cakes and the best ones. Cakes and books and men. It was definitely a good night out.

looked out the front window at the snow falling steadily. It was already deep, but it was getting deeper by the hour. Plows were going by regularly, but the road was still packed with a few inches of snow.

"What's wrong, Mommy?" Amber asked.

I shook my head. "Nothing, sweetheart. I'm just watching it snow."

"Do you think I'll have another snow day tomorrow?" she asked. Her eyes were wide watching the snow, and a smile turned her lips up.

I nodded. "I bet you will. Maybe Wednesday, too. It's supposed to snow all day tomorrow."

"Can we go out and play again?" she asked.

I loved when she got excited about simple things like playing in the snow. That was what it was supposed to be like as a kid. Play and laugh and have fun. I didn't have that, and it's what I always wanted to give my kids.

It was a dream Willow and I had together. She gave the dream up, so I felt like I was fighting for it for both of us. But lately, I wondered what I was fighting so hard for. If Willow didn't want the dream, and I couldn't have the dream, then why was I willing to risk my life for it?

"Mommy?" Amber said cautiously.

"Yeah, honey?"

"Are you okay? I asked if we can go out and play again."

I pulled her close and hugged her tight. "Sorry, Amber. I was thinking about something else." I glanced at the clock. "I need to get dinner started. But we'll definitely go outside a few times tomorrow. Is that okay?"

Amber shrugged and walked away with her shoulders drooped. I hated making her feel that way. It wasn't how any kid should ever feel.

"Do you want to help me figure out what to cook?"

She shrugged again.

"I bet Daddy would be excited to try something you helped with."

"Daddy?" she asked, her voice rising with her measured excitement.

I nodded, not ashamed at all that I was using him as a bribe. "Daddy said he was going to come over after work today. He's bringing us firewood and having dinner."

She jumped up and danced around in a little circle, throwing her arms in the air and wiggling her entire body. "Daddy's coming home tonight. Daddy's coming home tonight. Daddy's coming home tonight."

I realized what she was singing. My heart broke that I had to tell her she was wrong. He wasn't coming home. He was just coming for dinner.

A knock on the door and the door opening drew our attention.

"Hello?" Ramsey said as he let himself in. "It's snowing like crazy out there. Sorry."

I never cared if Ramsey let himself into the house, but he

said he wasn't living there, so he shouldn't walk in unannounced.

I smiled when he stuck his head around the corner. He grinned back and winked at me just before he caught a flying Amber as she barreled toward him.

"You're home, Daddy! I missed you."

"I missed you, too, sweet girl. How was your snow day with Mommy?"

"It was great!" Amber said, throwing her arms in the air. "We had breakfast, then we played in the snow, then we ate lunch, then we read a book, then we played in the snow some more, and then I drew a picture. I want you to have my picture. Do you want it?"

"Of course I do," Ramsey said. He hugged her close then set her down. "Let me get my stuff off so I don't drag snow and dirt through the house."

Amber stood and stared at him, her smile wide and her eyes bright. While Ramsey took off his boots and coat, I went to the kitchen to start dinner.

The two of them talked while Amber showed him the picture she drew of a snowball fight. I smiled at her excitement and wondered when she was going to be right. When Ramsey was going to come home for good.

They walked into the kitchen together as I slid dinner in the oven. It was the kind of day that called for comfort food, and I knew lasagna would hit the mark for all of us.

Ramsey wrapped his arms around me from behind and rested his head on my shoulder. "I missed you this weekend," he said quietly. He kissed my cheek then the top of my head.

I turned in his arms, the move so natural I barely thought about it. I wrapped my arms around his neck and lifted up to meet his lips. He kept the kiss short and chaste, but I could feel his restrained desire.

"Sorry I'm so late. My last client came down from

Massena. Today was the only day he had off work so he couldn't reschedule even though the weather was horrible."

I shook my head. "It's fine. You don't have to explain."

"I haven't always been good about telling you what's going on with work. I did bring the firewood. It's a little wet with all the snow, but I'll lay it out so it'll dry," he said.

"Can we build a fire?" Amber asked.

Ramsey shook his head. "The wood is too wet right now, honey. It'll smoke when we burn it."

"We should have enough in there for a fire tonight," I told him.

"Then, I guess we're on fire duty," Ramsey told Amber. He reached for her hand and the two of them left the kitchen.

I cleaned up the kitchen while they were in the other room. When dinner was ready, we ate in front of the fireplace again, letting the warmth and the conversation sink into us.

Until Amber asked, "Are you staying over tonight, Daddy?"

Ramsey and I exchanged a look. I opened and closed my mouth like a fish, but he just smiled.

"Mommy and I are working things out, Amber. We're talking and we're getting along. I probably won't stay tonight, but hopefully soon. Really soon. Because there's nothing I want more than to be back here with both of you full time."

Amber threw herself into Ramsey's arms, and I pushed down my desire to do the same. What he said was perfect. And I couldn't wait for the same thing, for Ramsey to be home with us for good.

We both put Amber to bed that night, and as soon as her door was closed, we were in each other's arms.

"Ramsey," I moaned softly.

He lifted me in his arms and wrapped my legs around his waist. He carried me down the hall, but I pulled back.

"You don't want—"

"Bedroom," I begged.

He paused. "Mel?"

"Ramsey, I need you. Please. It's all I've been able to think about. I want you. I want you inside me. I want you to touch me. I want you."

"Fuck, Mel," he groaned. He sealed his lips over mine and turned back to the bedroom. He closed the door behind us and locked it, then pressed me against it and himself against me.

I moaned and clawed at him while his kisses drove me insane. His tongue pulsed into my mouth, tasting me and teasing me. I tugged at his shirt until he set me down.

He was still dressed from work. The row of tiny buttons had our fingers fumbling to work quickly enough. I couldn't take it and grabbed the bottom and yanked. Only half the buttons popped, but that one move did so much to push us together.

"Fuck me, Mel," Ramsey groaned. His eyes blazed with hunger. He ripped the two sides apart, sending the rest of the buttons flying. He stripped his shirt off, and instantly, my hands were sliding up his chest.

I licked and kissed my way across his chest, taking my time to enjoy his body. I licked his abs and bit his nipples and when he tugged my lips to his, neither of us could stop until we were panting and breathless.

Ramsey walked me backward toward the bed. He stopped before my legs hit the mattress. His hands slid up my sides, pulling my shirt up and off. He bent and sucked one of my nipples through my bra. I moaned and held his head against me. He pulled the other cup to the side and rolled that nipple between his fingers.

"Ramsey," I begged. "Please."

He knew what I needed. He unclasped my bra and let it fall to the floor. Then his hands dragged my pants down my thighs. He pressed his nose to my crotch and inhaled deeply. My channel pulsed and flooded.

"I can't wait to taste you, Mel," he groaned, his rough voice making my knees weak.

He licked me through my panties, and every inch of me vibrated. He grabbed the edge of my panties with his teeth and pulled them down far enough to lick the seam of my thigh.

I spread my legs and shoved my panties down.

"Oh, yeah, that's better," he groaned. He pushed me back until I fell onto the bed. His hands pressed my thighs wide as his tongue swiped through my folds.

My hips rose off the bed. I clenched the sheets, desperate to hold onto something. His tongue circled my clit then pressed flat against it. Everything inside me built quickly. It had been far too long, and having Ramsey with me again was half the excitement.

"You feel so damn good," I moaned. "I've missed you."

"Me, too," he groaned. "I love you, Mel. You taste so fucking amazing."

He dove back in and thrust a finger deep inside me. My body clenched hard, my orgasm sweeping through me in an instant. I grabbed a pillow and bit down on it to stifle my scream.

Ramsey didn't let up. He added a second finger and sucked on my clit again. He built me up quickly until I leapt right over that edge again.

He slowed his teasing, licking me gently, his fingers lazily pulsing in and out of my body. He tasted me, licking every drop of my come, then spun his tongue around my clit again. His slow, gentle teasing made me hot. My body had time to adjust to every move he made, letting me feel every lick, every suck, every twist of his fingers.

"Ramsey," I cried softly.

He pulsed his fingers faster and teased my clit with a firm suck. Just that quickly, he was gone again, the gentle licks returning. Back and forth, gentle and firm, he teased me until I was panting and begging him to make me come.

He sucked hard on my clit and stroked hard into me. It didn't take long for my body to tighten around his fingers.

"Oh, God. Oh, God. Oh, God. Ramsey! Yes!"

My body convulsed with the power from my orgasm. Ramsey kept me going until I was wrung out and begging for him to stop.

He gentled his touch, kissing and licking me until I stopped twitching.

"Slide up," Ramsey commanded. He stripped off his clothes and crawled between my legs. He kissed between my thighs, making me jump, then kissed his way up my body.

His cock settled against me, and I wrapped my legs around him. He kissed me hard, letting me taste myself on him. I grabbed a hold of him and kissed him back, needing him.

He pulled back and sat on his knees. He stroked himself through my wet folds and eased inside.

"Oh, fuck," I moaned.

"Jesus, you feel so damn good," he groaned. "I love you, Mel."

"Ramsey," I cried, cupping his jaw. "Thank you."

He turned and kissed my palm. Inch by inch he filled me. He went slow, stretching my body with every stroke. It had been so long since we'd been together that it took a while, but he stared the entire time at where he entered me.

"I love disappearing inside you," he said softly. "Watching your body take me in…I've missed you so much, babe."

"Me, too," I said. All my emotions bubbled to the surface, and a tear leaked out. I closed my eyes and swiped at the tear before he could see, but he stilled.

"Mel?"

"It's fine," I said, not looking at him.

"Mel, don't hide from me. Let me see all of you."

"I think you can see all of me," I said wryly.

"Don't do that, Mel. Don't make jokes. Are you okay?"

I nodded. "I'm just so happy you're here. I…I didn't think we'd ever get here. I really thought we weren't going to be able to figure it out. Thank you, Ramsey."

He leaned down and kissed me. "I'm happy, too. I love you, Mel."

"I love you."

He kissed me while he pumped in and out of my body. The connection between us overwhelmed me again. I cried, but I didn't stop it, letting my tears run down my cheeks.

He kissed my tears away and held me, all the while stroking in and out.

"Mel," he groaned.

"I love you, Ramsey."

"I love you. I love you. I love you," he chanted. He thrust harder and harder until he grunted and stilled deep inside me.

I swore I could almost feel him release into me, and I held him closer, kissing his face until he rolled off me and pulled me onto his chest.

We laid there, panting. My head rested on his chest, listening to his heart throb beneath my ear. I closed my eyes and just breathed, feeling like everything was finally okay.

Ramsey shifted and kissed the side of my head. I wrapped my arm tighter around him, not ready to move yet.

"I know you have to get rid of the condom, but I just want to lay here for a minute," I said.

He stilled beneath me. He stopped breathing and the hand that was running delectable lines up and down my back froze. "I didn't wear a condom. I thought you were on the pill."

I bolted upright, grasping for the sheet to cover myself. "No. I went off the pill months ago."

"Why?"

"Because you left me! There was no reason for me to be on it, so I stopped. I've always hated taking it, you know that."

"Why didn't you tell me?"

"When? When was I supposed to tell you? At dinner with our daughter? Hey, Ramsey, by the way, I quit taking the pill because you left me and I'm not in the mood to fuck other men just yet. Pass the peas, Amber."

"How about before we had sex, Melody? You could have told me right before we had sex, when I was carrying you to bed and stripping your clothes off," he said, jumping out of bed.

I sat there and watched him get dressed. He jerked on his ripped shirt, then tugged up his boxer briefs. He stood and thrust his feet into his jeans. I'd always loved the way he looked in jeans. He didn't wear them often, but Ramsey filled out a pair of jeans like no other man.

He didn't even look at me before he walked out of the bedroom.

I grabbed my robe and followed him. He was mad at me, but I still didn't want him going out in the storm. They were predicting it would get worse overnight, and it wasn't safe for him to be on the road, even though he didn't have far to go.

"I'm sorry," I said first. "You're right. I should have told you, but I didn't think. I was just happy you were here. And I didn't think."

He turned back to me, his eyes stormy. "You didn't think? Are you sure about that?"

"What does that mean?" I asked.

"You've been dying to have another baby, Mel. Are you sure you didn't plan this whole thing so you could get pregnant again? Is that why you were crying? You finally got what you wanted?"

I opened my mouth to say something, then closed it again. I crossed my arms over my chest to protect myself from him. I'd never been so hurt in my life. Not even watching him walk out the door had hurt so badly.

"I guess it's good we're over if that's what you think of me."

"Mel," he hissed when I turned around.

I wasn't interested in anything else he had to say. I walked away, knowing that was the only thing I could do. Accept that things were over and my husband didn't love me anymore.

He called my name again, and I hurried to the bedroom, but the door across the hall opened before I got there.

"Mommy?" Amber said, rubbing her eyes.

I choked back the tears and pain and gave her a smile. "Yeah, honey. Are you okay?"

"I heard something."

"It's okay, baby," I said, taking her hand. "Let's go back to bed."

She nodded and let me lead her back to her bed. I knelt next to her bed and sang her a quiet song until she fell asleep again. I stayed there for a few more minutes, making sure she was okay, then quietly left her room.

I stood in the hallway, listening for sounds of Ramsey, but in my heart I knew the truth. He was gone. And this time, it was definitely for good.

RAMSEY

I would have slammed the door if it weren't for Amber. I didn't want her to know I was there so late. Hearing her get her hopes up about me moving back in was great, but knowing I'd crush it in one move kept me from doing anything other than silently leaving the house.

She wasn't the only one who'd be crushed. I was destroyed. The icy air and the overflowing sidewalks forced me to ignore the pain in my chest and focus on getting to my SUV. More snow fell in the few hours I was there, and my car was covered. I wasn't interested in sticking around to see if Melody would come out and try to stop me from leaving. She'd already disappointed me once, and this time, I didn't want her coming after me.

I cranked up the SUV and prayed the windshield wipers would get enough of the snow off that I could see without needing to scrape off the car. I blasted the defrost and crossed my fingers, sighing with relief when most of the snow sloughed off. Another few swipes and the windshield was clear enough for me to drive safely.

No one was on the roads as I made my way to Ian's.

Streetlights illuminated the quickly falling snow as the radio played some sappy love song that made me want to punch the dashboard.

I parked outside the boat house and hurried inside to avoid freezing. I didn't let myself think until I was in the apartment and knew I was alone.

Then it all hit me hard. Fear. Grief. Anger.

"Fuck!" I shouted at the top of my lungs. "Argh! Damn you, Melody!"

I grabbed the closest thing, a glass, and threw it against the wall. It shattered, glass exploding and splattering everywhere. I felt marginally better.

I walked away, leaving the glass on the floor, and grabbed a beer. As soon as I closed the fridge, I yanked it open and grabbed another. I wanted to carry the entire six-pack with me, but I needed to go to work in the morning.

I opened the first beer on my way to the shower. I stripped off all my clothes, needing to not smell Melody all over me. Clothes went into the hamper and beer went down my throat. Once I finished the first one, I got in the shower and scrubbed every inch of my body to erase her.

I wrapped a towel around my waist and opened the second beer. I carried it to the futon and turned on the TV. I flipped channels while I drank, hating myself for thinking Melody had changed.

She tricked me. I couldn't believe she did it. She wanted a baby, and instead of insisting we talk, I let my emotions and how much I loved her dictate my actions. I trusted her. And she lied, she talked me into bed, and she made me love her.

My heart fucking ached. My throat closed up. I wanted to...I don't know what I wanted to do. I wanted the pain to stop. A tear slid down my cheek, and I ruthlessly swiped it away. She didn't deserve my tears. If she got pregnant on accident, I could cry for her, but that wasn't what happened. She did this on purpose.

And because of it, I might lose her forever.

PENNY KNEW to leave me alone as soon as I walked in the next morning. I was barely functional, but I was there. She smiled and nodded, taking in my disheveled suit and red-rimmed eyes. I never appreciated her more than in that minute when she didn't ask anything, just kept working and said nothing.

I guzzled coffee and tried to get something done. Penny brought me lunch, again without a word, and closed the door to my office.

I had a meeting in the afternoon, but she sent me an email saying the meeting had been changed to the following week. I didn't know if she did it or they did, but I didn't care as long as I didn't have to talk to anyone.

I thought I was good to go, but Penny buzzed me just after four. "What?"

"Mr. Sinclair is on the phone. He was hoping he could speak to you," Penny said calmly.

"Fuck. Do me a favor. If you hear me yelling, disconnect the call and tell him there was a problem when he calls back."

"Um, okay."

I took a deep breath. "Thanks, Penny. Put him through."

She didn't say another word, just switched the call to my office.

"Mr. Sinclair," I said, hoping I sounded somewhere close to normal.

"Mr. Holland, Ramsey. Thank you for taking my call," Carter said.

"Of course. I've been trying to reach you."

"I know," he said with a sigh. "I'm sorry. I…when I got back, my wife wasn't happy about any of this. We just moved a few years ago. We have our dream house, and even considering relocating again was hard for her to talk about."

I couldn't reply. I wanted to, but I was afraid I'd say something nasty. He didn't deserve my anger, but he was going to be the one who got it if he said what I was afraid he was about to tell me.

"I had to think. I'm sorry I wasn't answering your calls. It wasn't easy to think about all this. I always knew my mom was adopted, but she never found out where she came from. She was curious, but she thought she'd have time to find out. For me, I think I wanted to hold on to that. To have that piece of her that she never got a chance to have. My wife… she didn't understand that."

"I'm sorry to hear that," I told him. I meant it, too. If nothing else, I could understand a man who didn't agree with his wife on how something should be.

"I am, too, but she was right. What I wanted was a connection. Family. Someone who shared something no one else could. But I don't have to live there to have that."

My breath hitched. "What are you saying, Carter?"

"I'm saying I don't want the farm, Ramsey. I'm sorry. If my cousin needs something, I'm happy to contribute. I don't have a lot of money, but I can pay him something. I don't want him to be left dealing with all this on his own, but it's just not for me."

I stood and paced my office. I ran a hand over my face and tried not to jump up and down. "No, um, I think he's okay. I was working with him on a loan and making sure he has everything set up."

"Oh, good," Carter breathed. "I don't mind, but I felt bad not wanting to help."

"Can I be honest with you, sir?"

"Of course."

"Colin, your cousin, he was going to do this on his own before he knew you existed. He's been holding out making too many decisions in case you wanted to be involved."

"I'm sorry. I should have called you before. I should have decided before. I just needed time to think about all of it."

"I understand. I really do. Not all decisions can be made quickly. I do need to ask you something else."

"Of course," Carter said, sounding more relaxed.

"For legal reasons, and I almost hate to ask you this, but for legal reasons, would you consider signing over your rights to Colin?"

"My rights?" Carter asked.

I cleared my throat. "Yes. I hate to say this at all, but things happen. People change their minds. Descendants make different decisions. I have a duty to my client to make sure he's protected."

"What do you need?" Carter asked.

Maybe I was feeling optimistic for the first time all day or maybe he really wanted to help. Either way, I couldn't stop yet. "Cleotha's will said she wanted her grandson to have full ownership of the farm. It didn't name names. We didn't know about you until Colin came to my office and I gave him a letter from her that said there were two of you. If you took him to court, a judge could say you own part of it. If you don't want this, I can draw up paperwork saying you surrender all rights to Colin."

"Yes, I'll sign. Of course. I don't want him to worry. I don't want him to ever wonder if someone is going to take something from him. My mother…she worried about who she would find if she went looking for her family. A part of her always feared it. I think that's why she never looked for her biological family. I don't want Colin, or anyone else in his family, to ever fear me."

I breathed a sigh of relief and wiped a hand across my face. "Thank you, Carter. Truly. That's…thank you."

"No, Ramsey, thank you. And I was wondering if I could ask you a favor."

"Of course," I told him.

"I, um, I'd really like to meet my cousin. I don't know if that's something he'd be open to, but if it is, I would really like a chance to meet him. Maybe see the farm, if you think he'd be willing."

The hope in his voice made me smile. "I have a feeling that won't be a problem at all. I'll talk to him, and if it's okay, I'll give him your number. You two can take it from there."

Carter sighed with relief. "Thank you," he said. "I…thank you."

I smiled. "You're welcome."

We chatted a few more minutes then hung up. I knew I needed to have a long conversation with Colin, but I wasn't up to it. At the same time, I was not willing to let it go another minute without telling him about his farm.

As soon as I hung up with Carter, I dialed Colin. He answered the phone on the first ring.

"Ramsey. Did you hear something?"

"I did. I just got off the phone with him. I want you to come in tomorrow to talk to me."

"Fuck," Colin breathed. "Son of a bitch. I really thought… Dammit. I got my hopes up."

"Colin," I said. "I want you to come tomorrow to talk about the loan application. Because you're the only one who needs to sign it."

"Wha…What?"

I chuckled. "He doesn't want your farm. He's going to sign it all over to you."

"No way! No fucking way! Are you kidding me?"

I laughed again. "I'm not kidding. The farm is all yours.

So, come in tomorrow, whatever time works for you, and we'll get everything taken care of so you can move forward."

"Yes. Hell, yes. Thank you, Ramsey. Thank you."

"I'll see you tomorrow, Colin."

"See you tomorrow, Ramsey. Thanks."

I nodded and hung up. For a few minutes, I was able to forget the pain I was going through. Then I ended the call and saw Amber and Melody smiling back at me from the background of my phone.

I locked my phone and set it face down on my desk. The urge to smash it to pieces was strong, but I couldn't. I stared at it for a long time before Penny knocked on the door.

"Yeah?"

Penny opened the door and stepped in. "I'm heading out. Mr. Jones called. He'll be here at ten."

I nodded. "Thank you, Penny."

She nodded and left without another word.

I stayed at work, unable to face my apartment alone. I hated the thought of having to find a new place to live, but I needed to. Ian was generous letting me stay at his place, but staying there forever was not going to happen. Not when I knew there was no chance I'd be able to go home again.

I waited until I was barely awake to go to Ian's and crashed when I got there. I slept like shit, but I slept, so I considered it a win.

I wasn't much better the next day, but I was determined to have a good meeting with Colin.

Penny kept her distance again, only letting me know when Colin arrived. I smoothed down my shirt and pasted on a smile. Colin had a huge grin on his face when he shook my hand.

"Man, I want to hug you," he said.

I chuckled. "I didn't do anything. I just happen to be the one who gets to deliver good news to you."

"Yeah, but you didn't give up. Thank you, Ramsey. Thank you. You saved my home."

He walked over and shook my hand, then pulled me into a hug with a firm slap on the back. I hugged him right back, happy I could at least do something right.

"Thank you."

I nodded. "You're welcome. Let's talk about your loan and the paperwork and get everything set up so you never have to worry about your home again."

Colin nodded and we dug into it all. Penny brought us in lunch two hours later, and we changed the subject from business for a few minutes.

"Your kid was pretty cute," Colin said with a grin. "I'm guessing she gets that from her mom?"

I laughed but it was forced. Just thinking about Melody hurt.

"That's not the face of a man who is rebuilding his marriage. What happened?"

I shook my head. "You don't want to know. Trust me."

He tilted his head to the side. "Yeah? Well, I asked. I've been told I can be a good listener. And I've never met your wife, so I'm not going to pass judgement. But you don't have to tell me anything."

I smiled and realized I was keeping it all bottled up and it was making me crazy. I'd been sitting on everything for two days, and I wasn't any less angry than when I walked out of the house Monday night.

"I left seven months ago because she wanted another baby, and her doctors said she could die if she got pregnant again. Over the last few weeks, we've been working things out. Trying to reconnect. Talking and flirting. I went over there Monday night, and she wanted to...anyway. But afterward, she told me she went off the pill."

"And?" Colin asked.

"And she could be pregnant. Right now, she could be pregnant."

Colin looked at me like I'd grown an extra head. He narrowed his eyes and tilted his head in question. "Explain it to me. Why is it her responsibility alone to manage the birth control? Is that something you two discussed?"

"No," I said. "But she's been on birth control since we lost Steven. We haven't used condoms in years. And she just expected that I had a condom. Why would I have them?"

"Maybe she thought you were with other women while you two have been apart."

I shook my head. "No, she knows I haven't been."

"Did you tell her?"

"No, but she knows. She knows me. I told her I missed her and that she's all I've been able to think about. There was no reason to buy condoms."

"Let me ask you a question. Are you more angry with her for not telling you or more angry at yourself for not asking?"

I sighed and shook my head again. "It isn't about the birth control. Not really. It's about her getting pregnant. She was the one who initiated sex. I think she wanted to have a baby so badly that she tricked me into sleeping with her."

Colin's eyebrows went up, and he whispered, "Whoa."

I nodded. "Exactly. That's why I'm mad. She had no right to do that. She knew how I felt. But instead of listening to me or thinking about our daughter, she decided she wanted to get pregnant again and nothing else mattered."

"Wow. Um, did you say all that to her?"

I nodded.

Colin leaned back in his chair. "Did you ever think maybe she got caught up in the moment like you did?"

I shook my head. "No. Melody isn't like that. She's level-headed and organized. She's a planner. She doesn't do caught up."

"You two never jumped each other in the backseat or started stripping each other's clothes off while you were walking in the door? What about oral sex while driving? Nothing that said you just couldn't wait another second to let logic take over?"

"Well, yeah. We've done all that."

"And you were always the one who started it? Your wife never once jumped you?"

"She has."

"So, maybe, just maybe, this one time, she did it again. She decided she just had to have you and couldn't wait another minute. And she didn't think about birth control because it wasn't something the two of you had thought about or talked about. If all that happened, and she is pregnant, and it was totally on accident, do you really want to spend all this time hating her, or would you rather spend it loving her?"

Dammit. "I don't like you very much right now."

Colin grinned. "I'm okay with that. But I'm not okay with you second guessing your marriage, so figure that one out first. Because if I'm right and you're wrong, you're going to regret it for the rest of your life."

I nodded because he was right. I knew Melody, and that wasn't the kind of person she was. She wouldn't trick me or trap me. She was the kindest person I'd ever known, and she wouldn't want a baby that was brought into the world under those circumstances.

Which meant I was an asshole, and I had a lot of groveling to do.

MELODY

"Do we have to go, Mommy?" Amber asked as I backed out of the driveway.

The snow finally stopped on Tuesday afternoon, and she went back to school Wednesday. That afternoon, my parents called and asked us to come to dinner Thursday. I wasn't any more excited about it than Amber, but it was a distraction for me.

I hadn't spoken to Ramsey. I didn't even try. A part of me wanted to explain to him that I wasn't trying to trick him, but a bigger part of me was angry that he would even think that about me.

"We haven't seen your grandparents since Christmas," I told Amber. "They want us to have dinner with them."

Amber sighed loudly but stopped arguing. My parents treated her much the same way they treated Willow and I growing up. Amber wasn't really important, and they barely acknowledged her. When she was little, she tried, but already at five, she'd given up on making a connection with them.

It bothered me, but I figured if she was already done with

them, maybe she wouldn't seek their approval her whole life like I had.

Willow's car was in the driveway when we arrived. Since I hadn't seen her since Ramsey came over, she didn't know about our fight Monday night. She would be pissed off all over again, but it would be nice to feel like maybe I wasn't completely screwing everything up again.

Amber gave Willow a hug and held onto her when we got inside. My parents said hello, but they didn't move to hug either of us. I asked my mom if I could help with dinner, and she said no. I almost rolled my eyes.

I was definitely in the anger stage of grief where everything annoyed me and I just wanted to yell all the time.

"What are we eating?" I asked.

"Hawaiian chicken with rice pilaf and vegetable medley," my mother said.

I forced a smile. We ate the same thing every time we went to their house. "Sounds good."

"It's ready," my mother said. "Since you're late, we can eat instead of visit first."

I nodded, refusing to feel guilty. We were late because we didn't want to be there. Small talk with my parents was unbearable. They only wanted to tell us what their friends and their friends' kids were doing. They never asked about Amber or Willow and me.

The only thing I appreciate at the moment was they wouldn't ask about Ramsey either.

We all sat at the table and passed serving dishes around. When everyone filled their plates, we started eating in silence.

"This is good, Mom," Willow said brightly. She had just as much of a troubled relationship with our parents as I did, but she hadn't given up trying to please our mother.

"Thank you, Willow."

Everyone was silent again. I ate my food and hoped we could get out of there before anyone said anything about Ramsey.

My parents made small talk, filling us in on everything everyone else they knew was doing. Willow and I rolled our eyes at each other when our parents weren't paying attention. It was so difficult to pretend I cared because I really had no interest. Half the people they talked about weren't even people I knew. And the rest were people I hadn't seen in years.

"How's Ramsey?" my dad asked toward the end of dinner.

I froze. I couldn't say much in front of Amber, but I didn't want to get her hopes up either.

"He's good. Daddy came over Monday, and he spends Fridays with us. He wants to move back in," Amber said.

Willow huffed a sigh. I just closed my eyes and prayed the ground would open up and swallow me.

"All our friends want to know when the two of you will work everything out," my mother said. "They agree with us that a husband and wife should do everything possible to work out their differences."

"We've tried, Mother," I said.

"Don't push her," Willow agreed. "They don't belong together."

"Willow!"

"No," Willow said. "I'm not going to sit here and listen to you berate yourself about him. He has proven time and time again that he's not right for you. And you've always bent to what he wants."

"Willow, stop," I said softly. It was a threat for Amber's sake, but also for mine. If she kept on, I might not be able to hold back the anger building inside me.

"Why? I know you don't want Mom and Dad to know your perfect little life isn't perfect. Ramsey shouldn't be with you. He never should have been. You're better off without him in your life."

"Well, you're going to get your wish," I blurted. "He left Monday night, and he's not coming back."

"Good. You can move on, and so can he."

"Why do you care?" I shouted. "Why do you care at all? You've always hated him."

"I love him!" Willow shouted.

The entire room went still.

"What?" I breathed.

Willow shook her head. "I love him. I've always loved him. You were never right for him. I told him the night you two got engaged that I was in love with him, and instead of telling me he felt the same way like I knew he did, he pushed me away. He said I was too young and then he proposed to you. Do you remember that?"

I nodded slowly. I could still see the smile on his face when he asked me to marry him. I had a year of college left, and he was starting law school, but we knew we wanted to be together. I didn't know he was going to propose, but I was so happy.

"He didn't have a ring," Willow said with a sneer. "He didn't intend to propose. He only married you because he felt guilty loving me. You were the replacement."

"What?" I asked. I knew she was wrong, but the pain I felt when he walked out swept through me all over again and teased my brain. Was she right? Did he really love her? Is that why they were so mean to each other all these years? "Did you...were you...?" I couldn't get the words out.

"I kissed him that night, and he kissed me back. Then he said he couldn't because of you, and the next time I saw him, he was on one knee in front of you. I told him he was making a mistake, but he argued you were the one he loved. It was never true," Willow said.

"That's why you always pushed me to push him away," I said. "You wanted me to end things with him. You wanted him for yourself."

"Of course! Because you two don't belong together."

"Yes, they do!" Amber shouted. "Don't say that about my mommy and daddy."

I looked at her, my chest heaving with anger and pain. Amber. My daughter. The one person in the room who actually mattered to me.

Tears streamed down her cheeks as she faced off with Aunt Willow, one of her favorite people in the world.

"I hate you! You broke up my mommy and daddy. You're mean, Aunt Willow. I hate you!"

I shoved my chair back and reached for Amber. I didn't look at anyone else as we rushed from the table. I grabbed my stuff and we left without a backward glance.

There was nothing left to say to anyone in that house.

I WAS STILL REELING from Willow's revelation on Saturday when I had to go to Robin's to set up for the party. I had everything ready to go, so thankfully, I could grab the bins and head out with Amber.

Amber was still not her normal self, but I hoped a party with her friends would help. She didn't deserve to hear what Willow said, and I hated my sister that much more for spewing her garbage in front of Amber.

Of course, it was all made worse when Ramsey canceled on Amber Friday night. She sat in her room the whole night instead of watching a movie or playing. I tried to coax her out, but she was shut down.

"Are you excited about Andrea's party?" I asked Amber on our way.

She shrugged.

"Amber, I'm sorry about Daddy not coming over last night."

Amber shrugged again.

I was losing my baby girl, right in front of my eyes. My hand went to my stomach and the fear I'd been feeling for days settled in. Amber was in pain. Not because anyone died, but because Ramsey and I were truly over. All the people in her life were leaving her. She'd lost her father and her aunt. The only one she had left was me, and if I was pregnant, she could lose me also.

The thought made me sick. I didn't want to leave her. I was all she had, and she was all I had. We were a team, and the thought of risking that was too much.

That dream I held onto so tightly, the one Willow and I shared, I finally saw it for what it was. A silly, childish wish that had no bearing on life as an adult. Willow tried to get me to hold onto it, but I didn't want to get pregnant again. I didn't want to leave Amber without a mom.

Willow probably expected to fill that role. She encouraged me to push Ramsey away, then she would step in when I was out of the picture. And if I got pregnant, well, then when I died or lost myself in a sea of misery, she could move right into my place with a family ready for her.

I couldn't believe my own sister, my best friend my whole life, did that to me.

I was still reeling when we pulled into Robin's driveway. Amber trudged to the door, looking like she wanted to be anywhere but there. Robin let us in with a tentative smile and told Amber where to find Andrea.

"Is she okay?" Robin asked when Amber walked away.

I shook my head. "No, not really."

"Are you?"

I shook my head again. "Nope."

"Do you want to talk about it?"

Robin and I were still forming a tentative friendship. I wasn't sure if she was being polite or if she was actually concerned. "Do you really want to know?"

She looked surprised that I would ask. "You don't have to tell me. I know I'm not the easiest person to get along with. I'm a control freak, and I take over things. I've always been that way, and it rubs a lot of people the wrong way."

"Yeah," I told her truthfully. "It really does."

She chuckled. "I've tried to tone it down, but when it comes to my kids, I can't help it."

"Kids? I thought you just had Andrea."

"Oh, well, for now," she said, cupping her belly.

I didn't notice before that it was round. I looked pregnant all the time, so I never assumed other people were. But with her hand on her belly and the look in her eyes, there was no mistaking she was pregnant.

She looked happy. Excited even. All week I'd been walking around in fear. I was terrified to be pregnant again. I didn't want it. If I was, I'd love the baby, but I was afraid of losing another baby, or of not being around to see my kids grow up.

A sob bubbled up and out. Robin's face went from joy to fear in an instant. I tried to stifle my tears, but they kept coming. Robin handed me a tissue, but it didn't do much. Another sob, more tears. I pressed a hand to my mouth, another to my stomach.

"Are you pregnant, too?" she asked, her eyes wide.

I shrugged. "I hope not."

"You don't want more kids?"

I shook my head. It was the first time I admitted it. I felt an immeasurable amount of guilt, but also a tiny bit of relief. "I don't. I might be pregnant, but I don't want to be. I'm not supposed to get pregnant or I might not survive. Ramsey and

I got carried away and neither of us thought about protection, and now I…I…I could die. I lost my last one. I don't want to be pregnant."

Robin pulled me in for a hug and held me tight for a long moment. Then she grabbed my shoulders and forced me to look at her. "You will get through this. You'll be okay. You have to believe that."

I shrugged. "I don't think I can. I'm alone. My husband thinks I tricked him to get pregnant. My sister is in love with him and has been trying to break us up so she can have him. And I don't have a lot of friends. I'm alone."

Robin smiled. "You're not alone. You have me. And I know you're close with Casey. And the rest of the moms from class will be there for you if you need them. You're not alone."

I smiled at her and hugged her again. "Thank you, Robin. Thank you. That means a lot."

She grinned. "One day at a time."

I nodded, and for the first time since Ramsey walked out the door, I actually believed I could handle things. One day at a time.

I PLANNED TO GO TO GIRLS' night out the next night, but I didn't have anyone to watch Amber. Ramsey and Willow were my two go-to people, and I wasn't speaking to either of them. I thought about calling Robin or Casey, but they had their own kids to get into bed on a Sunday night.

When I messaged Blake that I wouldn't be there, she said she understood and hoped I was okay. I replied that I wasn't but I would be and focused on getting Amber ready for bed.

Once Amber was down, I went back to the living room

and turned on the TV. A message dinged on my phone from Blake.

Are you up? Can I come in?

I replied asking if she was sending the text to the right person.

Yes. We decided to have GNO at your house if you're up for it. We have cake.

I went to the door and unlocked it, surprised to find all six of them on my porch.

"What are you guys doing here?" I asked, ushering them inside. "It's freezing out there."

"It is, but it's nice and warm in here," Laura said.

I'd started a fire earlier in the day and kept it going. The firewood Ramsey brought over was making me mad, so I wanted to use it up and be done with it. I wanted to be done with everything that had to do with Ramsey, to the point I was thinking of selling the house and moving into an apartment or condo or at least something much smaller.

"This is really nice," Elise said, looking around the house. She spotted a picture of Amber when she was a baby and smiled at it. "Adorable."

I grinned. "Thanks. Come in everyone. Amber is already asleep, so we have to be kind of quiet. I'm sorry about that."

"It's fine. We wanted to come here," Blake said. "We were worried about you."

"You were?" I asked.

They all nodded, and I lost it. I started crying right there in the middle of my living room surrounded by women I'd only talked to a handful of times.

Immediately, they surrounded me. Elise and Laura guided me to the couch. Blake went to the kitchen and got a glass of water. Karissa, Trinity, and Finley watched me carefully, as if they thought I was going to do worse than cry.

"What's going on?" Blake finally asked when I'd settled down enough to breathe.

"I've been really alone most of my life. Willow and I are… we're a team. We were a team. It was always just us against the world. Then Ramsey and I. Now, it's just me."

"You have us," Elise said. "I know we haven't been friends forever, but we're pretty good people."

"Thank you. All of you," I said, meeting all their eyes.

They found seats in the living room, and Karissa asked, "What's going on that you're all weepy. Are you pregnant or something?"

I breathed a mirthless laugh. "I might be."

"Really?" Karissa asked. "I was joking, but congratulations."

The others repeated the well wishes, but I shook my head. "I don't want to be pregnant. I…I don't want it."

"Why not?" Blake asked. "What happened?"

I took a breath and told them everything. From Ramsey and I having sex to his accusations. Then Willow's revelation. And finally, I told them about my business idea and party planning because the word vomit wouldn't stop.

"It's silly," I said, "but I love doing it. I love the joy on a child's face when they see a party that's just for them."

"That's not silly," Trinity said. "Not at all."

"I'm sorry about Ramsey and Willow," Blake said. "I really hoped you and Ramsey would work things out, but if he's going to say those things about you, you deserve better."

I nodded. "I do. That's what I've decided, too. I've spent a lot of years loving him, and I know that'll never change, but I can't be with someone who thinks so little of me."

"It's not easy walking away from someone you love," Elise said. "It's one of the hardest things in the world. Even when you know it's what's best for you. The good thing is you have people who care about you. People who will be there for you and Amber if you are pregnant."

"Thank you," I said. "I underestimated all of you, and judged you. And I'm sorry for that. I wasn't willing to let people in. My sister and I were taught not to show our feelings, and it's hard for me to let people see who I am. But I've finally learned that's not the right way to go through life. I'm lucky to have all of you."

"I judged you, too," Finley said. "I only saw you as Ramsey's girlfriend and wife, not as a person. I thought you were shallow, and Ramsey's been like a brother to me for a long time. But this…I never expected him to be so cruel. I'm sorry for that."

"Thanks, Finley. I appreciate that."

"Well, I don't know about all of you, but I need some cake after all that," Laura said.

We laughed and agreed. I didn't have a house full of kids, and I didn't have a husband, but I had a home and friends who were there for me when I needed them the most.

Family was what you made it, and I was creating a pretty great one.

23

RAMSEY

I went to O'Kelley's Thursday night knowing Melody would be home with Amber. I didn't want to risk running into her. We hadn't spoken or seen each other since we slept together, and it was killing me, but I knew if I saw her, I'd beg her to forgive me without thinking through how I needed to apologize. I loved her too much.

Hudson set a beer in front of me with a hard thud and walked away. I looked around, wondering what he was so pissed off about. It wasn't too crazy for a Thursday night, but something was bugging him.

I shrugged and drank my beer, barely paying attention to all the people around me. Only when Piper came over with a bill did I realize something was really messed up.

"Where's Hudson?" I asked her.

"In the back."

"Why isn't he out here?"

She avoided my gaze and shrugged. "I don't know."

I narrowed my eyes at her and nodded. She kept looking past me, so I sipped my beer until she walked away. She was the gatekeeper, which meant Hudson was pissed off at me for some reason.

When Piper was distracted with a table of customers, I snuck off my stool and carried my ticket to the back. Hudson's office door was closed, so I knocked on it.

"Yeah?"

I opened the door and glanced around to make sure no one else was in there, then closed the door behind me. "What the hell?"

He shook his head and clenched his jaw. Hudson was a big dude, and not one I wanted to fuck with. He was rough and aggressive when he needed to be, and I hadn't been in a fight since high school.

"What do you want?" he asked after a minute. He went back to staring at the paperwork on his desk.

"I want to know what the hell is wrong with you."

He scoffed. "Really? You want to know what's wrong with me?"

I nodded and crossed my arms over my chest.

Hudson shook his head. "Why did you do it?"

"Do what?"

"Sleep with Melody."

I tilted my head to the side and clamped my jaw shut. "She told you?" I asked through gritted teeth.

Hudson snorted. "Yeah, she told me. She's been crying her eyes out for days. I don't know what happened or why you decided to mess with her, but you need to leave her the hell alone."

"And since when do you get to tell me what to do with my wife?" I demanded.

Hudson stood and walked around his desk. "Since she became my friend, too. You want the right to call her your wife, then start acting like her fucking husband. You two haven't spoken in over a week because you're fucking scared.

You think you're the only one who's scared, but you haven't bothered to talk to her once. You just blame her and think she did this on purpose. She didn't, by the way, but instead of being there for her, you're throwing around accusations and abandoning her."

My fists clenched as tight as my stomach.

"My wife died. She actually fucking died. I don't have the choice to be there for her anymore, but I'd give anything to have just one day back. To be able to hold her and tell her I love her just one more time. You have that. You have no idea what's going to happen with Melody. And instead of grabbing on and holding her tight and never letting go, you're running scared and blaming her. You've been doing it since she lost the baby, and you're still doing it. You need to get the hell over yourself and man up. That or leave town so she doesn't keep her hopes up that you might actually show up for her."

His words hit me like a defenseless boxer. One blow after another threatened to take me down until I couldn't stand any longer. My knees gave out, and I sank to the floor. I put my head in my hands.

He was right. Just like Colin was right. I knew I was wrong, but I was still scared. I loved Melody, and I was terrified of losing her. If I pushed her away, I convinced myself it would hurt less, but it didn't matter. Without her, nothing mattered.

"You're right. And I'm going to fix it. I can't lose her. I don't want to."

"You better."

I nodded. I had a plan. I just needed to make it happen.

VALENTINE'S DAY. It was always our day. I hoped that would help, but convincing Melody to give me another chance after I was so horrible to her was not going to be easy. I needed to prove to her I was going to be there for her no matter what. And that I loved her. And that I was sorry for the things I said. Part one was being there for her and Amber.

I told Penny I was taking the day off and to cancel all my appointments. She wished me luck and said she'd handle everything. I knew she would, so I got dressed and drove straight to school.

Amber's class was having a Valentine's party. Melody was on the volunteer list, and I asked the teacher to put me down also. I also asked her to keep it a surprise so neither Amber nor Melody knew I would be there.

I showed up early, before the rest of the kids and parents. They were having a breakfast party with pancakes and morning treats since it was a half day. When Amber and Melody walked in, I was already cooking pancakes.

"Daddy!" Amber shouted. She raced over to me and wrapped her arms around my neck. "I didn't know you were coming."

I grinned and tapped her nose. "If you did, it wouldn't have been a surprise."

She hugged me again and refused to let go.

"Amber," Melody said, "you need to put your stuff away for school. Come on, honey."

"I want Daddy to help me," Amber said.

I leaned down until we were eye to eye and said, "Listen to Mommy, sweetheart. I'm not going anywhere. I'm making pancakes and I'm going to spend the whole day with you."

"You are?" she asked, her eyes wide. "But we have a half day."

I nodded. "I know. After school, the three of us are going to do something fun."

"Yay!" she shouted, throwing her hands in the air. She went and did as Melody asked and came back to help me with pancakes a minute later.

I watched Melody out of the corner of my eye. She spoke to the teacher, nodding at whatever Mrs. Anderson said. She kept glancing at me, but she never let her eyes linger for long. The pain on her face gutted me, but step one was all about making sure she knew I was there for them.

When I finished pancakes and everyone had eaten, Mrs. Anderson announced it was time for games. She turned it over to Melody, who stepped forward and addressed the class.

Watching her work turned me on. She commanded the room with a kind firmness that had all the kids and parents listening to her every word. She ran through the instructions with the kids then broke them up into teams.

Each of the parent volunteers, except me, managed one of the groups. There were five stations and at each station was a different game, letting the kids do a different activity each time they switched. I marveled at her ability to involve each kid.

One of the moms Melody didn't like went over to her and said something. Melody nodded and glanced at me. They were talking about me. The mom glared at me then hugged Melody.

What the hell?

The rest of the time they played games, the mom and Melody talked and laughed. They mostly ignored me, but Melody peeked my way more than once.

By the time school was over and it was time to go home, I knew Amber was excited to spend time together. But Melody…she looked like she'd rather do just about anything else.

"What are we going to do, Daddy?" Amber asked as she put her backpack on.

"Let's talk to Mommy and decide. I have a couple of ideas."

"Mommy, what do you want to do today?" Amber asked.

Melody smiled at Amber and crouched down in front of her. "I have work to do today, honey. Do you remember? You were going to help me. But I can do it myself. You go have fun with Daddy."

"What work was Amber going to help you with?" I asked.

"Will we see you tomorrow?" the mom Melody didn't like asked.

Melody nodded. "Definitely. Thanks again, Robin. I can't tell you how much I appreciate the help. You're a lifesaver."

Robin grinned. "Anything to help you get your business off the ground. Then you're independent and know you can take care of yourself." She gave me a parting glare and walked by.

"Business?" I asked, feeling like I had no idea what was going on. First Melody got a new job, now she owned a business. What else had I missed?

"Yeah, Mommy's party business. It's fun. I help her make up boxes of party stuff so people can have awesome birthday parties," Amber explained.

"Really?" I asked.

Melody nodded and thanked the teacher.

"When did you start a business? And why didn't you tell me?"

"There are a lot of things we haven't told each other lately, and a lot we have said," Melody said.

The barb was a good one, and one I deserved. It still stung.

"I'm going to go if you two are spending time together.

Amber's missed you, so have fun. I'll be home all afternoon whenever you need to get back to work."

"I'm not going back to work today."

Melody's eyes narrowed, but she didn't say anything. She nodded and walked away.

"Well," I told Amber, "that didn't go as planned."

"Why not?" Amber asked.

I sighed. "Because I haven't been very nice to Mommy. She's upset and hurt, and it's all my fault."

"I thought you were going to fix everything. You promised me you were going to."

I nodded and hugged Amber tight. "I am. I will."

AMBER and I went sledding at the park after we got lunch. I wanted to rush home and see Melody, but she needed space.

When Amber started dragging, we decided to go home and take a break. By the time I got to the house, she was passed out in the backseat and I had to carry her in.

Melody's car was there, so I knocked when I got to the door. She opened it a few seconds later. Her hair was a mess, and her eyes were red. I ached to sweep her into my arms like I'd done with Amber and make her feel better, but she crossed her arms and took a step back.

"Did she fall asleep?" Melody asked.

I nodded. "We went sledding. She had fun. It would have been better if you came with us."

"You can put her in her room," Melody said, ignoring my comment.

I stepped inside and let Melody close the door and pulled Amber's boots off before toeing mine off. I carried her to her room and laid her in her bed. I kissed her forehead and promised her I'd do everything I could to bring us all back together again.

When I went back to the living room, Melody was sitting on the couch in front of a bin full of party supplies.

"What are you doing?" I asked her.

"I'm working. Thanks for bringing Amber back. And for taking her today. She's missed you."

"I've missed her, too," I said. "And I've missed you."

She looked up at me, our gazes colliding. She held mine for a long moment, then looked away. "Well, thanks. I'm sure you have things to do today."

I shook my head. "Actually, I don't. I cleared my schedule so I could spent the day with you and Amber."

"Why?" she cried. "Why? Why bother, Ramsey? We both know our marriage is over. It's not going to change. I want you to spend time with Amber, and I hope you do, but don't walk in here and pretend you want to spend time with me. You told me what you really think of me, and I think it's best if you just leave. Now."

I expected her anger, but the pain in her voice hurt. Hudson was right. I broke her.

"I never should have said the things I said last time I was here. I was scared, and I'm sorry."

"Fine. You're forgiven," she said, not looking at me.

"Melody, don't be like that."

"What do you want from me, Ramsey? Do you want me to say it's okay that my husband of ten years thinks so little of me that he actually believed I would trick him into getting me pregnant? That he believed I would want a child that way? Do you want me to tell you I'm sorry for believing we could make it and asking you to come to bed with me? Do you want me to tell you I'm the whore and the deceptive bitch you think I am? What do you want, Ramsey? Tell me. What do you want?"

"Mommy?" Amber said softly from the hallway.

Melody and I both looked at her at the same time, but Melody moved first. She swiped her tears away and scooped Amber up.

"I'm sorry I woke you, sweetie. I shouldn't have been yelling."

"Why are you crying, Mommy?"

"I'm okay, Amber. I'm just sad right now."

Amber looked at me. "Did Daddy make you sad?"

Melody, always one to protect the people around her, shook her head. "No, honey. It's not Daddy's fault. Daddy loves you, but Daddy has to go right now. Go say bye."

Amber walked over to me once Melody put her down. She hugged me around my waist and said, "I love you, Daddy."

"I love you, too, sweetheart."

"Please don't make Mommy cry anymore," Amber said softly, looking up at me. "I don't like it when Mommy cries."

I glanced at Melody, but she wasn't looking at me. She only had eyes for Amber. "I'm going to try not to make Mommy cry."

Amber nodded. "Good because Aunt Willow made Mommy cry, and you made Mommy cry, and all Mommy does is cry. I want Mommy to stop crying."

"Aunt Willow?" I asked, glancing at Melody again.

"Amber," she said.

"Aunt Willow told Mommy she was in love with you and that the only reason you married Mommy was because Aunt Willow was too young. And she said that you should be with her instead of Mommy. Do you love Aunt Willow?"

I drew in a breath and shook my head. Melody might be ignoring me, but she was listening. "No. The only woman I've ever loved is Mommy. The only woman I ever will love is Mommy. I've made a lot of mistakes, but the one thing I did right is fall in love with your mommy. She's the best person I've ever known in my life, and I've made a lot of mistakes with her, but I'm hoping I can make up for those one day. I'm going to try."

"Come on, Amber," Melody said. Her voice was thick. "Daddy needs to go."

Amber looked at me, her eyes deadly serious, and said, "Don't mess it up."

I nodded and watched as they disappeared down the hall.

Step two did not go as planned.

MY LAST DITCH effort was a big, public apology like Hudson suggested. Melody never liked to be the center of attention, but I knew I couldn't hide the way I felt about her and expect her to forgive me. I knew getting Melody to trust me would take time, and I was willing to give her time, but I needed her to know I wasn't going anywhere.

I considered asking Willow to help me before Amber said they weren't speaking, but it never felt right. I hated that Willow hurt Melody, but she was not my priority. Melody and Amber were the ones who mattered to me. If Melody wanted to reconcile with her sister one day, that would be her choice, but Willow's toxic attitude almost destroyed my marriage. I wasn't going to bring it into our reunion.

Blake and Ian were watching Amber so Elise could get Melody to O'Kelley's. They all promised to help me because they cared about Melody. Knowing she'd connected with so many new people without me around was hard, but I was happy she hadn't been alone. And I was grateful for all the help I could get.

I hid in Hudson's office in a tux. Hudson walked into his office and shook his head. "You look like an idiot."

I flipped him off. "Thanks. If Melody likes it, I don't care."

"She doesn't care about stuff like this."

I knew, but wearing a tux would draw attention to me. O'Kelley's was a casual place, and dressed like I was meant everyone would see us and hear what I had to say.

"Is she here?" I asked.

"No, but Ian said she left the house, so she should be here soon."

I nodded and tried to squash the queasy feeling in my stomach. If this didn't work, I had no idea what to do.

Hudson left and promised to get me when Melody got there. I paced in his office for ten minutes before he returned. He wished me luck, then followed me out the door.

When I walked into the bar, the people closest to me stopped talking and looked at me. I waved the dozen roses I had in my hand and smiled at them, then kept moving.

I spotted Melody and Elise on the far side of the bar, near the dance floor. They were ordering drinks and hadn't seen me yet. I was able to get close before the murmurs of the crowd drew their attention.

Elise saw me first and raised an eyebrow. She pointed me out to Melody, and when she looked my way, tears filled her eyes.

I rushed to her side and eased onto the stool next to her. I took her hand and sighed. "I promised Amber I wouldn't make you cry again. Mel, please stop crying."

She shook her head. "Why are you doing this, Ramsey?"

"Because I love you. And I want you and everyone else to know that I screwed up. I said horrible things to you, and you didn't deserve them. I was wrong. I know who you are, and you're the most amazing woman I've ever met in my life. You're the best mother in the world. Amber is so lucky to have you. You've created a family while I was being an ass.

Everyone knows how amazing you are. And I hope you'll one day be willing to give me another chance."

She pressed her lips together in a smile. "I want to, Ramsey. I really do, but I just don't know if I can trust you."

"I know, Melody. And I understand. All day today, I've been trying to show you that I want to be there for you. I want to be there for Amber. I'm not walking away from our family again. But more than all that, I'm sorry. I want you to know I'm sorry for ever thinking you could do what I accused you of. You're the kindest, most honest and loving person I know. And I was a complete asshole for doubting that for even a second."

"It's okay," Melody said softly.

I shook my head. "It's not, Melody. It'll never be okay. But I will spend the rest of my life trying to make it up to you. Today was just the beginning."

"Ramsey, you don't have to do that."

"I want to, Mel. I want you to know I love you. I asked Ian, Blake, and Elise to help so you would know I love you. I'm not giving up on us. Not ever again."

Melody sucked in a breath. "I don't know how long it will take me to forgive you."

I nodded. "It doesn't matter. I'm going to be here. Waiting for you. I love you, and I still want to spend my life with you. I hope one day again, you'll feel the same way."

I kissed her cheek and lingered, memorizing everything I could about her. Pulling away was hard, but I knew I had to do it. I had to let Melody decide she wanted me. I was going to be there, but she needed to want me.

24

MELODY

"What are you going to do?" Elise asked as Ramsey walked away.

I looked at her and shook my head. "I don't know."

"Do you still love him?"

I nodded. "Yeah, of course."

"Then you should go after him."

I shook my head. "I can't. Not right now. I don't know if he's telling the truth. He can't erase all the pain he caused in one day. Yeah, it was a pretty great apology, but it's not good enough. Not yet."

Elise smiled and lifted her glass. "Good for you. I wasn't strong enough to say no with my ex. And I paid for it. Ramsey's a good guy, but you deserve to be treated better."

I nodded. Damn right I did.

Over the next week, Ramsey sent me messages on Book Boyfriends Wanted. He told me he loved me. He asked about Amber. He kept me informed about work. It was all the stuff I wanted him to do.

But he still hadn't said anything about the baby. And that was what I needed to hear. He said he'd be there for Amber and I, but he didn't say if he wanted the baby or if he would leave again if I was pregnant.

Thursday morning, almost a week after Ramsey's declaration, I woke up to find my period came overnight. I was so relieved I cried.

I dropped Amber off and sat in my car outside the school. I called Elise and Blake first and filled them in, then I called my OB/GYN and scheduled an appointment to talk about having my tubes tied.

When I got to O'Kelley's, I headed straight to the back to get some work done. The first day of my period was always the worst, and if I could work for a few hours then go home and rest, it would be much easier to deal with.

Hudson came back about an hour into my shift and asked me to help him up front. I said yes without thinking about it and followed him into the bar.

The bar was empty except one guy at a table in the corner. Hudson pointed for me to go to the table. I gave him a questioning look, but he just pointed. "Please, Mel," he said.

I narrowed my eyes, but I couldn't see the guy. I glanced back at Hudson, but he was gone. I walked over, more than a little uneasy.

His arm appeared first, then his shoulder. The side of his head and his profile, and my heart jumped.

Ramsey turned to look at me and stood when he saw me frozen a few feet away.

"Will you sit with me?"

I nodded and let him lead me to the table.

He looked amazing. He hadn't shaved in a couple days, the stubble dark against his skin. His dark hair was short, like he'd gotten it cut since I last saw him. His shoulders filled out his jacket as well as they ever did. His shirt was opened a few buttons at the top, showing off the top of his chest. His fingers were wound together, holding onto each other.

I took a deep breath and carried in his scent. I wanted to cry I missed him so much. I was supposed to be strong, but I couldn't help but wonder why I was still resisting him.

"I went to the house, but you weren't home."

"I have work to do."

"Will you tell me about your work?"

"It's not that exciting."

"Everything is exciting when it has to do with you," Ramsey said with a smile.

I sighed. "Listen, I know why you're here, okay. Someone told you. But I'm just…I'm not ready to talk about it yet, not with you."

"You don't have to talk about anything you don't want to," Ramsey said. He hung his head and closed his eyes, probably thanking God he wasn't going to have another kid with me.

"I should get back to work," I said and tried to stand.

"Melody, there's no one here. Hudson put the closed sign up. There's nothing for you to do right now."

I shook my head. "I can't just sit here right now, Ramsey."

"Then let me go with you. Let me take you somewhere."

I laughed. "You're off the hook, Ramsey. You can stop all this. I didn't get pregnant, so you're free. You don't have to worry about your obligation to me or to a baby or anything else."

"You're not pregnant?" he asked.

I shook my head. "No. That's why you're here. Because you know. Because you got what you wanted."

"No, Mel, all I wanted was you. I didn't know you weren't pregnant. It didn't matter to me. You were the only thing that mattered. This whole time, I've been worried about you. I don't want to lose you, and after Steven…I'm afraid to touch you. Afraid of everything."

"I'm not going to break."

"You did, though. When we lost Steven, you broke. You left us. You checked out completely and left us. I couldn't go through that again."

"You stopped seeing me as your wife. All I wanted when we lost Steven was for you to hold me and tell me you'd always love me. For you to tell me it wasn't my fault and that you didn't blame me. But I didn't get that."

"Melody," he groaned. He shifted then slid out of the booth and came over to my side.

I was trapped when he sat next to me. I didn't want to be trapped. I didn't want him to hold me. If he did, I'd let him back in.

"Come here," he said softly.

I shook my head.

"Please, Melody. I need you, too. Please."

He moved closer until I had no choice but to let him touch me. All the emotions I'd been feeling for two years rose to the surface and spilled over. My first tears fell as he wrapped his arms around me.

I clung to Ramsey, desperate to hold onto him as I sobbed. He held me the entire time, whispering apologies and loving words to me.

I didn't know I'd been holding on to so much until I cried it all out. The pain from Ramsey's words, the hurt he caused Amber, the loss of Willow from my life, and the baby we'd never get to raise.

All of it left me, drawn out by Ramsey's arms holding me close.

"Do you feel better?" he asked, wiping my tears.

I nodded. "I do. Thank you. I'm sorry I cried all over you."

"Never apologize for telling me how you feel. Please, Melody. That's what I'm here for."

"You used to be," I told him. "Before Steven, you were here. But after…"

"I'm never going to do that again. Any of it. I'm going to be here for you forever, Melody. I want to be here for you forever and always."

I smiled up at him and nodded. "I still love you. I always will."

"Me, too, Melody. And if you need more time—"

I shook my head. "I think I've had enough time to realize I work best when I'm with you."

"Yeah?" he asked.

I nodded. "Yeah. But things have changed since you moved out."

"Like what?"

I shrugged. "Like we're going to work together. And we're going to talk to each other. And I'm going to girls' night out with Blake and Elise and the others every Sunday, so you need to watch Amber."

He grinned. "I can handle all that."

"Good. Because I already lost one best friend. I can't lose a second."

He shook his head. "I'm not going anywhere."

"Good," I said.

I pulled him down for a kiss and smiled as he leaned me down on the bench. He nipped at my lip and said, "God, I've missed you."

"You have me now."

"And I'm not losing you again. I love you."

"I love you."

EPILOGUE

ELISE

Damn, it felt good to be outside. The fresh air, the sweet scent of sap, and the brisk spring day. I loved spring. It was a chance to start over. It was always a good thing.

"Hey," I said to Melody. She was the one who told me about the grand re-opening of Jones Family Maple Farm. Ramsey was working with the new owner and invited all of us to celebrate.

"Hey," Melody said, reaching for a hug.

Melody had become a hugger in the two months since we'd gotten to know each other. I had a tendency to shy away from physical contact with most people, but I didn't mind hugging Melody.

"Where are Amber and Ramsey?" I asked.

Melody shrugged. "They're around here somewhere. I told them I was going to check out the store."

"Sounds good. I'll come with you."

Melody grinned and looped her arm through mine. "When do you start on the tour boat?"

"Three weeks," I said. "I'm so ready. I don't mind waiting

tables and taking shifts in the gift shops, but I'd much rather be outside."

"We need to come on one of your tours this summer. We were saying we need to show Amber more of the River. She doesn't even know where Boldt Castle is."

I laughed. "Really?"

Melody nodded. "Yeah. Total parenting fail. She does know where the MacKellar Estate is, though."

"Well, that's better. Especially since it is in our town. If she didn't at least know that one I'd worry about you."

"What are you worried about?" Trinity asked, joining us.

"Melody and Ramsey want to take Amber on a tour this summer so she can see Boldt Castle. She doesn't know where it is," I told her.

"Seriously? Even I've been to Boldt Castle and I've only lived here ten months," Trinity said.

"She was really young before Steven, and then Ramsey and I were…well, you know. So, this summer is going to be it. She'll love it," Melody said.

"Absolutely."

"Melody," a man said from right behind us.

I jumped involuntarily. I hated that it happened, but I couldn't help it. I hated when people snuck up on me, and even worse when it was a man.

"Colin," Melody said with a smile. She reached up and hugged him.

He was gorgeous. Short, dark hair and rich, dark eyes. He grinned at us, his gaze scanning the three of us. I expected him to check out Trinity since she was the bombshell of the three of us, but his eyes lingered on me.

"How are you?" he said.

"Good," I answered the same time as Melody.

Melody chuckled and gave me a weird look. Crap. He wasn't talking to me.

"These are my friends, Trinity and Elise," Melody said, shoving me forward when she said my name. "Guys, this is Colin, the new owner."

"Nice to meet you," Trinity said, reaching to shake his hand. "I moved here the end of last spring. You're going to love the area. Lots to do and great people."

Colin nodded. "Thanks. I came here some growing up, but I haven't been back in a while. It's different than I remember, but things always are when you're a kid."

Trinity laughed. "True."

I couldn't tell if she was flirting with him or just talking. I'd never been good at flirting. It felt like a foreign language to me, one I never quite got the hang of. I could understand it when others did it, but my tongue got twisted up if I tried.

"How about you, Elise?" Colin asked. "Are you from here?"

I nodded. "Born and raised. Went to college in Rochester and came back here after. Lived here ever since."

Colin smiled. "I guess you like it here."

I nodded.

Colin narrowed his eyes at me then smiled at Melody again. "Well, I should go mingle. You ladies enjoy. I'm sure I'll see you all around sometime."

I nodded as Colin walked away. He glanced back, but I pretended I didn't see him.

"He's cute," Trinity said. "But he only had eyes for Elise."

I rolled my eyes. "Not even. You're the one with the curves that make men drool."

Trinity snorted. "Not all men. And definitely not that one."

I shook my head. It didn't matter how cute Colin was or if he was checking me out. Nothing was going to happen. He was too close. He was a friend of a friend, and if things went wrong, I was not going to put my friends in the position of choosing sides.

I already knew how well that turned out for me.

THANK **you** so much for reading Melody and Ramsey's story! I loved taking a peek inside a marriage. One of the first story ideas I ever had was about a marriage in trouble. I loved it because so often we feel like there's no romance once we're married, but there should be, dammit!

Elise and Colin's story is available now! Life in a small town is not what Colin expected. Not when everyone knows everything about him. Including that he's single. Elise has no interest in changing that little detail, but she can't help but be intrigued by and more than a little curious about the charming newcomer. Get His Curvy Treat today!

LOOKING for more from Melody and Ramsey? Subscribers get a free, exclusive bonus epilogue of Ramsey moving back home! Only available to subscribers! Sign up now!

LOVE A MARRIAGE IN TROUBLE STORY? Lizzy is determined to save her marriage. She enlists her best friend and sister to devise a plan to get Aaron to notice her again. But they're not the same people they once were, and Lizzy isn't sure her marriage can be saved. Read Work For It today.

ABOUT THE AUTHOR

USA TODAY Bestselling Author Mary E Thompson spent most of her childhood wishing she had a few less curves. She hid in the pages of books because her favorite characters never cared what size her clothes were. Now, neither does Mary, and she writes stories that celebrate women like her. Real women who have curves, chase dreams, and find love, because we should all be happy, no matter our dress size.

Mary spends her non-writing time with her husband and two kids, watching too much TV, cheering for her home-town football team (Go Bills!), and hiding chocolate from her family.

Visit https://MaryEThompson.com/ to sign up for Mary's newsletter, **Romancing the Curves**. Subscribers get free ebooks and other fun stuff, like exclusive, members only content and giveaways, plus are the first to know about new releases and sales!

www.ingramcontent.com/pod-product-compliance
Lightning Source LLC
Chambersburg PA
CBHW060922190726
48286CB00002B/599